HORACE WALPOLE: see Chronology, pp. vii–ix.

ROBERT L. MACK is currently an Assistant Professor of English at Vanderbilt University. He has edited a number of eighteenth-century texts, including Frances Burney's *The Wanderer*, the *Arabian Nights' Entertainments*, and a selection of *Oriental Tales*.

Villian

deal w/ Manfred was evil : Double Marriage Fredrich.

HORACE WALPOLE

The Castle of Otranto
and
Hieroglyphic Tales

Edited by
ROBERT L. MACK
Assistant Professor in the Department of English
Vanderbilt University

EVERYMAN
J.M. Dent
London
Charles E. Tuttle Co.
Rutland, Vermont

First published in Everyman in 1993

Introduction, notes, bibliography, selection of
criticism, chronology © J.M. Dent Ltd 1993

Made in Great Britain by
The Guernsey Press Co. Ltd, Guernsey, C.I.

for
J.M. Dent
Orion Publishing Group
Orion House
5 Upper St Martin's Lane
London WC2H 9EA
and
Charles E. Tuttle Co.
28 South Main Street
Rutland, Vermont
05701, USA

ISBN 0 460 87198 6

Everyman's Library
Reg. US Patent Office

CONTENTS

CHRONOLOGY OF THE
LIFE OF HORACE WALPOLE

1717, 24 September. Born Arlington Street, London. Third surviving son of Sir Robert Walpole and Catherine Shorter Walpole.

1721. Sir Robert Walpole becomes 'Prime Minister' in the wake of the bursting of the South Sea Bubble, a fraudulent, speculative trading scheme from which Sir Robert himself emerges a wealthy and powerful man.

1727, 26 April. At Eton. Begins close, lifelong friendships with George Selwyn, George Montagu, William Cole, and – most significantly – Thomas Gray. Together with Gray and Richard West and Thomas Ashton forms an informal confederacy known amongst themselves as the 'Quadruple Alliance'.

1734, 23 September. Leaves Eton, on the eve of his seventeenth birthday.

1735, 11 March. At King's College, Cambridge (Thomas Gray is at Peterhouse). Will leave at the end of 1738 without having taken a degree.

1737, 20 August. Death of Lady Walpole. Sir Robert soon marries his mistress, Maria Skerrett, who dies shortly thereafter in childbirth.

1739, 29 March. Embarks on Grand Tour to France and Italy accompanied by Thomas Gray.

1741, May. Quarrels while in Italy with Gray. They return to England separately.

1741, 12 September. Arrives at Dover. While abroad, elected to Parliament for a family borough (Callington) in Cornwall. He will remain MP for Callington until 1754, and will remain in Parliament (subsequently as Member for Castle Rising and King's Lynn) until 1768. His places in the

Exchequer and Custom House, procured for him by his father, secure him a comfortable income for the rest of his life.

1742. Sir Robert Walpole resigns as Prime Minister, is created Earl of Orford, and retires to his house, Houghton, in Norfolk.

1745, 28 March. Death of Sir Robert Walpole. In November Walpole is reconciled with Thomas Gray.

1747. Leases the small house he soon comes to call 'Strawberry Hill' near Twickenham, just over ten miles from London. He will purchase the house in June 1749. Earlier in the year publishes his first book, *Aedes Walpolianae*, a catalogue of his father's collection of pictures at Houghton, completed in August 1743.

1749. Begins remodelling Strawberry Hill as 'a little Gothic castle'. A library and 'refectory' will be added in 1754; a cloister, gallery, and tower in 1760–3.

1751. Begins writing his *Memoirs*.

1753, February. Contributes the first of nine papers to *The World*, a periodical published by Robert Dodsley.

1757, 25 June. Erects a printing press at Strawberry Hill, the first publication of which is *Two Odes by Mr Gray* (8 August). Later publications will include his own *Catalogue of Royal and Noble Authors* (April 1758), *Anecdotes of Painting in England* (1762–71), and a dramatic tragedy, *The Mysterious Mother* (15 March 1768).

1764, 11 April. Walpole's cousin Henry Seymour Conway dismissed from his post as Groom of the Bedchamber, and from the command of his military regiment. Walpole takes up Conway's defence in the popular press. Conway eventually (July 1765) installed in the new Whig government as a Secretary of State and Leader of the House of Commons.

1764, June. Begins writing *The Castle of Otranto*; he will complete the work on 6 August.

1764, 24 December. Publication of *The Castle of Otranto* (500 copies).

1765. Second edition of *The Castle of Otranto* (11 April). Leaves, in August, for the first of five visits to Paris, where he meets and becomes close friends with Mme du Deffand.

1766, August. Begins writing the *Hieroglyphic Tales*. The last of the tales appear to have been written around 1772. Third edition of *The Castle of Otranto*.

1768, February. Publication of *Historic Doubts on the Life and Reign of King Richard the Third*.

1781, 17 November. *The Count of Narbonne*, a dramatic adaptation of *The Castle of Otranto* written by Walpole's friend Robert Jephson, is successfully produced at Covent Garden.

1782. Fourth edition of *The Castle of Otranto*.

1785. Publication of *Hieroglyphic Tales*. Produces only seven copies, none of which circulate until after Walpole's death.

1786. Fifth edition of *The Castle of Otranto*.

1791, 5 December. Becomes the fourth Earl of Orford, following the death of his nephew George Walpole. Sixth edition (reprinting the fifth) of *The Castle of Otranto*.

1797, 2 March. Dies at his London home, aged eighty. Buried at Houghton.

1798. Publication of the *Works of Horatio Walpole, Earl of Orford*, in five volumes. The work is edited by Mary Berry, a close companion in his last years.

INTRODUCTION

The Castle of Otranto, arguably the most influential novel written in England in the latter half of the eighteenth century, was not an immediate critical success. The earliest reviewers of Horace Walpole's self-styled 'Gothic Story' objected both to the 'preposterous' nature of his narrative – to the fantastic gothic machinery of ghosts, skeletons, labyrinthine passages, and wild, picturesque landscapes – and to its author's initial attempt to pass the work off as an actual translation 'from the original Italian' of a medieval text written by one 'Onuphrio Muralto'.

The resentment at having been duped into believing that *Otranto* was a true antique text is perhaps understandable. John Langhorne, writing in the *Monthly Review* in May 1765 (following Walpole's acknowledgement in the second edition that the work was in fact his own), angrily insisted that the indulgence afforded to 'the foibles of a supposed antiquity' was not to be extended to his own 'cultivated period of learning', and bristled with injured pride at the notion that he had himself been taken in by an author who, though 'of a refined and polished genius', appeared nevertheless to be 'an advocate for re-establishing the barbarous superstitions of Gothic devilism'.[1]

The vehemence with which some of the novel's earliest critics argued against the very subject matter was even more striking. 'The publication of any work, at this time, composed of such rotten materials', an anonymous commentator in the *Critical Review* wrote, 'is a phenomenon we cannot account for.'[2] While reserving some faint praise for the 'surprising spirit and propriety' of certain portions of the narrative and for the delineation of individual characters, the same reviewer went on to assault the supposed 'absurdity' and 'monstrosity' of Walpole's overall fiction. He ridiculed the ostensible moral of the volume that 'the sins of the fathers are visited on their children to the third and fourth generations'.

Rather surprisingly, Walpole fared little better at the hands of some of his closest friends and correspondents. George 'Gilly' Williams, a regular visitor to Walpole's Twickenham home, commented scathingly in a letter to George Selwyn (another of Walpole's most frequent holiday guests) that *Otranto* was 'such a novel, that no boarding school Miss of thirteen could get half through without yawning'.[3] 'He says it was a dream', Williams adds by way of explanation, 'and I fancy one when he had some feverish disposition on him.' Even the comments of the poet Thomas Gray, another lifelong friend of Walpole's and one who was initially credited by some readers with having written the story himself, have frequently been misrepresented. 'I have received the C: of O:', Gray wrote casually from Pembroke College, Cambridge, soon after having been sent a copy of the first edition by Walpole, '& return you my thanks for it. [I]t engages our attention here, makes some of us cry a little, & all in general afraid to go to bed o' nights.'[4] Gray, whose own fears of public exposure were perhaps unmatched in an era noted for such authorial anxieties, was admittedly among those who had encouraged Walpole to publish the volume in the first place. Yet his understated remarks – often cited as evidence of the novel's overpowering ability to inspire the most profound fear and terror in its earliest readers – need to be taken within the larger context of his playful and often elaborately self-conscious correspondence with Walpole. The poet no doubt enjoyed the amusingly truncated 'C: of O:', and he clearly applauded the achievement of Walpole's fiction as a fanciful *jeu d'esprit*. Yet there is something very close to affectionate mockery in his suggestion that the College Fellows at Pembroke had been reduced to a group of weeping, trembling pedants huddled together for the sake of mutual security by the comforting light of the Senior Common Room. Gray may have approved of Walpole's tale, but he refused on some level to take it at all seriously.

Otranto was not, however, entirely without its serious and committed defenders even in the eighteenth century. The antiquary William Warburton, normally no great supporter of Walpole, in 1770 pronounced the novel 'a master-piece'. For him it was uniquely able among prose romances to 'effect the full purpose of the *ancient Tragedy*, that is, *to purge the passions by pity and terror.*'[5] Clara Reeve, though objecting to the marvellous in the story ('the machinery is so violent, that it destroys the effect it was intended to excite'), acknowledged in the preface to her *The Old English Baron* (1778) that her own novel was the 'literary offspring' of *Otranto*.[6]

Moreover, while *Otranto* may not immediately have won over the critics, Walpole's novel *was* a success where perhaps it counted most: with the general reading public. *Otranto* passed through numerous editions in Walpole's own lifetime. The first edition of five hundred copies was published on 24 December 1764, a second edition was readied for the press by 11 April the following year, and a third edition appeared in 1766; the novel has rarely, if ever, been out of print since. While the critics may have objected to Walpole's revival of a gothic spirit in romantic fiction, *Otranto* found an eager audience in readers already captivated by the work of the so-called 'Graveyard' poets (e.g. Thomas Parnell, Robert Blair, and Thomas Gray himself), by the wild Celtic lyricism of James Macpherson's Ossian poems (1760–3), and by the highly charged eroticism of the *Arabian Nights' Entertainments* (1704–17) and of the many other oriental tales in vogue throughout the eighteenth century.

Thus Walpole's novel was enormously popular, although it failed immediately to charm journals and reviews. It was in fact destined to play an extremely important role in the taxonomy and classification of English fiction in the period. The early years of the eighteenth century had witnessed a contest of sorts between the rival claims of the new realistic 'novel' (Daniel Defoe and, subsequently, Samuel Richardson and Henry Fielding), and the older prose 'romance'. The novel sought faithfully to reproduce a world known and familiar to its readers. The romance tended to offer sprawling and multi-episodic plots which tumbled riotously and often improbably across grand classical landscapes peopled by aristocratic lovers and martial heroes of mythic stature. It is an oversimplification to say that one 'kind' of fiction abruptly replaced the other in the affections of the critics: the novel is, properly speaking, a *part* of the larger romance tradition – making use of many of the same narrative techniques as its literary ancestor – and not a separate genre at all. Nevertheless it is true that by the time *Otranto* first appeared in 1764 the realism of the novel seemed – for better or for worse – to have carried the day. Charlotte Lennox's landmark work *The Female Quixote* (1752), for example, had seen its heroine forced to renounce the 'Romantick Heroism' of her wonderfully expansive French narrative models not only as 'absurd', but – because of their supposedly irresponsible representations of human passion – 'criminal'. What was demanded now by the self-declared arbiters of novelistic taste was a fiction which dealt with the conceivable, the probable, the known.

Walpole himself, who had since his earliest schooldays been an avid reader of French romances, in his preface to the second edition of *Otranto* openly laments such a development. He notes that in the scramble to copy a probable nature 'by a strict adherence to common life', the 'great resources of fancy' have consequently been 'dammed up'. His avowed aim in *Otranto* is 'to blend the two kinds of romance, the ancient and the modern', to blend a cast of characters who operate 'according to the rules of probability' with a plot which leaves the power of fancy and imagination 'at liberty to expatiate through the boundless realms of invention'. If *Otranto* was not to be included in the grand and newly respected novelistic tradition which demanded restraint, conformity, and, above all, a consciously realistic treatment of its subject matter, it lost no time in establishing – or at least significantly contributing to – a collateral line of narrative descent for the 'imagination and improbability' which seemed to have been so easily jettisoned with the traditions of prose romance.

Walpole's narrow escape route – the 'new route' he claims to have 'struck out' in his fiction – in a short time became a thoroughfare clogged with every possible vehicle of the romance imagination. Not so very long after the apparent repudiation of the fantasy and improbability of the romance by the official literary establishment, many romance traditions re-emerged in a powerful new form: the gothic. The mode became a fashionable one not only for novelists, but for poets – Blake, Wordsworth, Coleridge, and Byron among them – as well. In spite of all the critics had to say to the contrary, readers seemed to *demand* the looser and in some ways more natural, less predictable, and certainly more exotic structures of romantic narrative. And while *Otranto*'s many imitators fed the public's seemingly insatiable appetite for this supposedly new 'species' of writing,

Walter Scott's generous 1811 reappraisal of Walpole's story in turn set the tone for much of the subsequent, positive criticism of the novel itself. The critical tide had to some extent begun, even by the early nineteenth century, to turn in Walpole's favour. Scott was among the first to recognize the historical significance of Walpole's attempt to revive the traditions of romance, noting the form to have been one which had fallen into neglect 'so early as the reign of Queen Elizabeth'.[7] He noted too that Walpole's particular affinity for the gothic style in architecture and design as well as his abilities as an antiquarian and amateur genealogist rendered him especially suitable to undertake a modern gothic novel. Scott praised Walpole's use of the supernatural in the novel, his supposedly faithful delineation of the medieval character, and even his straightforward language and dialogue. He not only treated *Otranto* with the respect and serious consideration due to so influential a work but also, in a larger sense, welcomed its contribution to the tradition of the novel in English. One small but significant indication of the change in attitude first brought about by Scott's reassessment and of the degree to which *Otranto* was, by the end of the nineteenth century, being treated as a true achievement in prose fiction, can be seen by the number of instances (no less than nine) in which Walpole's decidedly slim volume is referred to as an authoritative source for illustrative quotations in the first edition of the *Oxford English Dictionary* (1857–1928). The novel initially rejected by the journals and periodicals as an absurd and idiosyncratic freak was finally recognized not only to have been a catalytic work in the English literary tradition, but was also, in time, enshrined as an eminently respectable exemplar of sound and standard English usage.

Today's readers have long grown familiar with the designation of *Otranto* as 'the first gothic novel'. Almost every serious study of the gothic as a literary mode begins with some examination of the influence of Walpole's volume on later novelists such as Clara Reeve, Ann Radcliffe, Matthew Lewis, William Beckford, and Charles Maturin.

While gothic novels can display a remarkable and even notorious diversity of plot and incident, the broad hallmarks of the gothic as a literary mode in the eighteenth and early nineteenth centuries are nevertheless relatively easy to identify.

Gothic novels tend to take place in the past and they tend also to be set in foreign countries, often in Italy and in Spain, where the supposed tyrannies and superstitions of the Roman Catholic Church provided English authors with fertile ground on which to explore the abuses of domestic and institutional authority. Eighteenth- and early nineteenth-century gothic fictions usually include some mention of supernatural phenomena, or of the appearance of spirits and other ghostly manifestations, or, as in *Otranto*, of walking skeletons and haunted castles. Some gothic authors, most notably Clara Reeve and Ann Radcliffe, seek ultimately to explain away the seemingly 'marvellous' aspects of their stories with rational explanations. Others, Walpole among them, seem to delight rather in rendering their fictions as unrealistic and fantastic as possible. Gothic heroes tend to be outcasts: gloomy, Byronic, mysterious, inscrutable. Gothic heroines tend to be threatened yet persistent, timid yet, when necessary, forceful and capable. The gothic villain is something of a hybrid between several of his romantic and poetic predecessors such as Spenser's Archimago and Milton's Satan, a dark manipulator (often a father or father figure) whose sinister and frequently incestuous machinations invariably lead to scenes of spectacular self-destruction. The typical gothic plot includes elements familiar to the most ancient romances: long buried secrets of social and domestic identity, a pattern of flight and persecution, ominous threats to the hero and/or heroine, and, most prominently, a providential design revealed in a dénouement which verges on the miraculous. The gothic landscape is the physical manifestation of the more dangerous sexual and psychological threats articulated in the fiction: labyrinthine dungeons, impenetrable castles, impassable mountains, dark cellars, and crenellated towers lit by a flash of lightning across the night sky. More than anything else, the dangerous and awesomely sublime physical environments of the gothic novel reflect its consuming and overwhelming concern with the threats of sexuality and desire. The gothic landscape is, ultimately, the landscape of the human mind.

A mode which delighted in defining itself so prominently with reference to its spectacular props and machinery – a mode which at once offered to chill and unsettle its readers and at the same time situated them in a rather surprisingly comfortable literary universe filled with reassuringly familiar narrative incidents and responses – was bound to open itself up to the threats of parody and burlesque. Authors such as William Beckford, E.S. Barrett, and, most memorably, Jane Austen, all poked affectionate fun at the predictable paraphernalia of the gothic. Although Walpole's volume was not, strictly speaking, the target of these later parodies, the most cursory reading of *Otranto* confirms that it would feel quite at home were it to be placed on a shelf alongside the later works of, say, Radcliffe or Beckford, or even alongside the parodies of Austen herself. *Otranto*, that is to say, contains almost all of the elements by which the gothic would later define itself.

Like many subsequent gothic fictions, *Otranto* tells the story of a buried secret and a dreaded revelation. The central plot concerns the usurpation by Manfred's grandfather, Don Ricardo, of the Castle and Lordship of Otranto. Two generations after his grandfather's treacherous poisoning of the aptly named 'Alfonso the Good', Manfred's own attempts to consolidate his misbegotten hold on the title by marrying his only son to the daughter of the Marquis of Vicenza (who holds the only other known claim to Otranto) brings tragedy to both houses. Manfred's knowledge of his grandfather's guilty secret is brought to light, and the true heir to Otranto is finally revealed in the form of the seeming peasant, Theodore. But at an enormous cost. By the end of the novel both of Manfred's children lie dead, his daughter Matilda having been killed by his own hand. Manfred himself and his long suffering wife Hippolita abdicate their titles and retire separately to religious retreats. The young Theodore succeeds to the principality and is finally married to Isabella, but Walpole makes it clear that they are to lead a mournful and melancholy existence. What was soon seen as the 'gothic' quality of the story is emphasized throughout. The giant 'dilated' ghost of 'Alfonso the Good' extends his angry presence throughout the narrative, and characters are made aware of his displeasure through a bizarre range of supernatural phenomena: an oversized helmet drops from the sky to kill Manfred's only son Conrad; a full-length portrait steps from its panel on the wall and beckons Manfred to follow; the decaying skeleton of a long dead hermit mysteriously appears to chasten the Marquis of Vicenza. The fundamental thematic concerns of the story – the manner in which the past impinges upon the present, the brutal and violent connection between sexuality and power, and the overwhelming conviction that the truth will finally be brought to light – are, again, those which to a large degree are at the centre of the gothic to this day.

   Walpole's own account of the remarkably swift composition of the novel in the summer of 1764 (he began writing in June and completed the work by 6 August), further confirms the notion that *Otranto* not only fulfilled what were in time to become the generic requirements of the gothic, but was also drawing deeply on the spontaneous and unconscious desires of its author in true gothic style. In a letter to his frequent correspondent William Cole written shortly after the novel was first published, Walpole explained how he had come to write the tale:

I waked one morning in the beginning of last June from a dream, of which all I could recover was, that I had thought myself in an ancient castle (a very natural dream for a head filled like mine with Gothic story) and that on the uppermost bannister of a great staircase I saw a gigantic hand in armour. In the evening I sat down and began to write, without knowing in the least what I intended to say or relate. The work grew on my hands and I grew fond of it – add that I was very glad to think of anything rather than politics – in short I was so engrossed with my tale, which I completed in less than two months, that one evening I wrote from the time I had drunk my tea, about six o'clock, till half an hour after one in the morning, when my hand and fingers were so weary, that I could not hold the pen to finish the sentence, but left Matilda and Isabella talking, in the middle of a paragraph.[8]

Elsewhere Walpole offered similar accounts of the novel's composition. Writing in a letter to Robert Jephson years after the novel was published, he again noted that he had had no preconceived plot in mind when he began writing – 'no, not even a plan', he protested, 'until some pages were written'.[9] Walpole would have his readers believe that *Otranto* emerged and took form almost of its own accord.

Yet we risk radically misinterpreting the tenor and the true generic significance of *Otranto* if we are content to classify it merely as *the* prototypical gothic fiction and leave it at that. Some very basic objections may be made against such pigeon-holing. To Walpole, of course, the terms 'Gothic' and 'Gothic story' themselves signified 'medieval' or 'chivalric' as opposed to modern and refined; wild, even barbarous, as opposed to civilized and culturally pure. There is, in fact, little if any anticipation in his own use of the word 'gothic' of the more specific *literary* meanings the term would acquire in the particular aesthetic vocabulary of the later eighteenth and early nineteenth centuries. Walpole's 'gothic', not at all surprisingly, looks to the past rather than to the future. *Otranto* is the literary equivalent of the fantastic architecture of his own Strawberry Hill home – an antiquarian 'folly', an attempt to revivify the past in a peculiarly English garb – in actual fact closer in light-hearted spirit and literary affiliation to the productions of Sidney and Spenser than to the work of later novelists such as Radcliffe or Lewis. It is fair to suggest that in consciously attempting to revive the narrative vivacity of the ancient romances, Walpole only inadvertently set the course and the standard for the new breed of terrific gothic horror novels which were to follow. In other words, while *Otranto* may indeed have originated the species of gothic fiction which flowered in such works as *The Mysteries of Udolpho* (1794) and *The Monk* (1795), it more actively and more consciously extended strains of narrative innovation which had long played an important role in the traditions of English literary history.

From what other directions, then, might the reader more profitably approach *Otranto*? One answer would be to read the work as a careful and deliberate parody of Shakespearean drama. When Walpole came finally to write a dramatic tragedy in 1768, he produced *The Mysterious Mother*, a profoundly bizarre piece which tells of the incestuous relationship between its young hero Edmund, Count of Narbonne, and his mother. Although Walpole justified the drama critically by linking it to classical tragedy, the reader of the play is struck most by the careful and deliberate Shakespearean environment that Walpole evokes in the drama. References to Shakespeare in *Otranto* similarly range from simple names (e.g. Hippolita, Isabella), to the slightest of allusions and seemingly casual linguistic echoes of particular passages (Duke Frederic's cry 'Angels of grace, protect me', for example, recalls Hamlet's exclamation, 'Angels and ministers of grace defend us'). It is even the case that he evokes the entire dramatic worlds of some of the most memorable of Shakespeare's plays, most notably *Hamlet* (1601), *Measure for Measure* (1604), *Macbeth* (1605), and the late romance

The Winter's Tale (1610). There is hardly a page of *Otranto* on which the reader is not 'referred' in some way to a Shakespearean original. Kristina Bedford has catalogued the extent to which Walpole's narrative is in fact *sustained* by a pattern of Shakespearean reference and allusion. It is a pattern which, she observes, 'constantly sends the reader back to its sources for elaboration'.[10]

Otranto is what some modern critics would call a 'writerly' as opposed to a 'readerly' text, always asking the reader actively to assist in creating the meaning of the work at hand. To understand Walpole's novel fully we need to look not so much outside the text for external or historical references (although, as the explanatory notes to the present edition testify, these too have an important role to play), but rather *inside* the tale, to allusions cryptically encoded in the language of the novel itself. So, for example, the setting and location of *Otranto* bears less resemblance to the historical lordship and Castle of Otranto (about which Walpole claimed to know nothing) than to, say, the Dunsinane of *Macbeth*, or the Elsinore of *Hamlet*. The compulsion of Manfred to repudiate and humiliate his wife Hippolita must likewise be understood not as an isolated, even melodramatic piece of narrative invention, but as an archetypal 'romance' dilemma, taking its specific textual cues from (among others) the situation and language of Leontes in *The Winter's Tale*.

Otranto is parody not in the sense that it seeks to deride or to mock the characteristics and language of Shakespearean drama, but parody rather in the more etymologically precise sense of the word. It is a literal *para-odos*, a complementary 'song' to be heard not in place of, but alongside its original. It asks its readers to carry their knowledge of the entire corpus of Shakespeare's drama to the work so that those very readers can themselves fill in the narrative gaps in the volume with the resonance of a shared theatrical tradition. That Walpole was himself keenly aware of the extent to which his own work was indebted to this larger tradition for its meaning is made evident in the preface to the second edition. Here Walpole justifies the conduct of the novel's characters with specific reference to the idiosyncratic decorum of Shakespeare's stage – a decorum which, he argues, stands as a striking example of theatrical fecundity in contrast with the narrow and not entirely impartial

strictures of Voltaire. Articulating the magnitude and significance of his indebtedness to Shakespeare, Walpole transformed
Otranto into a work of national significance, trumpeting the
claims of an English genius historically more in tune with the
greater strains of narrative romance than the current French
dramatic tradition which, he claimed, now only 'shackled' and
'cramped' its muse.

To the national purpose articulated so clearly in the preface to
the second edition may be added more specific, if at first less
obvious, political and personal subtexts. In these too we may
find alternative ways of interpreting Walpole's novel. It has
already been noted that Walpole completed *Otranto* in less than
three months in the summer of 1764. The previous year had
seen Walpole's beloved cousin, Henry Seymour Conway,
engaged in an ongoing dispute with the Court and with the
recently constituted Whig government of Lord Grenville. Walpole and Conway had, from their earliest youth, been close
friends and companions. Indeed, Walpole came very close to
idolizing his cousin. 'I have always loved you constantly,'
Walpole had once written, offering to extend his own relatively
modest income to his cousin in order to facilitate a marriage of
which he in fact disapproved, 'I loved you better than any-
body.'[11] Later in life he continually used his own position in
Parliament in order to further his cousin's more ambitious
political career. Conway's dispute with the government in 1763
specifically involved the validity of what were known as general
warrants, that is, warrants for the arrest of individuals which
fail to specify precisely who is to be arrested. At the time of the
quarrel Conway held both a civil appointment under the government as Groom of the Bedchamber, and a military appointment
as a commanding officer of a regiment of dragoons. Conway's
open defiance of the King, encouraged by Walpole, led to his
dismissal in April 1764 from both of these posts. Walpole was
stunned. He felt that the casual expulsion of a devoted officer
was a colossal example of the ingratitude of an ill assembled
government.

Claiming to feel personally the sting of each new attack on
Conway, Walpole leapt to his cousin's defence, offering him
financial assistance, working to unite the divided Opposition
to Grenville's government, and, most significantly, coming to

Conway's aid in print in the pamphlet skirmish which had ensued soon after the dismissal. Even Walpole's closest associates (most of whom had rarely shared his enthusiasm for his cousin) were taken aback by the vehemence of his defence, failing to perceive the extent to which Walpole felt himself personally responsible for his cousin's situation and also the extent to which he believed Conway's disgrace to be a thinly veiled attack on his own political reputation.

It was perhaps natural that during such a period of uncertainty and upheaval – the most intense period of political activity he would ever experience – Walpole should look to find some solace and consolation in the mere activity of creative endeavour. He had, after all, confessed to Cole in his account of the novel's composition that at the time he was 'very glad to think of *anything* rather than politics'. The almost 'stream-of-consciousness' *Otranto* would certainly have been a means of escape – a way of working through the anxieties of political pressure without outwardly appearing to confront them. Yet the specific accusations and counteraccusations which characterized the debate over Conway's dismissal in the popular press shed an even more fascinating light on precisely why the most stressful and intense period of political activity in Walpole's career should in turn have created the conditions for his most sustained creative work. Walpole's impassioned defence of his cousin was in fact seen by government apologists as little less than an embarrassing public statement of his own not entirely appropriate love for Conway. 'I should go on to take notice of how extremely personal he grows in the prosecution of his subject,' the pamphleteer William Guthrie wrote of Walpole's *Counter-Address* in Conway's defence published in June 1764:

How pathetically he dwells on the ingenuous modesty of the general, on his extraordinary humility, on the twenty-seven years that he served, the six regular battles he was engaged in, beside the many bye battles or smaller actions, the heroes under whom he was formed, and the decorum which has graced every period in his fortune, if I did not recollect the unhappy situation of my Author, *C'est une affaire du coeur*: 'Tis his first love who has been so barbarously used.[12]

'*C'est une affaire du coeur*': Walpole's 'unhappy situation' is openly mocked in Guthrie's reply. The pamphleteer had earlier suggested that Walpole was 'by nature maleish, by disposition female, so haltingly between the two, that it would very much puzzle a common observer to assign him his true sex', and that the defence of Conway was so personal that one would have thought the arrow to have 'come forth from a female quiver'.[13] 'They have nothing better to say than that I am in love with you,' Walpole wrote resignedly to Conway in the following September, '[and] have been so these past twenty years.'[14]

Walpole himself seemed to recognize on some level that *Otranto* was produced within a crucible of passion which was both political *and* personal. It is little wonder that the forces and turbulent affections which motivated Walpole's spirited public defence of his cousin should seek expression which, while yet cryptic and encoded, should somehow body forth a more brutally honest, if yet dimly perceived assessment of the true nature of his affections.

There are some rather obvious points of connection between the narrative of *Otranto* and Walpole's own life. The son of the most powerful man in the kingdom – as Horace's father Sir Robert assuredly was throughout almost all of the boy's youth and young manhood – produces a phantasmagoric and dream-like novel in which the centre stage is held by a feared and tyrannical father only too glad to see his son brutally killed. The leap to reading a valid, semi-autobiographical subtext in the work is not an unreasonable one. Walpole seems in some ways to conjure the overwhelming figure of Sir Robert/Manfred only to punish and to exorcise him. Attending to the affairs of the nation, the elder Walpole must have had little time for his fragile and sickly child, although there is enough evidence to suggest that his preoccupations with politics and finance did not amount to any kind of systematic or considered neglect. Yet, as George E. Haggerty has pointed out, 'it hardly seems likely . . . that the sexually aberrant father/husband figure in *Otranto* is meant *solely* as a revenge for paternal neglect'.[15] Haggerty chooses rather to emphasize Walpole's own understandable identification and 'emotional involvement' with the figure of Manfred himself – a character who 'attempts to challenge the limits of convention and is summarily destroyed'.[16] He further suggests that the author's self-destructive impulses embodied in the story are emblematic of an early stage in the history of homosexual fiction, a stage in which the virtual impossibility of the kind of 'self-acceptance' and 'self-assertion' available to later, openly gay writers, led to narratives which embodied the unfortunate but historically inescapable self-loathing of their authors. Thus in *Otranto* Manfred's 'sexual frenzy and violent self-assertion' – and his ultimate downfall – are in some significant ways connected to the younger Walpole's own 'suppressed or misdirected anger and self-contempt'.[17]

It is indeed very probable that Walpole was homosexual. It is equally probable that his fictions should reflect this orientation. In the middle of a crisis which threatened to expose the deepest and most personal secrets of his heart to a callous and careless public scrutiny, Walpole produces a novel in which a potential sexual transgressor is driven to his spectacular downfall and punishment. Yet while several of the fictional strands in *Otranto* themselves remain bleak and unpromising, the fundamental impulse embodied in the text is not entirely one of self-destruction and self-loathing. At the end of the novel the 'truths' which have at great cost been revealed in the course of time have at least set matters straight. *Veritas filia temporis*: time *will* bring truth and justice to light. We tend to forget that the ending of Walpole's novel is a quintessentially comic one, in which the confusions of social, domestic, dynastic and sexual identity are unravelled and made clear. The Manfred whom Walpole exorcises in the course of his fiction is perhaps not only the tremendous and imposing father figure of his youth, but the fictional Manfred as well who hides behind guilty secrets and deceptions. The conclusion of *Otranto* seems to point suggestively towards a world in which the truth cannot only be exhumed and brought to light, but recognized, acknowledged, and perhaps some day (like the marriage of Theodore and Isabella anticipated at the end of the novel) even celebrated.

*   *   *   *

Walpole's collection of *Hieroglyphic Tales* was first printed at his own Strawberry Hill Press, at his home in Twickenham in 1785. He produced only seven copies of the six-tale collection, none of which appear to have circulated in his lifetime. One of those seven copies, a set of proofs now in the British Library, contains some additional manuscript notes and comments on the stories, including the observation that the prime virtue of such tales is the fact that they are 'written extempore and without any plan'.[18] The tales finally brought together in Walpole's printed collection (at least one 'hieroglyphic tale' remained unprinted in his lifetime) seem to have been composed between 1766 and 1772, and several were written with particular readers in mind. The third story, entitled 'The Dice Box, A Fairy Tale', for example, is playfully noted to have been 'translated' from a French original for the amusement of Caroline Campbell, the young niece of Lady Ailesbury (who in 1747 had married Walpole's cousin Conway). Similarly, the fourth story, 'The Peach in Brandy, A Milesian Tale', is said to have been written originally for Anne Liddel, whom Walpole had admired for years prior to her marriage to John Fitzpatrick, second Earl of Upper Ossory, in 1769. Walpole even notes that the Count and Countess's daughter, Anne, is 'the subject of [the] story'. The other tales appear to have been written with an eye to a larger audience, although again Walpole seems to have been disinclined to permit the volume the most modest circulation. When pressed in 1779 about the tales by the Reverend William Cole (who had been under the impression that the stories had been the recent by-product of one of Walpole's confining illnesses) the author confessed that he did possess in his drawers some 'strange things . . . even wilder than the *Castle of Otranto*, and called *Hieroglyphic Tales*'.[19] Other references to the collection in Walpole's correspondence, however, are rare. The few friends who did read the *Tales* seem unable to have made much sense of them; the most understanding and indulgent of Walpole's correspondents were perhaps too polite to comment on the volume at all. The stories first printed in 1785 were included by Mary Berry – one of those who knew the collection in its original form – in the collected *Works* of 1798. Their appearance then attracted little attention, however. Charles Burney, reviewing the *Works* in the *Monthly Review* in October 1798, could only comment that the *Tales* contained 'a great many odd fancies', and many allusions which were 'extremely sarcastic, personal, and sometimes profane'.[20]

The *Hieroglyphic Tales* are, indeed, as Walpole noted, 'even wilder' than *The Castle of Otranto*; in some respects the collection is *The Castle of Otranto* writ large. If Walpole's purpose in the earlier story was to revive the traditions of romance in the form of an elaborately parodic 'Gothic story' – to resist the restrictions he rightly felt were being imposed on prose fiction and retain the form's expansive narrative heritage – the

Hieroglyphic Tales take that purpose several steps further. Although the preface to the volume quickly dispenses with the pretence of treating critical matters with any degree of seriousness ('The "Hieroglyphic Tales"', the fictitious translator and editor announces with mock solemnity, 'were undoubtedly written a little before the creation of the world, and ... preserved, by oral tradition, in ... an uninhabited island, not yet discovered'), the brief postscript which Walpole appended to the volume offers at least some explanation for the frenetic and kaleidoscopic collection of stories which has preceded it. Walpole first confesses that the stories are 'mere whimsical trifles, written chiefly for private amusement'. 'They deserve at most', he goes on to explain, 'to be considered as an attempt to vary the stale and beaten class of stories and novels, which, though works of invention, are almost always devoid of imagination.' He further confesses an impatience with a genre which, though fettered by no rules, 'and by no obligation of speaking truth', should nevertheless have produced works of 'so little fancy, so little variety, and so little novelty'. The *Hieroglyphic Tales* attempt to infuse some of this fancy, variety, and novelty back into story-telling.

The epigraph to Walpole's volume from Crébillon's *Le Sopha* (1745) suggests that the reader is about to encounter things which are 'absurd' and 'beyond belief'. Yet few readers are prepared for just *how* absurd Walpole is intent on becoming here. The individual stories Walpole tells are by turns amusing, shocking, allusively ingenious and disturbing.[21] At times the author seems intent on satirizing particular moments in European history, and the precise historical references included in some of the tales can be, as might be expected from someone possessing Walpole's fascination with ecclesiastical and antiquarian lore, remarkably esoteric. There are many other instances, however, (particularly in Tales 4 and 5), in which the focus of the narrative becomes far more personal, rooted in family histories and circumstances barely elucidated by the frequently anecdotal explanatory glosses. 'Despite a wealth of literary and historical allusion', as one of Walpole's twentieth-century editors, Kenneth Gross, has pointed out, 'and many *moments* of sharp, ironic criticism, Walpole's hieroglyphics do not invite us to read them as ciphers of an integrated satiric argument'.[22] There is no coherent satiric 'ethic' at work in the tales – no single base from which Walpole is controlling his parodies – and the appropriateness of Walpole's name for the collection becomes apparent only as we make our way through the volume. These are 'hieroglyphics' not so much in the sense that they contain a hidden, symbolic meaning which can ultimately be deciphered or decoded by the diligent reader, but rather in the sense that they are tales which insist on *remaining* 'devices' and 'inscriptions' difficult to make out, elusive literary enigmas, the satiric and parodic agendas of which remain tantalizingly beyond our grasps. While *Otranto* reached into a gothic and romantic past for its peculiar novelty and vivacity, the *Tales* extend their inclusive reach into every conceivable area of narrative invention. The preface's claim that the *Tales* are 'incontestably the most ancient in the world' is to some degree a truthful one; Walpole here plunders not only romantic narrative to breathe new life into the fictions of his own day, but he also exploits the wildest possibilities of personal anecdote, epistolary correspondence, fairy tales, classical epics, political histories and chronicles, oriental tales, travel narratives, and dynastic histories – to name only a few. 'An entire world of invention lies open for your use and enjoyment,' Walpole seems to say, 'why not take advantage of it?' The wild surrealism of these generically slippery tales – their extreme self-consciousness – anticipates the work of modern and postmodern artists in our own century. Walpole's purpose, however, remains much the same here as in his earlier gothic novel. Desiring always to liberate rather than enclose, to expand rather than confine, the *Hieroglyphic Tales* further the aims first set out in *Otranto* to extend the frontiers of prose fiction.

Robert Mack
1992

NOTE ON THE TEXTS

The text of *The Castle of Otranto* reproduced here originally appeared in the second volume (ii.1–90) of the collected *Works of Horatio Walpole, Earl of Orford* (June 1798). Although Walpole had frequently protested that his writings were little more than inconsequential 'trifles' ('they will soon obtain that oblivion', he wrote in 1792, 'out of which I wish I had never endeavoured to emerge' [*Corr.* 4.230]), he nevertheless took a great deal of care in the manner in which they were presented to the public; the impressive, illustrated quarto volumes published in the year following his death were designed at least in part to preserve his own tales and stories for posterity in much the same way that his chronicles, political memoirs, and personal correspondence were meant to offer future generations a privileged and comprehensive picture of his time. (He had 'everything in the world', he once commented of his *Memoirs* to his cousin Henry Conway, 'to tell posterity' [*Corr.* 38.59].)

The notion of bringing together his collected 'works' had been on Walpole's mind for some time. In a letter to George Nicol – the prestigious bookseller to King George III who had published elaborate editions of Shakespeare and Milton, and who in 1792 had proposed issuing an edition of Walpole's writings – the author had protested that he would 'no more hear of a splendid and ornamented edition of my trifling writings, than I would dress my old, emaciated, infirm person in rich and gaudy clothes' (*Corr.* 42.371–3). In the same letter, however, Walpole notes that he had himself begun publishing a collected edition of his writings in 1768, when he claims to have learned that a 'little printer' had already prepared an inferior edition which was to be published (the author predicted) 'the moment the breath should be out of my body'. 'I could not doubt', he goes on to observe, 'but that in a posthumous edition some babes that had been laid to me, but were no babes of mine, would be produced as my issue.' Walpole's anxiety to avoid being credited with works he did not write is expressed more formally and at greater length in the advertisement finally prefaced to the collected *Works*:

As I have been an author in various ways and in various forms, somebody or other might think of collecting my works. To prevent this, and at the same time to avoid having pieces attributed to me which I never wrote, and to condemn, by suppressing as far as I can, some which do not deserve publication, I have determined to leave this collection behind me. The approbation bestowed on some part, authorises me to think that they are not unworthy of being preserved in this manner . . . .

(*Works* i.xxi)

The collected *Works* which finally appeared in 1798 was thus designed to forestall the ambitions of those 'little printers' who were only too ready to take advantage of Walpole's reputation. The five-volume edition, though nominally edited by Walpole's Twickenham neighbour Robert Berry, was in fact prepared for the press by Berry's young daughter, Mary. Regardless of their difference in age (she was forty-six years younger than the author), Mary Berry was one of Walpole's closest companions in his last years. She notes in the preface to the first volume of the *Works* that Walpole assisted her in the task of preparing the text for publication. 'The completion of this work he entrusted to the editor,' Berry graciously notes, 'to whom he also bequethed [*sic*] all the notes, additions, and alterations which he had himself collected and arranged. Lord Orford may therefore still be considered as his own editor' (*Works* i.vi). The text of *Otranto* included in the *Works* made only minor orthographical and typographical emendations to earlier editions. The first edition (five hundred copies) of *The Castle of Otranto* had been printed on 24 December 1764. It had frequently been reprinted in the late eighteenth century and had by the time of Walpole's death been translated into French (1767) and Italian (1794), and published throughout Europe.

Walpole's collection of *Hieroglyphic Tales* was first printed at his Strawberry Hill Press in 1785. The text of the first edition was reprinted in Volume IV of the collected *Works* (iv. 319–52) and the text of that later edition (collated with Walpole's own proofs for the first edition copy [BM C. 28. b. 7.] now in the British Museum) has been reprinted here. In the case of both works obvious misprints have been silently corrected, and the eighteenth-century long 's' (f) had been modernized. Idiosyncracies of grammar, italicization, punctuation, and spelling remain unchanged. Walpole's manuscript notes to his first edition of the *Hieroglyphic Tales* and several of his original notes to the tales subsequently omitted from the *Works* have been included in the explanatory notes to the present edition.

SELECT BIBLIOGRAPHY

Texts, Editions, and Bibliography

Robert Berry [Mary Berry] (ed.), *The Works of Horatio Walpole, Earl of Orford* (London, 1798).

Kenneth Gross (ed.), *Hieroglyphic Tales* (Los Angeles, 1982).

A.T. Hazen, *A Bibliography of Horace Walpole* (New Haven, 1948).

W.S. Lewis (ed.), *The Castle of Otranto* (Oxford, 1964).

——(ed.), *The Yale Edition of the Correspondence of Horace Walpole* (New Haven, 1937–83).

Biographies

Brian Fothergill, *The Strawberry Hill Set: Horace Walpole and His Circle* (London, 1984).

Martin Kallich, *Horace Walpole* (New York, 1971).

R.W. Ketton-Cremer, *Horace Walpole: A Biography* (New York, 1940).

W.S. Lewis, *Horace Walpole* (New York, 1961).

Warren H. Smith, *Horace Walpole: Writer, Politician, and Connoisseur* (New Haven, 1967).

Critical Works Related to The Castle of Otranto *and* the 'Gothic'

Edith Birkhead, *The Tale of Terror: A Study of the Gothic Romance* (London, 1921).

Kate Ferguson Ellis, *The Contested Castle: Gothic Novels and the Subversion of Domestic Ideology* (Urbana: University of Illinois Press, 1989).

Robert Kiely, *The Romantic Novel in England* (Cambridge, Mass., 1972).

David Punter, *The Literature of Terror: A History of Gothic Fictions from 1765 to the Present Day* (London, 1980).

Eve Kosofsky Sedgwick, *The Coherence of Gothic Conventions* (New York, 1980).

J.M.S. Tompkins, *The Popular Novel in England, 1770–1800* (London, 1932).

Devendra P. Varma, *The Gothic Flame* (New York, 1957).

Introductions, Articles, and Anthologies

Chris Baldick, 'Introduction' to *The Oxford Book of Gothic Tales* (Oxford, 1992), xi–xxiii.

Kristina Bedford, ' "This Castle Hath a Pleasent Seat": Shakespearean Allusion in *The Castle of Otranto*', *English Studies In Canada*, xiv (1988), 415–33.

Carol M. Dole, 'Three Tyrants in *The Castle of Otranto*', *English Language Notes*, xxvi (1988), 26–35.

Leigh Ehlers, 'The Gothic World as Stage: Providence and Character in *The Castle of Otranto*', *Wascana Review*, xiv (1979), 17–30.

George E. Haggerty, 'Literature and Homosexuality in the Late Eighteenth Century: Walpole, Beckford, and Lewis', *Studies in the Novel*, xviii (1986), 341–52.

Peter Sabor (ed.), *Horace Walpole: The Critical Heritage* (London, 1987).

Maria M. Tatar, 'The House of Fiction: Toward a Definition of the Uncanny', *Comparative Literature*, xxxiii (1981), 167–82.

EDITOR'S NOTE ON FURTHER READING

Having completed *The Castle of Otranto*, readers further interested in the relation of Walpole's volume to later gothic fiction might wish first to get some idea of the development of the gothic novel in the late eighteenth and early nineteenth centuries. The best place to begin is with the original works themselves. The immensely popular novels of Walpole's 'successor', Ann Radcliffe, including *The Romance of the Forest* (1791), *The Mysteries of Udolpho* (1794), and *The Italian* (1797), remain widely available in several inexpensive popular editions, as do later gothic landmarks such as Matthew Lewis's *The Monk* (1795), and Charles Maturin's *Melmoth the Wanderer* (1820). Another place to begin would be Jane Austen's *Northanger Abbey* (1818), one of that author's earliest works (though published posthumously) which parodies the gothic mode, and offers some genial and well intentioned criticisms of the gothic in the early nineteenth century. One might then move on to a critical work such as David Punter's *The Literature of Terror* (noted above) for an overview both of the difficulties in defining the gothic as a literary mode and of the developments throughout the nineteenth and twentieth centuries of a wide range of gothic 'types' in literature and film. Punter's accessible and straightforward analysis is well supplemented by Eve Kosofsky Sedgwick's *The Coherence of Gothic Conventions* and Kate Ferguson Ellis's *The Contested Castle* (also noted above), both of which examine the gothic mode from slightly less conventional, less literary-historical points of view. Readers interested in Walpole himself can turn to R.W. Ketton-Cremer's biography, *Horace Walpole*. The only real way to get a genuine feel for what Walpole was like as an individual is through his correspondence – a collection which remains the most elegant and well crafted body of letters in the language. Before tackling the immense and authoritative multi-volume edition of Walpole's *Correspondence* noted in the bibliography, however, the general reader might want to begin with the more manageable *Selection of the Letters of Horace Walpole*, also edited by W.S. Lewis (London, 1926). Other single-volume selections of Walpole's *Correspondence* are also available.

→ supernatural coincidence.

THE CASTLE OF OTRANTO

Synopsis

On the day appointed for his wedding to the Marquis of Vicenza's daughter Isabella, the sickly son of Manfred prince of Otranto, Conrad, is suddenly killed by a tremendous, over-sized helmet which falls from the sky and crushes him. The helmet is thought by many spectators to resemble that which usually rests on a statue of Alfonso the Good, a former prince of Otranto, in the nearby church of St Nicholas. Abruptly dismissing any such connection, Manfred imprisons a young peasant who has dared to note the similarity between the two helmets.

Now Manfred decides to rid himself of his wife Hippolita, and pursue Isabella for himself – remaining faithful to his plan to consolidate his hold on his title by sealing a family tie between himself and the Marquis, who has the only other possible claim to Otranto. His fears regarding the stability of his dynasty are further exacerbated by an ancient, cryptic prophecy which hangs over his house, declaring that 'the Castle and Lordship of Otranto should pass from the present family whenever the real owner should be grown too large to inhabit it'. Isabella, however, is horrified at Manfred's advances. With the help of Theodore, the peasant who had soon managed to escape his confinement, she flees via an underground passage to seek sanctuary in the church of St Nicholas. Pursuing Isabella, Manfred discovers Theodore, and again imprisons him in the castle. Manfred's daughter Matilda and her servant Bianca overhear Theodore lamenting his situation, and wonder at his true identity; Matilda is puzzled too by the reasons for Isabella's sudden disappearance.

On the following morning father Jerome arrives from the church of St Nicholas to confront Manfred regarding Isabella's accusations. He also informs him that she demands to be returned to the care of her guardians so that she may learn more concerning the fate of her father, who is believed to have died in the Crusades. Manfred tells Jerome that his reasons for pursuing Isabella are noble and justified, and pretends to a genuine concern that his near relation to Hippolita has led him to have moral qualms regarding the propriety of their marriage. He has decided to have Theodore executed. Jerome pleads unsuccessfully for Manfred to spare the young man's life. Yet just as the fatal blow is about to be delivered, Theodore's shirt slips from his shoulder, revealing a birthmark which identifies him as the long lost child of father Jerome, who now tells Manfred that, before taking orders, he was the Count of Falconara. Manfred postpones Theodore's execution, but separates him from his father, whom he banishes from the castle.

A herald arrives from Frederic, Marquis of Vicenza, demanding the return of Isabella and challenging Manfred's claim to the title and lordship of Otranto. Manfred reflects on the truth of the challenge, recalling that his claim to Otranto has unjustly usurped the more legitimate line of Frederic. He promises the herald that he will extend a courteous reception to the Marquis. The knight arrives in full armour with a cavalcade of retainers who together carry a tremendous sword. They listen silently while the obsequious Manfred outlines his plans to marry Isabella himself and unite the two lines. Father Jerome bursts in upon the gathering, however, to inform Manfred that Isabella has fled from the church and is nowhere to be found. The knights quickly go in search of her. Matilda takes advantage of the confusion in the castle to free Theodore, who promptly joins the search for Isabella.

They find her in a labyrinth of caves near the castle which were formerly the retreat of religious hermits. Theodore reveals himself to her and suggests that they take refuge from those seeking her on Manfred's behalf deeper inside the caverns. At the mouth of the cave Theodore wounds a knight in search of Isabella – only to learn that his victim is in fact Isabella's father. Frederic, who believes himself to be mortally wounded, asks to be carried back to Manfred's castle.

At Otranto the doctors who examine Frederic declare that none of his wounds are life-threatening. He tells Hippolita of his adventures in the Holy Land, and of his encounter with an aged, venerable hermit who revealed to him the location of the enormous sabre which had been carried by his knights into the courtyard of Otranto. He had learned of Isabella's captivity through a dream, and had hurried to Otranto to rescue her.

Both Matilda and Isabella are attracted to the young Theodore, though Isabella, thinking Theodore prefers Matilda, is determined to overcome her passion. Hippolita has meanwhile proposed to Manfred that Matilda should be married to lord Frederic, thus averting destruction of her own line by uniting the two rival houses. Manfred proposes a double marriage to Frederic: Frederic would marry Matilda, and Manfred himself – should Hippolita consent to a divorce – marry Isabella. Father Jerome objects to the arrangement, but his counsel is scornfully rejected by Manfred.

Lord Frederic is soon intent on the possession of Matilda, but is challenged by the appearance of the skeleton of the holy hermit who warned him of the plight of Isabella in the first place. The skeleton enjoins Frederic to temper his heedless pursuit of carnal pleasures. One of Manfred's attendants informs his lord that he has observed Theodore and an unidentified young lady speaking together at the tomb of Alfonso, in the church of St Nicholas. Manfred hastens to the church and, believing in his jealous fury that the lady declaring her love for Theodore is Isabella, stabs her. As she falls Manfred sees that it is not Isabella he has attacked, but his own daughter, Matilda. As Matilda dies, the castle of Otranto is shaken to its very foundations by a tremendous clap of thunder. The giant, dilated form of Alfonso appears at the centre of the ruins, declaring: 'Behold in Theodore the true heir of Alfonso.'

Manfred acknowledges that his grandfather, Ricardo, poisoned Alfonso in the Holy Land, and produced a forged will declaring him to be Alfonso's heir. Now father Jerome explains Theodore's specific claim to the title. Father Jerome's own wife, whom he had married as the Count of Falconara, was Alfonso's daughter: Theodore is thus the legitimate heir to Otranto. Manfred abdicates the title and retires to a nearby convent; his wife joins a neighbouring order. Theodore eventually marries Isabella, finding her to be the one person with whom he can indulge in melancholy discussion of his true love, Matilda.

THE CASTLE OF OTRANTO

A Gothic Tale

PREFACE

To the First Edition

The following work was found in the library of an ancient catholic family in the north of England. It was printed at Naples, in the black letter, in the year 1529.[n] How much sooner it was written does not appear. The principal incidents are such as were believed in the darkest ages of christianity; but the language and conduct have nothing that savours of barbarism. The style is the purest Italian. If the story was written near the time when it is supposed to have happened, it must have been between 1095, the æra of the first crusade, and 1243, the date of the last, or not long afterwards.[n] There is no other circumstance in the work that can lead us to guess at the period in which the scene is laid: the names of the actors are evidently fictitious, and probably disguised on purpose: yet the Spanish names of the domestics seem to indicate that this work was not composed until the establishment of the Arragonian kings in Naples had made Spanish appellations familiar in that country.[n] The beauty of the diction, and the zeal of the author, [moderated however by singular judgment] concur to make me think that the date of the composition was little antecedent to that of the impression. Letters were then in their most flourishing state in Italy, and contributed to dispel the empire of superstition, at that time so forcibly attacked by the reformers. It is not unlikely that an artful priest might endeavour to turn their own arms on the innovators; and might avail himself of his abilities as an author to confirm the populace in their ancient errors and superstitions. If this was his view, he has certainly acted with signal address. Such a work as the following would enslave a hundred vulgar minds beyond half the books of controversy that have been written from the days of Luther[n] to the present hour.

This solution of the author's motives is however offered as a mere conjecture. Whatever his views were, or whatever effects the execution of them might have, his work can only be laid before the public at present as a matter of entertainment. Even as such, some apology for it is necessary. Miracles, visions, necromancy, dreams, and other preternatural events, are exploded now even from romances.[n] That was not the case when our author wrote; much less when the story itself is supposed to have happened. Belief in every kind of prodigy was so established in those dark ages, that an author would not be faithful to the *manners* of the times who should omit all mention of them. He is not bound to believe them himself, but he must represent his actors as believing them.

If this *air* of the *miraculous* is excused, the reader will find nothing else unworthy of his perusal. Allow the possibility of the facts, and all the actors comport themselves as persons would do in their situation. There is no bombast, no similies, flowers, digressions, or unnecessary descriptions. Every thing tends directly to the catastrophe. Never is the reader's attention relaxed. The rules of the drama are almost observed throughout the conduct of the piece. The characters are well drawn, and still better maintained. Terror, the author's principal engine, prevents the story from ever languishing; and it is so often contrasted by pity, that the mind is kept up in a constant vicissitude of interesting passions.

Some persons may perhaps think the characters of the domestics too little serious for the general cast of the story; but besides their opposition to the principal personages, the art of the author is very observable in his conduct of the subalterns.[n] They discover many passages essential to the story, which could not well be brought to light but by their *naïveté* and simplicity: in particular, the womanish terror and foibles of Bianca, in the last chapter, conduce essentially towards advancing the catastrophe.

It is natural for a translator to be prejudiced in favour of his adopted work. More impartial readers may not be so much struck with the beauties of this piece as I was. Yet I am not blind to my author's defects. I could wish he had grounded his plan on a more useful moral than this; that *the sins of fathers are visited on their children to the third and fourth generation.*[n] I doubt whether in his time, any more than at present, ambition curbed its appetite of dominion from the dead of so remote a punishment. And yet this moral is weakened by that less direct insinuation, that even such anathema may be diverted by devotion to saint Nicholas.[n] Here the interest of the monk plainly gets the better of the judgment of the author. However, with all its faults, I have no doubt but the English reader will be pleased with a sight of this performance. The piety that reigns throughout, the lessons of virtue that are inculcated, and the rigid purity of the sentiments, exempt this work from the censure to which romances are but too liable. Should it meet with the success I hope for, I may be encouraged to re-print the original Italian, though it will tend to depreciate my own labour. Our language falls far short of the charms of the Italian, both for variety and harmony. The latter is peculiarly excellent for simple narrative. It is difficult in English *to relate* without falling too low or rising too high; a fault obviously occasioned by the little care taken to speak pure language in common conversation. Every Italian or Frenchman of any rank piques himself on speaking his own tongue correctly and with choice. I cannot flatter myself with having done justice to my author in this respect: his style is as elegant as his conduct of the passions is masterly. It is pity that he did not apply his talents to what they were evidently proper for, the theatre.[n]

I will detain the reader no longer but to make one short remark. Though the machinery is invention, and the names of the actors imaginary, I cannot but believe that the ground-work of the story is founded on truth. The scene is undoubtedly laid in some real castle.[n] The author seems frequently, without design, to describe particular parts. *The chamber*, says he, *on the right hand; the door on the left hand; the distance from the chapel to Conrad's apartment:* these and other passages are strong presumptions that the author had some certain building in his eye. Curious persons, who have leisure to employ in such researches, may possibly discover in the Italian writers the foundation on which our author has built. If a catastrophe, at all resembling that which he describes, is believed to have given rise to this work, it will contribute to interest the reader, and will make The Castle of Otranto a still more moving story.

PREFACE

To the Second Edition

The favourable manner in which this little piece has been received by the public, calls upon the author to explain the grounds on which he composed it. But before he opens those motives, it is fit that he should ask pardon of his readers for having offered his work to them under the borrowed personage of a translator. As diffidence of his own abilities, and the novelty of the attempt, were his sole inducements to assume that disguise, he flatters himself he shall appear excusable. He resigned his performance to the impartial judgment of the public; determined to let it perish in obscurity, if disapproved; nor meaning to avow such a trifle, unless better judges should pronounce that he might own it without a blush.

It was an attempt to blend the two kinds of romance, the ancient and the modern.[n] In the former all was imagination and improbability: in the latter, nature is always intended to be, and sometimes has been, copied with success. Invention has not been wanting; but the great resources of fancy have been dammed up, by a strict adherence to common life. But if in the latter species Nature has cramped imagination, she did but take her revenge, having been totally excluded from old romances. The actions, sentiments, conversations, of the heroes and heroines of ancient days were as unnatural as the machines employed to put them in motion.

The author of the following pages thought it possible to reconcile the two kinds. Desirous of leaving the powers of fancy at liberty to expatiate through the boundless realms of invention, and thence of creating more interesting situations, he wished to conduct the mortal agents in his drama according to the rules of probability; in short, to make them think, speak and act, as it might be supposed mere men and women would do in extraordinary positions. He had observed, that in all inspired writings, the personages under the dispensation of miracles, and witnesses to the most stupendous phenomena, never lose sight of their human character: whereas in the productions of romantic story, an improbable event never fails to be attended by an absurd dialogue. The actors seem to lose their senses the moment the laws of nature have lost their tone. As the public have applauded the attempt, the author must not say he was entirely unequal to the task he had undertaken: yet if the new route he has struck out shall have paved a road for men of brighter talents, he shall own with pleasure and modesty, that he was sensible the plan was capable of receiving greater embellishments than his imagination or conduct of the passions could bestow on it.

With regard to the deportment of the domestics, on which I have touched in the former preface, I will beg leave to add a few words. The simplicity of their behaviour, almost tending to excite smiles, which at first seem not consonant to the serious cast of the work, appeared to me not only not improper, but was marked designedly in that manner. My rule was nature. However grave, important, or even melancholy, the sensations of princes and heroes may be, they do not stamp the same affections on their domestics: at least the latter do not, or should not be made to express their passions in the same dignified tone. In my humble opinion, the contrast between the sublime of the one, and the *naïveté* of the other, sets the pathetic of the former in a stronger light. The very impatience which a reader feels, while delayed by the coarse pleasantries of vulgar actors from arriving at the knowledge of the important catastrophe he expects, perhaps heightens, certainly proves that he has been artfully interested in, the depending event. But I had higher authority than my own opinion for this conduct. That great master of nature, Shakespeare, was the model I copied. Let me ask if his tragedies of Hamlet and Julius Cæsar would not lose a considerable share of their spirit and wonderful beauties, if the humour of the grave-diggers, the fooleries of Polonius, and the clumsy jests of the Roman citizens were omitted, or vested in heroics ?ⁿ Is not the eloquence of Antony, the nobler and affectedly-unaffected oration of Brutus, artificially exalted by the rude bursts of nature from the mouths of their auditors ? These touches remind one of the Grecian sculptor, who, to convey the idea of a Colossus within the dimensions of a seal, inserted a little boy measuring his thumb.ⁿ

No, says Voltaire in his edition of Corneille, this mixture of buffoonery and solemnity is intolerable.ⁿ—Voltaire is a genius* – but not of Shakespeare's magnitude. Without recurring to disputable authority, I appeal from Voltaire to himself. I shall not avail myself of his former encomiums on our mighty poet; though the French critic has twice translated the same speech in Hamlet, some years ago in admiration, latterly in derision; and I am sorry to find that his judgment grows weaker, when it ought to be farther matured. But I shall make use of his own words, delivered on the general topic of the theatre, when he was neither thinking to recommend or decry Shakespeare's practice; consequently at a moment when Voltaire was impartial. In the preface to his Enfant prodigue, that exquisite piece of which I declare my admiration, and which, should I live twenty years longer, I trust I should never attempt to ridicule, he has these words, speaking of comedy, [but equally applicable

---

* The following remark is foreign to the present question, yet excusable in an Englishman, who is willing to think that the severe criticisms of so masterly a writer as Voltaire on our immortal countryman, may have been the effusions of wit and precipitation, rather than the result of judgment and attention. May not the critic's skill in the force and powers of our language have been as incorrect and incompetent as his knowledge of our history ? Of the latter his own pen has dropped glaring evidence. In his preface to Thomas Corneille's Earl of Essex, monsieur de Voltaire allows that the truth of history has been grossly perverted in that piece. In excuse he pleads, that when Corneille wrote, the noblesse of France were much unread in English story; but now, says the commentator, that they study it, such misrepresentations would not be suffered—Yet forgetting that the period of ignorance is lapsed, and that it is not very necessary to instruct the knowing, he undertakes from the overflowing of his own reading to give the nobility of his own country a detail of queen Elizabeth's favourites – of whom, says he, Robert Dudley was the first, and the earl of Leicester the second.— Could one have believed that it could be necessary to inform monsieur de Voltaire himself, that Robert Dudley and the earl of Leicester were the same person ?

to tragedy, if tragedy is, as surely it ought to be, a picture of human life; nor can I conceive why occasional pleasantry ought more to be banished from the tragic scene, than pathetic seriousness from the comic] *On y voit un melange de serieux et de plaisanterie, de comique et de touchant*; souvent même une seule avanture *produit tous ces contrastes. Rien n'est si commun qu'une maison dans laquelle* un pere gronde, une fille occupée de sa passion pleure; *le fils se moque des deux, et quelques parens prennent part differemment à la scene, &c. Nous n'infer-ons pas de là que toute comedie doive avoir des scenes de bouffonnerie et des scenes attendrissantes: il y a beaucoup de tres bonnes pieces où il ne regne que de la gayeté; d'autres toutes serieuses; d'autres melangées: d'autres où l'attendrisse-ment va jusques aux larmes:* il ne faut donner l'exclusion à aucun genre: *et si l'on me demandoit, quel genre est le meilleur, je repondrois, celui qui est le mieux traité.*[n] Surely if a comedy may be *toute serieuse*, tragedy may now and then, soberly, be indulged in a smile. Who shall proscribe it? Shall the critic, who in self-defence declares that *no kind* ought to be excluded from comedy, give laws to Shakespeare?

I am aware that the preface from whence I have quoted these passages does not stand in monsieur de Voltaire's name, but in that of his editor; yet who doubts that the editor and author were the same person?[n] Or where is the editor, who has so happily possessed himself of his author's style and brilliant ease of argument? These passages were indubitably the genuine senti-ments of that great writer. In his epistle to Maffei, prefixed to his Merope, he delivers almost the same opinion, though I doubt with a little irony. I will repeat his words, and then give my reason for quoting them. After translating a passage in Maffei's Merope, monsieur de Voltaire adds, *Tous ces traits sont naïfs: tout y est convenable à ceux que vous introduisez sur la scene, et aux mœurs que vous leur donnez. Ces familiarités naturelles eussent eté, à ce que je crois, bien reçues dans Athenes; mais Paris et notre parterre veulent une autre espece de simplicité.*[n] I doubt, I say, whether there is not a grain of sneer in this and other passages of that epistle; yet the force of truth is not damaged by being tinged with ridicule. Maffei was to represent a Grecian story: surely the Athenians were as competent judges of Grecian manners, and of the propriety of introducing them, as the parterre of Paris. On the contrary, says Voltaire [and I cannot but admire his reasoning] there were but ten thousand citizens at Athens, and Paris has near eight hundred thousand inhabitants, among whom one may reckon thirty thousand judges of dramatic works.—Indeed!—But allowing so numerous a tribunal, I believe this is the only instance in which it was ever pretended that thirty thousand persons, living near two thousand years after the æra in question, were, upon the mere face of the poll, declared better judges than the Grecians themselves of what ought to be the manners of a tragedy written on a Grecian story.

I will not enter into a discussion of the *espece de simplicité*, which the *parterre* of Paris demands, nor of the shackles with which *the thirty thousand judges* have cramped their poetry, the chief merit of which, as I gather from repeated passages in The New Commentary on Corneille, consists in vaulting in spite of those fetters; a merit which, if true, would reduce poetry from the lofty effort of imagination, to a puerile and most contemptible labour – *difficiles nugæ*[n] with a witness! I cannot help however mentioning a couplet, which to my English ears always sounded as the flattest and most trifling instance of circumstantial propriety; but which Voltaire, who has dealt so severely with nine parts in ten of Corneille's works, has singled out to defend in Racine;

> *De son appartement cette porte est prochaine,*
> *Et cette autre conduit dans celui de la reine.*[n]

In English,
To Cæsar's closet through this door you come,
And t'other leads to the queen's drawing-room.

Unhappy Shakespeare! hadst thou made Rosencrans inform his compeer Guildenstern of the ichnography[n] of the palace of Copenhagen, instead of presenting us with a moral dialogue between the prince of Denmark and the grave-digger, the illuminated pit of Paris would have been instructed *a second time* to adore thy talents.

The result of all I have said, is to shelter my own daring under the cannon of the brightest genius this country, at least, has produced. I might have pleaded, that having created a new species of romance, I was at liberty to lay down what rules I thought fit for the conduct of it : but I should be more proud of having imitated, however faintly, weakly, and at a distance, so masterly a pattern, than to enjoy the entire merit of invention, unless I could have marked my work with genius as well as with originality. Such as it is, the public have honoured it sufficiently, whatever rank their suffrages allot to it.[n]

SONNET

To the Right Honourable
LADY MARY COKE[n]

The gentle maid, whose hapless tale
These melancholy pages speak;
Say, gracious lady, shall she fail
To draw the tear adown thy cheek?

No; never was thy pitying breast
Insensible to human woes;
Tender, though firm, it melts distrest
For weaknesses it never knows.

Oh! guard the marvels I relate
Of fell ambition scourg'd by fate,
    From reason's peevish blame:
Blest with thy smile, my dauntless sail
I dare expand to fancy's gale,
    For sure thy smiles are fame.

H. W.

CHAPTER 1

Manfred, prince of Otranto, had one son and one daughter : the latter, a most beautiful virgin, aged eighteen, was called Matilda. Conrad, the son, was three years younger, a homely youth, sickly, and of no promising disposition; yet he was the darling of his father, who never showed any symptoms of affection to Matilda. Manfred had contracted a marriage for his son with the marquis of Vicenza's daughter, Isabella; and she had already been delivered by her guardians into the hands of Manfred, that he might celebrate the wedding as soon as Conrad's infirm state of health would permit. Manfred's impatience for this ceremonial was remarked by his family and neighbours. The former, indeed, apprehending the severity of their prince's disposition, did not dare to utter their surmises on this precipitation. Hippolita, his wife, an amiable lady, did sometimes venture to represent the danger of marrying their only son so early, considering his great youth, and greater infirmities; but she never received any other answer than reflections on her own sterility, who had given him but one heir. His tenants and subjects were less cautious in their discourses : they attributed this hasty wedding to the prince's dread of seeing accomplished an ancient prophecy, which was said to have pronounced, *That the castle and lordship of Otranto should pass from the present family, whenever the real owner should be grown too large to inhabit it.* It was difficult to make any sense of this prophecy; and still less easy to conceive what it had to do with the marriage in question. Yet these mysteries, or contradictions, did not make the populace adhere the less to their opinion.

Young Conrad's birth-day was fixed for his espousals. The

company was assembled in the chapel of the castle, and every thing ready for beginning the divine office, when Conrad himself was missing. Manfred, impatient of the least delay, and who had not observed his son retire, dispatched one of his attendants to summon the young prince. The servant, who had not staid long enough to have crossed the court to Conrad's apartment, came running back breathless, in a frantic manner, his eyes staring, and foaming at the mouth. He said nothing, but pointed to the court. The company were struck with terror and amazement. The princess Hippolita, without knowing what was the matter, but anxious for her son, swooned away. Manfred, less apprehensive than enraged at the procrastination of the nuptials, and at the folly of his domestic, asked imperiously, what was the matter? The fellow made no answer, but continued pointing towards the court-yard; and at last, after repeated questions put to him, cried out, Oh, the helmet! the helmet! In the mean time some of the company had run into the court, from whence was heard a confused noise of shrieks, horror, and surprise. Manfred, who began to be alarmed at not seeing his son, went himself to get information of what occasioned this strange confusion. Matilda remained endeavouring to assist her mother, and Isabella staid for the same purpose, and to avoid showing any impatience for the bridegroom, for whom, in truth, she had conceived little affection.

The first thing that struck Manfred's eyes was a group of his servants endeavouring to raise something that appeared to him a mountain of sable plumes. He gazed without believing his sight. What are ye doing? cried Manfred, wrathfully: Where is my son? A volley of voices replied, Oh, my lord! the prince! the prince! the helmet! the helmet! Shocked with these lamentable sounds, and dreading he knew not what, he advanced hastily—But what a sight for a father's eyes! – He beheld his child dashed to pieces, and almost buried under an enormous helmet, an hundred times more large than any casque[n] ever made for human being, and shaded with a proportionable quantity of black feathers.

The horror of the spectacle, the ignorance of all around how this misfortune happened, and above all, the tremendous

phænomenon before him, took away the prince's speech. Yet
his silence lasted longer than even grief could occasion. He fixed
his eyes on what he wished in vain to believe a vision; and
seemed less attentive to his loss, than buried in meditation on
the stupendous object that had occasioned it. He touched, he
examined the fatal casque; nor could even the bleeding mangled
remains of the young prince divert the eyes of Manfred from the
portent before him. All who had known his partial fondness for
young Conrad, were as much surprised at their prince's insens-
ibility, as thunderstruck themselves at the miracle of the helmet.
They conveyed the disfigured corpse into the hall, without
receiving the least direction from Manfred. As little was he
attentive to the ladies who remained in the chapel: on the
contrary, without mentioning the unhappy princesses his wife
and daughter, the first sounds that dropped from Manfred's lips
were, Take care of the lady Isabella.

The domestics, without observing the singularity of this
direction, were guided by their affection to their mistress to
consider it as peculiarly addressed to her situation, and flew to
her assistance. They conveyed her to her chamber more dead
than alive, and indifferent to all the strange circumstances she
heard, except the death of her son. Matilda, who doted on her
mother, smothered her own grief and amazement, and thought
of nothing but assisting and comforting her afflicted parent.
Isabella, who had been treated by Hippolita like a daughter, and
who returned that tenderness with equal duty and affection, was
scarce less assiduous about the princess; at the same time
endeavouring to partake and lessen the weight of sorrow which
she saw Matilda strove to suppress, for whom she had conceived
the warmest sympathy of friendship. Yet her own situation
could not help finding its place in her thoughts. She felt no
concern for the death of young Conrad, except commiseration;
and she was not sorry to be delivered from a marriage which
had promised her little felicity, either from her destined bridegroom, or from the severe temper of Manfred, who, though he
had distinguished her by great indulgence, had imprinted her
mind with terror, from his causeless rigour to such amiable
princesses as Hippolita and Matilda.

While the ladies were conveying the wretched mother to her bed, Manfred remained in the court, gazing on the ominous casque, and regardless of the crowd which the strangeness of the event had now assembled round him. The few words he articulated tended solely to enquiries, whether any man knew from whence it could have come? Nobody could give him the least information. However, as it seemed to be the sole object of his curiosity, it soon became so to the rest of the spectators, whose conjectures were as absurd and improbable as the catastrophe itself was unprecedented. In the midst of their senseless guesses a young peasant, whom rumour had drawn thither from a neighbouring village, observed that the miraculous helmet was exactly like that on the figure in black marble of Alfonso the Good, one of their former princes, in the church of St Nicholas. Villain! What sayest thou? cried Manfred, starting from his trance in a tempest of rage, and seizing the young man by the collar: How darest thou utter such treason? Thy life shall pay for it. The spectators, who as little comprehended the cause of the prince's fury as all the rest they had seen, were at a loss to unravel this new circumstance. The young peasant himself was still more astonished, not conceiving how he had offended the prince: yet recollecting himself, with a mixture of grace and humility, he disengaged himself from Manfred's gripe, and then, with an obeisance which discovered more jealousy of innocence, than dismay, he asked with respect, of what he was guilty? Manfred, more enraged at the vigour, however decently exerted, with which the young man had shaken off his hold, than appeased by his submission, ordered his attendants to seize him, and, if he had not been withheld by his friends whom he had invited to the nuptials, would have poignarded[n] the peasant in their arms.

During this altercation some of the vulgar spectators had run to the great church which stood near the castle, and came back open-mouthed, declaring the helmet was missing from Alfonso's statue. Manfred, at this news, grew perfectly frantic; and, as if he sought a subject on which to vent the tempest within him, he rushed again on the young peasant, crying, Villain! monster! sorcerer! 'tis thou hast slain my son! The mob, who wanted some object within the scope of their capacities on whom they might discharge their bewildered reasonings, caught the words from the mouth of their lord, and re-echoed, Ay, ay, 'tis he, 'tis he: he has stolen the helmet from good Alfonso's tomb, and dashed out the brains of our young prince with it: — never reflecting how enormous the disproportion was between the marble helmet that had been in the church, and that of steel before their eyes; nor how impossible it was for a youth, seemingly not twenty, to wield a piece of armour of so prodigious a weight.

The folly of these ejaculations brought Manfred to himself: yet whether provoked at the peasant having observed the resemblance between the two helmets, and thereby led to the farther discovery of the absence of that in the church; or wishing to bury any fresh rumour under so impertinent a supposition; he gravely pronounced that the young man was certainly a necromancer, and that till the church could take cognizance of the affair, he would have the magician, whom they had thus detected, kept prisoner under the helmet itself, which he ordered his attendants to raise, and place the young man under it; declaring he should be kept there without food, with which his own infernal art might furnish him.

It was in vain for the youth to represent against this preposterous sentence: in vain did Manfred's friends endeavour to divert him from this savage and ill-grounded resolution. The generality were charmed with their lord's decision, which to their apprehensions carried great appearance of justice, as the magician was to be punished by the very instrument with which he had offended: nor were they struck with the least compunction at the probability of the youth being starved, for they firmly believed that by his diabolical skill he could easily supply himself with nutriment.

Manfred thus saw his commands even cheerfully obeyed; and appointing a guard with strict orders to prevent any food being conveyed to the prisoner, he dismissed his friends and attendants, and retired to his own chamber, after locking the gates of the castle, in which he suffered none but his domestics to remain.

In the mean time, the care and zeal of the young ladies had brought the princess Hippolita to herself, who amidst the transports of her own sorrow frequently demanded news of her lord, would have dismissed her attendants to watch over him, and at last enjoined Matilda to leave her, and visit and comfort her father. Matilda, who wanted no affectionate duty to Manfred, though she trembled at his austerity, obeyed the orders of Hippolita, whom she tenderly recommended to Isabella; and enquiring of the domestics for her father, was informed that he was retired to his chamber, and had commanded that nobody should have admittance to him. Concluding that he was immersed in sorrow for the death of her brother, and fearing to renew his tears by the sight of his sole remaining child, she hesitated whether she should break in upon his affliction; yet solicitude for him, backed by the commands of her mother, encouraged her to venture disobeying the orders he had given; a fault she had never been guilty of before. The gentle timidity of her nature made her pause for some minutes at his door. She heard him traverse his chamber backwards and forwards with disordered steps; a mood which increased her apprehensions. She was however just going to beg admittance, when Manfred suddenly opened the door; and as it was now twilight, concurring with the disorder of his mind, he did not distinguish the person, but asked angrily who it was? Matilda replied trembling, My dearest father, it is I, your daughter. Manfred, stepping back hastily, cried, Begone, I do not want a daughter; and, flinging back abruptly, clapped the door against the terrified Matilda.

She was too well acquainted with her father's impetuosity to venture a second intrusion. When she had a little recovered the shock of so bitter a reception, she wiped away her tears, to prevent the additional stab that the knowledge of it would give to Hippolita, who questioned her in the most anxious terms on the health of Manfred, and how he bore his loss. Matilda assured her he was well, and supported his misfortune with manly fortitude. But will he not let me see him? said Hippolita mournfully: Will he not permit me to blend my tears with his, and shed a mother's sorrows in the bosom of her lord? Or do you deceive me, Matilda? I know how Manfred doted on his son: Is not the stroke too heavy for him? Has he not sunk under it? – You do not answer me – Alas, I dread the worst! – Raise me, my maidens: I will, I will see my lord. Bear me to him instantly; he is dearer to me even than my children. Matilda made signs to Isabella to prevent Hippolita's rising; and both these lovely young women were using their gentle violence to stop and calm the princess, when a servant on the part of Manfred arrived, and told Isabella that his lord demanded to speak with her.

With me! cried Isabella. Go, said Hippolita, relieved by a message from her lord: Manfred cannot support the sight of his own family. He thinks you less disordered than we are, and dreads the shock of my grief. Console him, dear Isabella, and tell him I will smother my own anguish rather than add to his.

It was now evening; the servant who conducted Isabella bore a torch before her. When they came to Manfred, who was walking impatiently about the gallery, he started and said hastily, Take away that light, and begone. Then shutting the door impetuously, he flung himself upon a bench against the wall, and bade Isabella sit by him. She obeyed trembling. I sent for you, lady, said he, – and then stopped under great appearance of confusion. My lord! – Yes, I sent for you on a matter of great moment, resumed he: – Dry your tears, young lady – you have lost your bridegroom: – yes, cruel fate, and I have lost the hopes of my race! – But Conrad was not worthy of your beauty. – How! my lord, said Isabella; sure you do not suspect me of not feeling the concern I ought? My duty and affection would have always – Think no more of him, interrupted Manfred; he was a sickly puny child, and heaven has perhaps taken him away that I might not trust the honours of my house on so frail a foundation. The line of Manfred calls for numerous supports. My foolish fondness for that boy blinded the eyes of my prudence – but it is better as it is. I hope in a few years to have reason to rejoice at the death of Conrad.

Words cannot paint the astonishment of Isabella. At first she apprehended that grief had disordered Manfred's understanding. Her next thought suggested that this strange discourse was designed to ensnare her: she feared that Manfred had perceived her indifference for his son: and in consequence of that idea she replied, Good my lord, do not doubt my tenderness; my heart would have accompanied my hand. Conrad would have engrossed all my care; and wherever fate shall dispose of me, I shall always cherish his memory, and regard your highness and the virtuous Hippolita as my parents. Curse on Hippolita! cried Manfred: forget her from this moment, as I do. In short, lady, you have missed a husband undeserving of your charms: they shall now be better disposed of. Instead of a sickly boy, you shall have a husband in the prime of his age, who will know how to value your beauties, and who may expect a numerous offspring. Alas, my lord, said Isabella, my mind is too sadly engrossed by the recent catastrophe in your family to think of another marriage. If ever my father returns, and it shall be his pleasure, I shall obey, as I did when I consented to give my hand to your son: but until his return permit me to remain under your hospitable roof, and employ the melancholy hours in assuaging yours, Hippolita's, and the fair Matilda's affliction.

I desired you once before, said Manfred angrily, not to name that woman; from this hour she must be a stranger to you, as she must be to me: — in short, Isabella, since I cannot give you my son, I offer you myself. — Heavens! cried Isabella, waking from her delusion, what do I hear! You, my lord! You! My father in law! the father of Conrad! the husband of the virtuous and tender Hippolita! — I tell you, said Manfred imperiously, Hippolita is no longer my wife; I divorce her from this hour. Too long has she cursed me by her unfruitfulness: my fate depends on having sons, — and this night I trust will give a new date to my hopes. At those words he seized the cold hand of Isabella, who was half-dead with fright and horror. She shrieked, and started from him. Manfred rose to pursue her; when the moon, which was now up, and gleamed in at the opposite casement, presented to his sight the plumes of the fatal helmet, which rose to the height of the windows, waving backwards and forwards in a tempestuous manner, and accompanied with a hollow and rustling sound. Isabella, who gathered courage from her situation, and who dreaded nothing so much as Manfred's pursuit of his declaration, cried, Look, my lord! see heaven itself declares against your impious intentions! – Heaven nor hell shall impede my designs, said Manfred, advancing again to seize the princess. At that instant the portrait of his grandfather, which hung over the bench where they had been sitting, uttered a deep sigh and heaved its breast. Isabella, whose back was turned to the picture, saw not the motion, nor knew whence the sound came, but started and said, Hark, my lord! what sound was that? and at the same time made towards the door. Manfred, distracted between the flight of Isabella, who had now reached the stairs, and his inability to keep his eyes from the picture, which began to move, had however advanced some steps after her, still looking backwards on the portrait, when he saw it quit its pannel, and descend on the floor with a grave and melancholy air. Do I dream? cried Manfred returning, or are the devils themselves in league against me? Speak, infernal spectre! Or, if thou art my grandsire, why dost thou too conspire against thy wretched descendant, who too dearly pays for – Ere he could finish the sentence the vision sighed again, and made a sign to Manfred to follow him. Lead on! cried Manfred; I will follow thee to the gulph of perdition.[n] The spectre marched sedately, but dejected, to the end of the gallery, and turned into a chamber on the right hand. Manfred accompanied him at a little distance, full of anxiety and horror, but resolved. As he would have entered the chamber, the door was clapped-to with violence by an invisible hand. The prince, collecting courage from this delay, would have forcibly burst open the door with his foot, but found that it resisted his utmost efforts. Since hell will not satisfy my curiosity, said Manfred, I will use the human means in my power for preserving my race; Isabella shall not escape me.

That lady, whose resolution had given way to terror the moment she had quitted Manfred, continued her flight to the bottom of the principal staircase. There she stopped, not knowing whither to direct her steps, nor how to escape from the impetuosity of the prince. The gates of the castle she knew were locked, and guards placed in the court. Should she, as her heart prompted her, go and prepare Hippolita for the cruel destiny that awaited her, she did not doubt but Manfred would seek her there, and that his violence would incite him to double the injury he meditated, without leaving room for them to avoid the impetuosity of his passions. Delay might give him time to reflect on the horrid measures he had conceived, or produce some circumstance in her favour, if she could for that night at least avoid his odious purpose.—Yet where conceal herself! How avoid the pursuit he would infallibly make throughout the castle! As these thoughts passed rapidly through her mind, she recollected a subterraneous passage which led from the vaults of the castle to the church of saint Nicholas. Could she reach the altar before she was overtaken, she knew even Manfred's violence would not dare to profane the sacredness of the place; and she determined, if no other means of deliverance offered, to shut herself up for ever among the holy virgins, whose convent was contiguous to the cathedral. In this resolution, she seized a lamp that burned at the foot of the staircase, and hurried towards the secret passage.

The lower part of the castle was hollowed into several intricate cloisters; and it was not easy for one under so much anxiety to find the door that opened into the cavern. An awful silence reigned throughout those subterraneous regions, except now and then some blasts of wind that shook the doors she had passed, and which grating on the rusty hinges were re-echoed through that long labyrinth of darkness. Every murmur struck her with new terror; – yet more she dreaded to hear the wrathful voice of Manfred urging his domestics to pursue her. She trod as softly as impatience would give her leave, – yet frequently stopped and listened to hear if she was followed. In one of those moments she thought she heard a sigh. She shuddered, and recoiled a few paces. In a moment she thought she heard the step of some person. Her blood curdled; she concluded it was Manfred. Every suggestion that horror could inspire rushed into her mind. She condemned her rash flight, which had thus exposed her to his rage in a place where her cries were not likely to draw any body to her assistance. – Yet the sound seemed not to come from behind; – if Manfred knew where she was, he must have followed her : she was still in one of the cloisters, and the steps she had heard were too distinct to proceed from the way she had come. Cheered with this reflection, and hoping to find a friend in whoever was not the prince ; she was going to advance, when a door that stood a-jar, at some distance to the left, was opened gently ; but ere her lamp, which she held up, could discover who opened it, the person retreated precipitately on seeing the light.

Isabella, whom every incident was sufficient to dismay, hesitated whether she should proceed. Her dread of Manfred soon outweighed every other terror. The very circumstance of the person avoiding her, gave her a sort of courage. It could only be, she thought, some domestic belonging to the castle. Her gentleness had never raised her an enemy, and conscious innocence made her hope that, unless sent by the prince's order to seek her, his servants would rather assist than prevent her flight. Fortifying herself with these reflections, and believing, by what she could observe, that she was near the mouth of the subterraneous cavern, she approached the door that had been opened ; but a sudden gust of wind that met her at the door extinguished her lamp, and left her in total darkness.

Words cannot paint the horror of the princess's situation. Alone in so dismal a place, her mind imprinted with all the terrible events of the day, hopeless of escaping, expecting every moment the arrival of Manfred, and far from tranquil on knowing she was within reach of somebody, she knew not whom, who for some cause seemed concealed thereabouts, all these thoughts crowded on her distracted mind, and she was ready to sink under her apprehensions. She addressed herself to every saint in heaven, and inwardly implored their assistance. For a considerable time she remained in an agony of despair. At last, as softly as was possible, she felt for the door, and, having found it, entered trembling into the vault from whence she had heard the sigh and steps. It gave her a kind of momentary joy to perceive an imperfect ray of clouded moonshine gleam from the roof of the vault, which seemed to be fallen in, and from whence hung a fragment of earth or building, she could not distinguish which, that appeared to have been crushed inwards.

She advanced eagerly towards this chasm, when she discerned a human form standing close against the wall.

She shrieked, believing it the ghost of her betrothed Conrad. The figure advancing, said in a submissive voice, Be not alarmed, lady; I will not injure you. Isabella, a little encouraged by the words and tone of voice of the stranger, and recollecting that this must be the person who had opened the door, recovered her spirits enough to reply, Sir, whoever you are, take pity on a wretched princess standing on the brink of destruction: assist me to escape from this fatal castle, or in a few moments I may be made miserable for ever. Alas! said the stranger, what can I do to assist you? I will die in your defence; but I am unacquainted with the castle, and want—Oh! said Isabella, hastily interrupting him, help me but to find a trap-door that must be hereabout, and it is the greatest service you can do me; for I have not a minute to lose. Saying these words she felt about on the pavement, and directed the stranger to search likewise for a smooth piece of brass inclosed in one of the stones. That, said she, is the lock, which opens with a spring, of which I know the secret. If I can find that, I may escape – if not, alas, courteous stranger, I fear I shall have involved you in my misfortunes: Manfred will suspect you for the accomplice of my flight, and you will fall a victim to his resentment. I value not my life, said the stranger; and it will be some comfort to lose it in trying to deliver you from his tyranny. Generous youth, said Isabella, how shall I ever requite—As she uttered those words, a ray of moonshine streaming through a cranny of the ruin above shone directly on the lock they sought – Oh, transport! said Isabella, here is the trap-door! and taking out a key, she touched the spring, which starting aside discovered an iron ring. Lift up the door, said the princess. The stranger obeyed; and beneath appeared some stone steps descending into a vault totally dark. We must go down here, said Isabella: follow me; dark and dismal as it is, we cannot miss our way; it leads directly to the church of saint Nicholas – But perhaps, added the princess modestly, you have no reason to leave the castle, nor have I farther occasion for your service; in a few minutes I shall be safe from Manfred's rage – only let me know to whom I am so much obliged. I will never quit you, said the stranger eagerly, till I have placed you in safety − nor think me, princess, more generous than I am: though you are my principal care—The stranger was interrupted by a sudden noise of voices that seemed approaching, and they soon distinguished these words: Talk not to me of necromancers; I tell you she must be in the castle; I will find her in spite of enchantment. − Oh, heavens! cried Isabella, it is the voice of Manfred! Make haste, or we are ruined! and shut the trap-door after you. Saying this, she descended the steps precipitately; and as the stranger hastened to follow her, he let the door slip out of his hands: it fell, and the spring closed over it. He tried in vain to open it, not having observed Isabella's method of touching the spring, nor had he many moments to make an essay. The noise of the falling door had been heard by Manfred, who, directed by the sound, hastened thither, attended by his servants with torches. It must be Isabella, cried Manfred before he entered the vault; she is escaping by the subterraneous passage, but she cannot have got far. − What was the astonishment of the prince, when, instead of Isabella, the light of the torches discovered to him the young peasant, whom he thought confined under the fatal helmet! Traitor! said Manfred, how camest thou here? I thought thee in durance above in the court. I am no traitor, replied the young man boldly, nor am I answerable for your thoughts. Presumptuous villain! cried Manfred, dost thou provoke my wrath? Tell me; how hast thou escaped from above? Thou hast corrupted thy guards, and their lives shall answer it. My poverty, said the peasant calmly, will disculpate[n] them: though the ministers of a tyrant's wrath, to thee they are faithful, and but too willing to execute the orders which you unjustly imposed upon them. Art thou so hardy as to dare my vengeance? said the prince − but tortures shall force the truth from thee. Tell me, I will know thy accomplices. There was my accomplice! said the youth smiling, and pointing to the roof. Manfred ordered the torches to be held up, and perceived that one of the cheeks of the enchanted casque had forced its way through the pavement of the court, as his servants had let it fall over the peasant, and had broken through into the vault, leaving a gap through which the peasant had pressed himself some minutes before he was found by Isabella. Was that the way by which thou didst descend? said Manfred. It was, said the youth. But what noise was that, said Manfred, which I heard as I entered the cloister? A door clapped, said the peasant: I heard it as well as you. What door? said Manfred hastily. I am not acquainted with your castle, said the peasant; this is the first time I ever entered it, and this vault the only part of it within which I ever was. But I tell thee, said Manfred, [wishing to find out if the youth had discovered the trap-door] it was this way I heard the noise: my servants heard it too. — My lord, interrupted one of them officiously, to be sure it was the trap-door, and he was going to make his escape. Peace! blockhead, said the prince angrily; if he was going to escape, how should he come on this side? I will know from his own mouth what noise it was I heard. Tell me truly; thy life depends on thy veracity. My veracity is dearer to me than my life, said the peasant; nor would I purchase the one by forfeiting the other. Indeed! young philosopher! said Manfred contemptuously: tell me then, what was the noise I heard? Ask me what I can answer, said he, and put me to death instantly if I tell you a lie. Manfred, growing impatient at the steady valour and indifference of the youth, cried, Well then, thou man of truth! answer; was it the fall of the trap-door that I heard? It was, said the youth. It was! said the prince; and how didst thou come to know there was a trap-door here? I saw the plate of brass by a gleam of moonshine, replied he. But what told thee it was a lock? said Manfred: How didst thou discover the secret of opening it? Providence, that delivered me from the helmet, was able to direct me to the spring of a lock, said he. Providence should have gone a little farther, and have placed thee out of the reach of my resentment, said Manfred: when Providence had taught thee to open the lock, it abandoned thee for a fool, who did not know how to make use of its favours. Why didst thou not pursue the path pointed out for thy escape? Why didst thou shut the trap-door before thou hadst descended the steps? I might ask you, my lord, said the peasant, how I, totally unacquainted with your castle, was to know that those steps led to any outlet? but I scorn to evade your questions. Wherever those steps lead to, perhaps I should have explored the way – I could not have been in a worse situation than I was. But the truth is, I let the trap-door fall : your immediate arrival followed. I had given the alarm – what imported it to me whether I was seized a minute sooner or a minute later ? Thou art a resolute villain for thy years, said Manfred – yet on reflection I suspect thou dost but trifle with me : thou hast not yet told me how thou didst open the lock. That I will show you, my lord, said the peasant ; and taking up a fragment of stone that had fallen from above, he laid himself on the trap-door, and began to beat on the piece of brass that covered it ; meaning to gain time for the escape of the princess. This presence of mind, joined to the frankness of the youth, staggered Manfred. He even felt a disposition towards pardoning one who had been guilty of no crime. Manfred was not one of those savage tyrants who wanton in cruelty unprovoked. The circumstances of his fortune had given an asperity to his temper, which was naturally humane ; and his virtues were always ready to operate, when his passion did not obscure his reason.

While the prince was in this suspense, a confused noise of voices echoed through the distant vaults. As the sound approached, he distinguished the clamour of some of his domestics, whom he had dispersed through the castle in search of Isabella, calling out, Where is my lord ? Where is the prince ? Here I am, said Manfred, as they came nearer ; have you found the princess ? The first that arrived replied, Oh, my lord ! I am glad we have found you. – Found me ! said Manfred : have you found the princess ? We thought we had, my lord, said the fellow looking terrified – but – But what ? cried the prince : has she escaped ? – Jaquez and I, my lord – Yes, I and Diego, interrupted the second, who came up in still greater consternation – Speak one of you at a time, said Manfred ; I ask you, where is the princess ? We do not know, said they both together : but we are frightened out of our wits. – So I think, blockheads, said Manfred : what is it has scared you thus ? – Oh, my lord ! said Jaquez, Diego has seen such a sight ! your highness would not believe our eyes. – What new absurdity is this ? cried Manfred – Give me a direct answer, or by heaven – Why, my lord, if it please your highness to hear me, said the poor fellow; Diego and I — Yes, I and Jaquez, cried his comrade — Did not I forbid you to speak both at a time? said the prince: You, Jaquez, answer; for the other fool seems more distracted than thou art; what is the matter? My gracious lord, said Jaquez, if it please your highness to hear me; Diego and I, according to your highness's orders, went to search for the young lady; but being comprehensive[n] that we might meet the ghost of my young lord, your highness's son, God rest his soul, as he has not received christian burial — Sot! cried Manfred in a rage, is it only a ghost then that thou hast seen? Oh, worse! worse! my lord! cried Diego: I had rather have seen ten whole ghosts. — Grant me patience! said Manfred; these blockheads distract me — Out of my sight, Diego! And thou, Jaquez, tell me in one word, art thou sober? art thou raving? Thou wast wont to have some sense: has the other sot frightened himself and thee too? Speak; what is it he fancies he has seen? Why, my lord, replied Jaquez trembling, I was going to tell your highness, that since the calamitous misfortune of my young lord, God rest his soul! not one of us your highness's faithful servants, indeed we are, my lord, though poor men; I say, not one of us has dared to set a foot about the castle, but two together: so Diego and I, thinking that my young lady might be in the great gallery, went up there to look for her, and tell her your highness wanted something to impart to her. — O blundering fools! cried Manfred: and in the mean time she has made her escape, because you were afraid of goblins! Why, thou knave! she left me in the gallery; I came from thence myself. — For all that, she may be there still for aught I know, said Jaquez; but the devil shall have me before I seek her there again! — Poor Diego! I do not believe he will ever recover it! Recover what? said Manfred; am I never to learn what it is has terrified these rascals? But I lose my time; follow me, slave! I will see if she is in the gallery. — For heaven's sake, my dear good lord, cried Jaquez, do not go to the gallery! Satan himself I believe is in the great chamber next to the gallery. — Manfred, who hitherto had treated the terror of his servants as an idle panic, was struck at this new circumstance. He recollected the apparition of the portrait, and the sudden closing of the door at the end of the gallery – his voice faltered, and he asked with disorder, what is in the great chamber? My lord, said Jaquez, when Diego and I came into the gallery, he went first, for he said he had more courage than I. So when we came into the gallery, we found nobody. We looked under every bench and stool; and still we found nobody. – Were all the pictures in their places? said Manfred. Yes, my lord, answered Jaquez; but we did not think of looking behind them. – Well, well! said Manfred; proceed. When we came to the door of the great chamber, continued Jaquez, we found it shut. – And could not you open it? said Manfred. Oh! yes, my lord, would to heaven we had not! replied he – Nay, it was not I neither, it was Diego: he was grown fool-hardy, and would go on, though I advised him not – If ever I open a door that is shut again – Trifle not, said Manfred shuddering, but tell me what you saw in the great chamber on opening the door. – I! my lord! said Jaquez, I saw nothing; I was behind Diego; – but I heard the noise. – Jaquez, said Manfred in a solemn tone of voice, tell me, I adjure thee by the souls of my ancestors, what it was thou sawest; what it was thou heardest? It was Diego saw it, my lord, it was not I, replied Jaquez; I only heard the noise. Diego had no sooner opened the door, than he cried out and ran back – I ran back too, and said, Is it the ghost? The ghost! No, no, said Diego, and his hair stood on end – it is a giant, I believe; he is all clad in armour, for I saw his foot and part of his leg, and they are as large as the helmet below in the court. As he said these words, my lord, we heard a violent motion and the rattling of armour, as if the giant was rising; for Diego has told me since, that he believes the giant was lying down, for the foot and leg were stretched at length on the floor. Before we could get to the end of the gallery, we heard the door of the great chamber clap behind us, but we did not dare turn back to see if the giant was following us – Yet now I think on it, we must have heard him if he had pursued us – But for heaven's sake, good my lord, send for the chaplain and have the castle exorcised, for, for certain, it is enchanted. Ay, pray do, my lord, cried all the servants at once, or we must leave your highness's service. – Peace, dotards! said Manfred, and follow me; I will

know what all this means. We! my lord! cried they with one
voice; we would not go up to the gallery for your highness's
revenue. The young peasant, who had stood silent, now spoke.
Will your highness, said he, permit me to try this adventure?
My life is of consequence to nobody: I fear no bad angel, and
have offended no good one. Your behaviour is above your
seeming, said Manfred; viewing him with surprise and admiration – hereafter I will reward your bravery – but now,
continued he with a sigh, I am so circumstanced, that I dare
trust no eyes but my own – However, I give you leave to
accompany me.

　Manfred, when he first followed Isabella from the gallery, had
gone directly to the apartment of his wife, concluding the
princess had retired thither. Hippolita, who knew his step, rose
with anxious fondness to meet her lord, whom she had not seen
since the death of their son. She would have flown in a transport
mixed of joy and grief to his bosom; but he pushed her rudely
off, and said, Where is Isabella? Isabella! my lord! said the
astonished Hippolita. Yes, Isabella; cried Manfred imperiously;
I want Isabella. My lord, replied Matilda, who perceived how
much his behaviour had shocked her mother, she has not been
with us since your highness summoned her to your apartment.
Tell me where she is, said the prince; I do not want to know
where she has been. My good lord, said Hippolita, your
daughter tells you the truth: Isabella left us by your command,
and has not returned since: – but, my good lord, compose
yourself: retire to your rest: this dismal day has disordered you.
Isabella shall wait your orders in the morning. What, then you
know where she is? cried Manfred: tell me directly, for I will
not lose an instant – And you, woman, speaking to his wife,
order your chaplain to attend me forthwith. Isabella, said
Hippolita calmly, is retired I suppose to her chamber: she is not
accustomed to watch at this late hour. Gracious my lord,
continued she, let me know what has disturbed you: has Isabella
offended you? Trouble me not with questions, said Manfred,
but tell me where she is. Matilda shall call her, said the princess
– sit down, my lord, and resume your wonted fortitude. – What,
art thou jealous of Isabella, replied he, that you wish to be

present at our interview? Good heavens! my lord, said Hippolita, what is it your highness means? Thou wilt know ere many minutes are passed, said the cruel prince. Send your chaplain to me, and wait my pleasure here. At these words he flung out of the room in search of Isabella; leaving the amazed ladies thunder-struck with his words and frantic deportment, and lost in vain conjectures on what he was meditating.

Manfred was now returning from the vault, attended by the peasant and a few of his servants whom he had obliged to accompany him. He ascended the stair-case without stopping till he arrived at the gallery, at the door of which he met Hippolita and her chaplain. When Diego had been dismissed by Manfred, he had gone directly to the princess's apartment with the alarm of what he had seen. That excellent lady, who no more than Manfred doubted of the reality of the vision, yet affected to treat it as a delirium of the servant. Willing, however, to save her lord from any additional shock, and prepared by a series of griefs not to tremble at any accession to it; she determined to make herself the first sacrifice, if fate had marked the present hour for their destruction. Dismissing the reluctant Matilda to her rest, who in vain sued for leave to accompany her mother, and attended only by her chaplain, Hippolita had visited the gallery and great chamber: and now, with more serenity of soul than she had felt for many hours, she met her lord, and assured him that the vision of the gigantic leg and foot was all a fable; and no doubt an impression made by fear, and the dark and dismal hour of the night, on the minds of his servants: She and the chaplain had examined the chamber, and found every thing in the usual order.

Manfred, though persuaded, like his wife, that the vision had been no work of fancy, recovered a little from the tempest of mind into which so many strange events had thrown him. Ashamed too of his inhuman treatment of a princess, who returned every injury with new marks of tenderness and duty, he felt returning love forcing itself into his eyes – but not less ashamed of feeling remorse towards one, against whom he was inwardly meditating a yet more bitter outrage, he curbed the yearnings of his heart, and did not dare to lean even towards pity. The next transition of his soul was to exquisite villainy. Presuming on the unshaken submission of Hippolita, he flattered himself that she would not only acquiesce with patience to a divorce, but would obey, if it was his pleasure, in endeavouring to persuade Isabella to give him her hand — But ere he could indulge this horrid hope, he reflected that Isabella was not to be found. Coming to himself, he gave orders that every avenue to the castle should be strictly guarded, and charged his domestics on pain of their lives to suffer nobody to pass out. The young peasant, to whom he spoke favourably, he ordered to remain in a small chamber on the stairs, in which there was a pallet-bed,[n] and the key of which he took away himself, telling the youth he would talk with him in the morning. Then dismissing his attendants, and bestowing a sullen kind of half-nod on Hippolita, he retired to his own chamber.

CHAPTER 2

Matilda, who by Hippolita's order had retired to her apartment, was ill-disposed to take any rest. The shocking fate of her brother had deeply affected her. She was surprised at not seeing Isabella: but the strange words which had fallen from her father, and his obscure menace to the princess his wife, accompanied by the most furious behaviour, had filled her gentle mind with terror and alarm. She waited anxiously for the return of Bianca, a young damsel that attended her, whom she had sent to learn what was become of Isabella. Bianca soon appeared, and informed her mistress of what she had gathered from the servants, that Isabella was no where to be found. She related the adventure of the young peasant, who had been discovered in the vault, though with many simple additions from the incoherent accounts of the domestics; and she dwelled principally on the gigantic leg and foot which had been seen in the gallery-chamber. This last circumstance had terrified Bianca so much, that she was rejoiced when Matilda told her that she would not go to rest, but would watch till the princess should rise.

The young princess wearied herself in conjectures on the flight of Isabella, and on the threats of Manfred to her mother. But what business could he have so urgent with the chaplain? said Matilda. Does he intend to have my brother's body interred privately in the chapel? Oh! madam, said Bianca, now I guess. As you are become his heiress, he is impatient to have you married: he has always been raving for more sons; I warrant he is now impatient for grandsons. As sure as I live, madam, I shall see you a bride at last. Good madam, you won't cast off your faithful Bianca: you won't put Donna Rosara over me, now you are a great princess? My poor Bianca, said Matilda, how fast your thoughts amble! I a great princess! What hast thou seen in Manfred's behaviour since my brother's death that bespeaks any increase of tenderness to me? No, Bianca, his heart was ever a stranger to me – but he is my father, and I must not complain. Nay, if heaven shuts my father's heart against me, it over-pays my little merit in the tenderness of my mother – O that dear mother! Yes, Bianca, 'tis there I feel the rugged temper of Manfred. I can support his harshness to me with patience; but it wounds my soul when I am witness to his causeless severity towards her. Oh, madam, said Bianca, all men use their wives so, when they are weary of them. – And yet you congratulated me but now, said Matilda, when you fancied my father intended to dispose of me. I would have you a great lady, replied Bianca, come what will. I do not wish to see you moped in a convent, as you would be if you had your will, and if my lady your mother, who knows that a bad husband is better than no husband at all, did not hinder you. – Bless me! what noise is that? Saint Nicholas forgive me! I was but in jest. It is the wind, said Matilda, whistling through the battlements in the tower above: you have heard it a thousand times. Nay, said Bianca, there was no harm neither in what I said: it is no sin to talk of matrimony – And so, madam, as I was saying; if my lord Manfred should offer you a handsome young prince for a bridegroom, you would drop him a curtsy, and tell him you would rather take the veil. Thank heaven! I am in no such danger, said Matilda: you know how many proposals for me he has rejected. – And you thank him, like a dutiful daughter, do you, madam? – But come, madam; suppose, to-morrow morning he was to send for you to the great council-chamber, and there you should find at his elbow a lovely young prince, with large black eyes, a smooth white forehead, and manly curling locks like jet; in short, madam, a young hero resembling the picture of the good Alfonso in the gallery, which you sit and gaze at for hours together. – Do not speak lightly of that picture, interrupted Matilda sighing: I know the adoration with which I look at that picture is uncommon – but I am not in love with a coloured pannel. The character of that virtuous prince, the veneration with which my mother has inspired me for his memory, the orisons[n] which I know not why she has enjoined me to pour forth at his tomb, all have concurred to persuade me that somehow or other my destiny is linked with something relating to him. – Lord! madam, how should that be? said Bianca: I have always heard that your family was no way related to his: and I am sure I cannot conceive why my lady, the princess, sends you in a cold morning, or a damp evening, to pray at his tomb: he is no saint by the almanack.[n] If you must pray, why does not she bid you address yourself to our great saint Nicholas? I am sure he is the saint I pray to for a husband. Perhaps my mind would be less affected, said Matilda, if my mother would explain her reasons to me: but it is the mystery she observes, that inspires me with this – I know not what to call it. As she never acts from caprice, I am sure there is some fatal secret at bottom – nay, I know there is: in her agony of grief for my brother's death she dropped some words that intimated as much. – Oh, dear madam, cried Bianca, what were they? No, said Matilda: if a parent lets fall a word, and wishes it recalled, it is not for a child to utter it. What! was she sorry for what she had said? asked Bianca. – I am sure, madam, you may trust me. – With my own little secrets, when I have any, I may, said Matilda; but never with my mother's: a child ought to have no ears or eyes but as a parent directs. Well! to be sure, madam, you was born to be a saint, said Bianca, and there's no resisting one's vocation:[n] you will end in a convent at last. But there is my lady Isabella would not be so reserved to me: she will let me talk to her of young men; and when a handsome cavalier has come to the castle, she has owned to me that she wished your brother Conrad resembled him. Bianca, said the princess, I do not allow you to mention my friend disrespect-fully. Isabella is of a cheerful disposition, but her soul is pure as virtue itself. She knows your idle babbling humour, and perhaps has now and then encouraged it, to divert melancholy, and to enliven the solitude in which my father keeps us. – Blessed Mary! said Bianca starting, there it is again! – Dear madam, do you hear nothing? – This castle is certainly haunted! – Peace! said Matilda, and listen! I did think I heard a voice – but it must be fancy; your terrors I suppose have infected me. Indeed! indeed! madam, said Bianca, half-weeping with agony, I am sure I heard a voice. Does any body lie in the chamber beneath? said the princess. Nobody has dared to lie there, answered Bianca, since the great astrologer that was your brother's tutor drowned himself. For certain, madam, his ghost and the young prince's are now met in the chamber below — for heaven's sake let us fly to your mother's apartment! I charge you not to stir, said Matilda. If they are spirits in pain, we may ease their sufferings by questioning them.[n] They can mean no hurt to us, for we have not injured them — and if they should, shall we be more safe in one chamber than in another? Reach me my beads; we will say a prayer, and then speak to them. Oh, dear lady, I would not speak to a ghost for the world, cried Bianca. — As she said those words, they heard the casement of the little chamber below Matilda's open. They listened attentively, and in few minutes thought they heard a person sing, but could not distinguish the words. This can be no evil spirit, said the princess in a low voice: it is undoubtedly one of the family — open the window, and we shall know the voice. I dare not indeed, madam, said Bianca. Thou art a very fool, said Matilda, opening the window gently herself. The noise the princess made was however heard by the person beneath, who stopped, and, they concluded, had heard the casement open. Is any body below? said the princess: if there is, speak. Yes, said an unknown voice. Who is it? said Matilda. A stranger, replied the voice. What stranger? said she; and how didst thou come there at this unusual hour, when all the gates of the castle are locked? I am not here willingly, answered the voice — but pardon me, lady, if I have disturbed your rest: I knew not that I was overheard. Sleep had forsaken me: I left a restless couch, and came to waste the irksome hours with gazing on the fair approach of morning, impatient to be dismissed from this castle. Thy words and accents, said Matilda, are of a melancholy cast: if thou art unhappy, I pity thee. If poverty afflicts thee, let me know it; I will mention thee to the princess, whose beneficent soul ever melts for the distressed; and she will relieve thee. I am indeed unhappy, said the stranger; and I know not what wealth is: but

I do not complain of the lot which heaven has cast for me: I am
young and healthy, and am not ashamed of owing my support
to myself – yet think me not proud, or that I disdain your
generous offers. I will remember you in my orisons, and will
pray for blessings on your gracious self and your noble mistress
– If I sigh, lady, it is for others, not for myself. Now I have it,
madam, said Bianca whispering to the princess. This is certainly
the young peasant; and by my conscience he is in love!—Well,
this is a charming adventure! – Do, madam, let us sift him.[n] He
does not know you, but takes you for one of my lady Hippolita's
women. Art thou not ashamed, Bianca? said the princess: what
right have we to pry into the secrets of this young man's heart?
He seems virtuous and frank, and tells us he is unhappy: are
those circumstances that authorize us to make a property of
him? How are we entitled to his confidence? Lord! madam,
how little you know of love! replied Bianca: why, lovers have
no pleasure equal to talking of their mistress. And would you
have *me* become a peasant's confidante? said the princess. Well
then, let me talk to him, said Bianca: though I have the honour
of being your highness's maid of honour, I was not always so
great: besides, if love levels ranks, it raises them too: I have a
respect for any young man in love. – Peace, simpleton! said the
princess. Though he said he was unhappy, it does not follow
that he must be in love. Think of all that has happened to-day,
and tell me if there are no misfortunes but what love causes.
Stranger, resumed the princess, if thy misfortunes have not been
occasioned by thy own fault, and are within the compass of the
princess Hippolita's power to redress, I will take upon me to
answer that she will be thy protectress. When thou art dismissed
from this castle, repair to holy father Jerome at the convent
adjoining to the church of saint Nicholas, and make thy story
known to him, as far as thou thinkest meet: he will not fail to
inform the princess, who is the mother of all that want her
assistance. Farewell: it is not seemly for me to hold farther
converse with a man at this unwonted hour. May the saints
guard thee, gracious lady! replied the peasant – but oh, if a
poor and worthless stranger might presume to beg a minute's
audience farther – am I so happy? – the casement is not shut –

might I venture to ask – Speak quickly, said Matilda; the morning dawns apace:ⁿ should the labourers come into the fields and perceive us – What wouldst thou ask? – I know not how – I know not if I dare, said the young stranger faltering – yet the humanity with which you have spoken to me emboldens – Lady! dare I trust you? – Heavens! said Matilda, what dost thou mean? with what wouldst thou trust me? Speak boldly, if thy secret is fit to be entrusted to a virtuous breast. – I would ask, said the peasant, recollecting himself, whether what I have heard from the domestics is true, that the princess is missing from the castle? What imports it to thee to know? replied Matilda. Thy first words bespoke a prudent and becoming gravity. Dost thou come hither to pry into the secrets of Manfred? Adieu. I have been mistaken in thee. – Saying these words, she shut the casement hastily, without giving the young man time to reply. I had acted more wisely, said the princess to Bianca with some sharpness, if I had let thee converse with this peasant: his inquisitiveness seems of a piece with thy own. It is not fit for me to argue with your highness, said Bianca; but perhaps the questions I should have put to him, would have been more to the purpose, than those you have been pleased to ask him. Oh, no doubt, said Matilda; you are a very discreet personage! May I know what you would have asked him? A by-stander often sees more of the game than those that play, answered Bianca.ⁿ Does your highness think, madam, that his question about my lady Isabella was the result of mere curiosity? No, no, madam; there is more in it than you great folks are aware of. Lopez told me, that all the servants believe this young fellow contrived my lady Isabella's escape – Now, pray, madam, observe—You and I both know that my lady Isabella never much fancied the prince your brother. – Well! he is killed just in the critical minute – I accuse nobody. A helmet falls from the moon – so my lord your father says; but Lopez and all the servants say that this young spark is a magician, and stole it from Alfonso's tomb. – Have done with this rhapsody of impertinence, said Matilda. Nay, madam, as you please, cried Bianca – yet it is very particular though, that my lady Isabella should be missing the very same day, and this young sorcerer

should be found at the mouth of the trap-door – I accuse nobody
– but if my young lord came honestly by his death – Dare not
on thy duty, said Matilda, to breathe a suspicion on the purity
of my dear Isabella's fame. – Purity, or not purity, said Bianca,
gone she is: a stranger is found that nobody knows: you
question him yourself: he tells you he is in love, or unhappy, it
is the same thing – nay, he owned he was unhappy about others;
and is any body unhappy about another, unless they are in love
with them? And at the very next word he asks innocently, poor
soul! if my lady Isabella is missing. – To be sure, said Matilda,
thy observations are not totally without foundation – Isabella's
flight amazes me: the curiosity of this stranger is very particular
– yet Isabella never concealed a thought from me. – So she told
you, said Bianca, to fish out your secrets – but who knows,
madam, but this stranger may be some prince in disguise? – Do,
madam, let me open the window, and ask him a few questions.
No, replied Matilda, I will ask him myself, if he knows aught of
Isabella: he is not worthy that I should converse farther with
him. She was going to open the casement, when they heard the
bell ring at the postern-gate[n] of the castle, which is on the right
hand of the tower, where Matilda lay. This prevented the
princess from renewing the conversation with the stranger.

After continuing silent for some time; I am persuaded, said
she to Bianca, that whatever be the cause of Isabella's flight, it
had no unworthy motive. If this stranger was accessary to it, she
must be satisfied of his fidelity and worth. I observed, did not
you, Bianca? that his words were tinctured with an uncommon
infusion of piety. It was no ruffian's speech: his phrases were
becoming a man of gentle birth. I told you, madam, said Bianca,
that I was sure he was some prince in disguise. – Yet, said
Matilda, if he was privy to her escape, how will you account for
his not accompanying her in her flight? Why expose himself
unnecessarily and rashly to my father's resentment? As for that,
madam, replied she, if he could get from under the helmet, he
will find ways of eluding your father's anger. I do not doubt but
he has some talisman[n] or other about him. – You resolve every
thing into magic, said Matilda – but a man who has any
intercourse with infernal spirits does not dare to make use of

those tremendous and holy words which he uttered. Didst thou not observe with what fervour he vowed to remember *me* to heaven in his prayers? Yes, Isabella was undoubtedly convinced of his piety. — Commend me to the piety of a young fellow and a damsel that consult to elope! said Bianca. No, no, madam; my lady Isabella is of another-guess mould[n] than you take her for. She used indeed to sigh and lift up her eyes in your company, because she knows you are a saint — but when your back was turned — You wrong her, said Matilda; Isabella is no hypocrite: she has a due sense of devotion, but never affected a call she has not. On the contrary, she always combated my inclination for the cloister: and though I own the mystery she has made to me of her flight confounds me; though it seems inconsistent with the friendship between us; I cannot forget the disinterested warmth with which she always opposed my taking the veil: she wished to see me married, though my dower would have been a loss to her and my brother's children. For her sake I will believe well of this young peasant. Then you do think there is some liking between them? said Bianca. — While she was speaking, a servant came hastily into the chamber, and told the princess that the lady Isabella was found. Where? said Matilda. She has taken sanctuary in saint Nicholas's church, replied the servant: father Jerome has brought the news himself: he is below with his highness. Where is my mother? said Matilda. She is in her own chamber, madam, and has asked for you.

Manfred had risen at the first dawn of light, and gone to Hippolita's apartment, to enquire if she knew ought of Isabella. While he was questioning her, word was brought that Jerome demanded to speak with him. Manfred, little suspecting the cause of the friar's arrival, and knowing he was employed by Hippolita in her charities, ordered him to be admitted, intending to leave them together, while he pursued his search after Isabella. Is your business with me or the princess? said Manfred. With both, replied the holy man. The lady Isabella — What of her? interrupted Manfred eagerly — is at saint Nicholas's altar, replied Jerome. That is no business of Hippolita, said Manfred with confusion: let us retire to my chamber, father; and inform me how she came thither. No, my lord, replied the good man with an air of firmness and authority that daunted even the resolute Manfred, who could not help revering the saint-like virtues of Jerome: my commission is to both; and, with your highness's good-liking, in the presence of both I shall deliver it – But first, my lord, I must interrogate the princess, whether she is acquainted with the cause of the lady Isabella's retirement from your castle. – No, on my soul, said Hippolita; does Isabella charge me with being privy to it? – Father, interrupted Manfred, I pay due reverence to your holy profession; but I am sovereign here, and will allow no meddling priest to interfere in the affairs of my domestic." If you have aught to say, attend me to my chamber – I do not use to let my wife be acquainted with the secret affairs of my state; they are not within a woman's province. My lord, said the holy man, I am no intruder into the secrets of families. My office is to promote peace, to heal divisions, to preach repentance, and teach mankind to curb their headstrong passions. I forgive your highness's uncharitable apostrophe: I know my duty, and am the minister of a mightier prince than Manfred. Hearken to him who speaks through my organs. Manfred trembled with rage and shame. Hippolita's countenance declared her astonishment, and impatience to know where this would end: her silence more strongly spoke her observance of Manfred.

The lady Isabella, resumed Jerome, commends herself to both your highnesses; she thanks both for the kindness with which she has been treated in your castle: she deplores the loss of your son, and her own misfortune in not becoming the daughter of such wise and noble princes, whom she shall always respect as *parents*: she prays for uninterrupted union and felicity between you: [Manfred's colour changed] but as it is no longer possible for her to be allied to you, she entreats your consent to remain in sanctuary till she can learn news of her father; or, by the certainty of his death, be at liberty, with the approbation of her guardians, to dispose of herself in suitable marriage. I shall give no such consent, said the prince; but insist on her return to the castle without delay: I am answerable for her person to her guardians, and will not brook her being in any hands but my own. Your highness will recollect whether that can any longer be proper, replied the friar. I want no monitor, said Manfred colouring. Isabella's conduct leaves room for strange suspicions – and that young villain, who was at least the accomplice of her flight, if not the cause of it – The cause! interrupted Jerome: was a *young* man the cause? This is not to be borne! cried Manfred. Am I to be bearded[n] in my own palace by an insolent monk? Thou art privy, I guess, to their amours. I would pray to heaven to clear up your uncharitable surmises, said Jerome, if your highness were not satisfied in your conscience how unjustly you accuse me. I do pray to heaven to pardon that uncharitableness: and I implore your highness to leave the princess at peace in that holy place, where she is not liable to be disturbed by such vain and worldly fantasies as discourses of love from any man. Cant not to me, said Manfred, but return, and bring the princess to her duty. It is my duty to prevent her return hither, said Jerome. She is where orphans and virgins are safest from the snares and wiles of this world; and nothing but a parent's authority shall take her thence. I am her parent, cried Manfred, and demand her. She wished to have you for her parent, said the friar; but heaven, that forbad that connexion, has for ever dissolved all ties betwixt you: and I announce to your highness – Stop! audacious man, said Manfred, and dread my displeasure. Holy father, said Hippolita, it is your office to be no respecter of persons:[n] you must speak as your duty prescribes: but it is my duty to hear nothing that it pleases not my lord I should hear. I will retire to my oratory, and pray to the blessed Virgin to inspire you with her holy counsels, and to restore the heart of my gracious lord to its wonted peace and gentleness. Excellent woman! said the friar. – My lord, I attend your pleasure.

Manfred, accompanied by the friar, passed to his own apartment; where shutting the door, I perceive, father, said he, that Isabella has acquainted you with my purpose. Now hear my resolve, and obey. Reasons of state, most urgent reasons, my own and the safety of my people, demand that I should have a son. It is in vain to expect an heir from Hippolita. I have made choice of Isabella. You must bring her back; and you must do more. I know the influence you have with Hippolita: her conscience is in your hands. She is, I allow, a faultless woman: her soul is set on heaven, and scorns the little grandeur of this world: you can withdraw her from it entirely. Persuade her to consent to the dissolution of our marriage, and to retire into a monastery – she shall endow one if she will; and she shall have the means of being as liberal to your order as she or you can wish. Thus you will divert the calamities that are hanging over our heads, and have the merit of saving the principality of Otranto from destruction. You are a prudent man; and though the warmth of my temper betrayed me into some unbecoming expressions, I honour your virtue, and wish to be indebted to you for the repose of my life and the preservation of my family.

The will of heaven be done! said the friar. I am but its worthless instrument. It makes use of my tongue to tell thee, prince, of thy unwarrantable designs. The injuries of the virtuous Hippolita have mounted to the throne of pity. By me thou art reprimanded for thy adulterous intention of repudiating her: by me thou are warned not to pursue the incestuous design on thy contracted daughter. Heaven, that delivered her from thy fury, when the judgments so recently fallen on thy house ought to have inspired thee with other thoughts, will continue to watch over her. Even I, a poor and despised friar, am able to protect her from thy violence. – I, sinner as I am, and uncharitably reviled by your highness as an accomplice of I know not what amours, scorn the allurements with which it has pleased thee to tempt mine honesty. I love my order; I honour devout souls; I respect the piety of thy princess – but I will not betray the confidence she reposes in me, nor serve even the cause of religion by foul and sinful compliances – But forsooth! the welfare of the state depends on your highness having a son. Heaven mocks the short-sighted views of man. But yester-morn, whose house was so great, so flourishing as Manfred's? – Where is young Conrad now? – My lord, I respect your tears – but I mean not to check them – Let them flow, prince! they will weigh more with heaven towards the welfare of thy subjects, than a marriage, which, founded on lust or policy, could never prosper. The sceptre, which passed from the race of Alfonso to thine, cannot be preserved by a match which the church will never allow. If it is the will of the Most High that Manfred's name must perish, resign yourself, my lord, to its decrees; and thus deserve a crown that can never pass away. – Come, my lord, I like this sorrow – Let us return to the princess: she is not apprized of your cruel intentions; nor did I mean more than to alarm you. You saw with what gentle patience, with what efforts of love, she heard, she rejected hearing the extent of your guilt. I know she longs to fold you in her arms, and assure you of her unalterable affection. Father, said the prince, you mistake my compunction: true, I honour, Hippolita's virtues; I think her a saint; and wish it were for my soul's health to tie faster the knot that has united us. – But alas! father, you know not the bitterest of my pangs! It is some time that I have had scruples on the legality of our union: Hippolita is related to me in the fourth degree[n] – It is true, we had a dispensation; but I have been informed that she had also been contracted to another. This it is that sits heavy at my heart: to this state of unlawful wedlock I impute the visitation that has fallen on me in the death of Conrad! – Ease my conscience of this burden; dissolve our marriage, and accomplish the work of godliness which your divine exhortations have commenced in my soul.

How cutting was the anguish which the good man felt, when he perceived this turn in the wily prince! He trembled for Hippolita, whose ruin he saw was determined; and he feared, if Manfred had no hope of recovering Isabella, that his impatience for a son would direct him to some other object, who might not be equally proof against the temptation of Manfred's rank. For some time the holy man remained absorbed in thought. At length, conceiving some hope from delay, he thought the wisest conduct would be to prevent the prince from despairing of recovering Isabella. Her the friar knew he could dispose, from her affection to Hippolita, and from the aversion she had expressed to him for Manfred's addresses, to second his views, till the censures of the church could be fulminated against a divorce. With this intention, as if struck with the prince's scruples, he at length said, My lord, I have been pondering on what your highness has said; and if in truth it is delicacy of conscience that is the real motive of your repugnance to your virtuous lady, far be it from me to endeavour to harden your heart! The church is an indulgent mother; unfold your griefs to her: she alone can administer comfort to your soul, either by satisfying your conscience, or, upon examination of your scruples, by setting you at liberty, and indulging you in the lawful means of continuing your lineage. In the latter case, if the lady Isabella can be brought to consent—Manfred, who concluded that he had either over-reached[n] the good man, or that his first warmth had been but a tribute paid to appearance, was overjoyed at this sudden turn, and repeated the most magnificent promises, if he should succeed by the friar's mediation. The well-meaning priest suffered him to deceive himself, fully determined to traverse[n] his views, instead of seconding them.

Since we now understand one another, resumed the prince, I expect, father, that you satisfy me in one point. Who is the youth that we found in the vault? He must have been privy to Isabella's flight: tell me truly; is he her lover? or is he an agent for another's passion? I have often suspected Isabella's indifference to my son: a thousand cirumstances crowd on my mind that confirm that suspicion. She herself was so conscious of it, that, while I discoursed her in the gallery, she outran my suspicions, and endeavoured to justify herself from coolness to Conrad. The friar, who knew nothing of the youth but what he had learnt occasionally from the princess, ignorant what was become of him, and not sufficiently reflecting on the impetuosity of Manfred's temper, conceived that it might not be amiss to sow the seeds of jealousy in his mind: they might be turned to some use hereafter, either by prejudicing the prince against Isabella, if he persisted in that union; or, by diverting his attention to a wrong scent, and employing his thoughts on a visionary intrigue, prevent his engaging in any new pursuit. With this unhappy policy, he answered in a manner to confirm Manfred in the belief of some connection between Isabella and the youth. The prince, whose passions wanted little fuel to throw them into a blaze, fell into a rage at the idea of what the friar suggested. I will fathom to the bottom of this intrigue, cried he; and quitting Jerome abruptly, with a command to remain there till his return, he hastened to the great hall of the castle, and ordered the peasant to be brought before him.

Thou hardened young impostor! said the prince, as soon as he saw the youth; what becomes of thy boasted veracity now? It was Providence, was it, and the light of the moon, that discovered the lock of the trap-door to thee? Tell me, audacious boy, who thou art, and how long thou hast been acquainted with the princess – and take care to answer with less equivocation than thou didst last night, or tortures shall wring the truth from thee. The young man, perceiving that his share in the flight of the princess was discovered, and concluding that any thing he should say could no longer be of service or detriment to her, replied, I am no impostor, my lord; nor have I deserved opprobrious language. I answered to every question your highness put to me last night with the same veracity that I shall speak now: and that will not be from fear of your tortures, but because my soul abhors a falsehood. Please to repeat your questions, my lord; I am ready to give you all the satisfaction in my power. You know my questions, replied the prince, and only want time to prepare an evasion. Speak directly; who art thou? and how long hast though been known to the princess? I am a labourer at the next village, said the peasant; my name is Theodore. The princess found me in the vault last night: before that hour I never was in her presence. – I may believe as much or as little as I please of this, said Manfred; but I will hear thy own story, before I examine into the truth of it. Tell me, what reason did the princess give thee for making her escape? Thy life depends on thy answer. She told me, replied Theodore, that she was on the brink of destruction; and that, if she could not escape from the castle, she was in danger in a few moments of being made miserable for ever. And on this slight foundation, on a silly girl's report, said Manfred, thou didst hazard my displeasure? I fear no man's displeasure, said Theodore, when a woman in distress puts herself under my protection. – During this examination, Matilda was going to the apartment of Hippolita. At the upper end of the hall, where Manfred sat, was a boarded gallery with latticed windows,[n] through which Matilda and Bianca were to pass. Hearing her father's voice, and seeing the servants assembled round him, she stopped to learn the occasion. The prisoner soon drew her attention: the steady and composed manner in which he answered, and the gallantry of his last reply, which were the first words she heard distinctly, interested her in his favour. His person was noble, handsome and commanding, even in that situation: but his countenance soon engrossed her whole care. Heavens! Bianca, said the princess softly, do I dream? or is not that youth the exact resemblance of Alfonso's picture in the gallery? She could say no more, for her father's voice grew louder at every word. This bravado, said he, surpasses all thy former insolence. Thou shalt experience the wrath with which thou darest to trifle. Seize him, continued Manfred, and bind him – the first news the princess hears of her champion shall be, that he has lost his head for her sake. The injustice of which thou art guilty towards me, said Theodore, convinces me that I have done a good deed in delivering the princess from thy tyranny. May she be happy, whatever becomes of me! – This is a lover! cried Manfred in a rage: a peasant within sight of death is not animated by such sentiments. Tell me, tell me, rash boy, who thou art, or the rack shall force thy secret from thee. Thou hast threatened me with death already, said the youth, for the truth I have told thee: if that is all the encouragement I am to expect for sincerity, I am not tempted to indulge thy vain curiosity farther. Then thou wilt not speak? said Manfred. I will not, replied he. Bear him away into the court-yard, said Manfred; I will see his head this instant severed from his body. – Matilda fainted at hearing those words. Bianca shrieked, and cried, Help! help! the princess is dead! Manfred started at this ejaculation, and demanded what was the matter. The young peasant, who heard it too, was struck with horror, and asked eagerly the same question; but Manfred ordered him to be hurried into the court, and kept there for execution, till he had informed himself of the cause of Bianca's shrieks. When he learned the meaning, he treated it as a womanish panic; and ordering Matilda to be carried to her apartment, he rushed into the court, and, calling for one of his guards, bade Theodore kneel down and prepare to receive the fatal blow.

The undaunted youth received the bitter sentence with a resignation that touched every heart but Manfred's. He wished earnestly to know the meaning of the words he had heard relating to the princess; but, fearing to exasperate the tyrant more against her, he desisted. The only boon he deigned to ask was, that he might be permitted to have a confessor, and make his peace with heaven. Manfred, who hoped by the confessor's means to come at the youth's history, readily granted his request: and being convinced that father Jerome was now in his interest, he ordered him to be called and shrieve the prisoner. The holy man, who had little foreseen the catastrophe that his imprudence occasioned, fell on his knees to the prince, and adjured him in the most solemn manner not to shed innocent blood. He accused himself in the bitterest terms for his indiscretion, endeavoured to disculpate the youth, and left no method untried to soften the tyrant's rage. Manfred, more incensed than appeased by Jerome's intercession, whose retractation now made him suspect he had been imposed upon by both, commanded the friar to do his duty, telling him he would not allow the prisoner many minutes for confession. Nor do I ask many, my lord, said the unhappy young man. My sins, thank heaven! have not been numerous; nor exceed what might be expected at my years. Dry your tears, good father, and let us dispatch: this is a bad world; nor have I had cause to leave it with regret. Oh! wretched youth! said Jerome; how canst thou bear the sight of me with patience? I am thy murderer! It is I have brought this dismal hour upon thee! – I forgive thee from my soul, said the youth, as I hope heaven will pardon me. Hear my confession, father; and give me thy blessing. How can I prepare thee for thy passage, as I ought? said Jerome. Thou canst not be saved without pardoning thy foes – and canst thou forgive that impious man there? I can, said Theodore; I do. – And does not this touch thee, cruel prince? said the friar. I sent for thee to confess him, said Manfred sternly; not to plead for him. Thou didst first incense me against him – his blood be upon thy head! – It will! it will! said the good man in an agony of sorrow. Thou and I must never hope to go where this blessed youth is going. – Dispatch! said Manfred: I am no more to be moved by the whining of priests, than by the shrieks of women. What! said the youth, is it possible that my fate could have occasioned what I heard? Is the princess then again in thy power? – Thou dost but remember me of my wrath, said Manfred: prepare thee, for this moment is thy last. The youth, who felt his indignation rise, and who was touched with the sorrow which he saw he had infused into all the spectators, as well as into the friar, suppressed his emotions, and, putting off his doublet and unbuttoning his collar, knelt down to his prayers. As he stooped, his shirt slipped down below his shoulder, and discovered the mark of a bloody arrow. Gracious heaven! cried the holy man starting, what do I see? It is my child! my Theodore!

The passions that ensued must be conceived; they cannot be painted. The tears of the assistants were suspended by wonder, rather than stopped by joy. They seemed to enquire in the eyes of their lord what they ought to feel. Surprise, doubt, tenderness, respect, succeeded each other in the countenance of the youth. He received with modest submission the effusion of the old man's tears and embraces: yet afraid of giving a loose to hope, and suspecting from what had passed the inflexibility of Manfred's temper, he cast a glance towards the prince, as if to say, Canst thou be unmoved at such a scene as this?

Manfred's heart was capable of being touched. He forgot his anger in his astonishment; yet his pride forbad his owning himself affected. He even doubted whether this discovery was not a contrivance of the friar to save the youth. What may this mean? said he. How can he be thy son? Is it consistent with thy profession or reputed sanctity to avow a peasant's offspring for the fruit of thy irregular amours? – Oh God! said the holy man, dost thou question his being mine? Could I feel the anguish I do, if I were not his father? Spare him! good prince, spare him! and revile me as thou pleasest. – Spare him! spare him! cried the attendants, for this good man's sake! – Peace! said Manfred sternly: I must know more, ere I am disposed to pardon. A saint's bastard may be no saint himself. – Injurious lord! said Theodore: add not insult to cruelty. If I am this venerable man's son, though no prince as thou art, know, the blood that flows in my veins – Yes, said the friar, interrupting him, his blood is noble: nor is he that abject thing, my lord, you speak him. He is my lawful son; and Sicily can boast of few houses more ancient than that of Falconara – But alas! my lord, what is blood? what is nobility? We are all reptiles, miserable sinful creatures. It is piety alone that can distinguish us from the dust whence we sprung, and whither we must return. – Truce to your sermon, said Manfred; you forget you are no longer friar Jerome, but the count of Falconara. Let me know your history; you will have time to moralize hereafter, if you should not happen to obtain the grace of that sturdy criminal there. Mother of God! said the friar, is it possible my lord can refuse a father the life of his only, his long lost child? Trample me, my lord, scorn, afflict me, accept my life for his, but spare my son! – Thou canst feel then, said Manfred, what it is to lose an only son? A little hour ago thou didst preach up resignation to me: *my* house, if fate so pleased, must perish – but the count of Falconara – Alas! my lord, said Jerome, I confess I have offended; but aggravate not an old man's sufferings. I boast not of my family, nor think of such vanities – it is nature that pleads for this boy; it is the memory of the dear woman that bore him – Is she, Theodore, is she dead? – Her soul has long been with the blessed, said Theodore. Oh how? cried Jerome, tell me – No – she is happy! Thou art all my care now! – Most dread lord! will you – will you grant me my poor boy's life? Return to thy convent, answered Manfred; conduct the princess hither; obey me in what else thou knowest; and I promise thee the life of thy son.—Oh! my lord, said Jerome, is honesty the price I must pay for this dear youth's safety? – For me! cried Theodore: let me die a thousand deaths, rather than stain thy conscience. What is it the tyrant would exact of thee? Is the princess safe from his power? Protect her, thou venerable old man! and let all his wrath fall on me. Jerome endeavoured to check the impetuosity of the youth; and ere Manfred could reply, the trampling of horses was heard, and a brazen trumpet, which hung without the gate of the castle, was suddenly sounded. At the same instant the sable plumes on the enchanted helmet, which still remained at the other end of the court, were tempestuously agitated, and nodded thrice, as if bowed by some invisible wearer.

CHAPTER 3

Manfred's heart misgave him when he beheld the plumage on the miraculous casque shaken in concert with the sounding of the brazen trumpet. Father! said he to Jerome, whom he now ceased to treat as count of Falconara, what mean these portents? If I have offended – [the plumes were shaken with greater violence than before] Unhappy prince that I am! cried Manfred – Holy father! will you not assist me with your prayers? – My lord, replied Jerome, heaven is no doubt displeased with your mockery of its servants. Submit yourself to the church; and cease to persecute her ministers. Dismiss this innocent youth; and learn to respect the holy character I wear: heaven will not be trifled with: you see – [the trumpet sounded again] I acknowledge I have been too hasty, said Manfred. Father, do you go to the wicket,[n] and demand who is at the gate. Do you grant me the life of Theodore? replied the friar. I do, said Manfred; but enquire who is without.

Jerome, falling on the neck of his son, discharged a flood of tears, that spoke the fulness of his soul. You promised to go to the gate, said Manfred. I thought, replied the friar, your highness would excuse my thanking you first in this tribute of my heart. Go, dearest sir, said Theodore, obey the prince; I do not deserve that you should delay his satisfaction for me.

Jerome, enquiring who was without, was answered, A herald. From whom? said he. From the knight of the gigantic sabre, said the herald: and I must speak with the usurper of Otranto. Jerome returned to the prince, and did not fail to repeat the message in the very words it had been uttered. The first sounds struck Manfred with terror; but when he heard himself styled usurper, his rage rekindled, and all his courage revived. Usurper ! – Insolent villain ! cried he, who dares to question my title ? Retire, father; this is no business for monks: I will meet this presumptuous man myself. Go to your convent, and prepare the princess's return: your son shall be a hostage for your fidelity; his life depends on your obedience. – Good heaven ! my lord, cried Jerome, your highness did but this instant freely pardon my child – have you so soon forgot the interposition of heaven ? – Heaven, replied Manfred, does not send heralds to question the title of a lawful prince – I doubt whether it even notifies its will through friars – but that is your affair, not mine. At present you know my pleasure; and it is not a saucy herald that shall save your son, if you do not return with the princess.

It was in vain for the holy man to reply. Manfred commanded him to be conducted to the postern-gate, and shut out from the castle: and he ordered some of his attendants to carry Theodore to the top of the black tower, and guard him strictly; scarce permitting the father and son to exchange a hasty embrace at parting. He then withdrew to the hall, and, seating himself in princely state, ordered the herald to be admitted to his presence.

Well, thou insolent ! said the prince, what wouldst thou with me ? I come, replied he, to thee, Manfred, usurper of the principality of Otranto, from the renowned and invincible knight, the knight of the gigantic sabre: in the name of his lord, Frederic marquis of Vicenza, he demands the lady Isabella, daughter of that prince, whom thou hast basely and traitorously got into thy power, by bribing her false guardians during his absence: and he requires thee to resign the principality of Otranto, which thou hast usurped from the said lord Frederic, the nearest of blood to the last rightful lord Alfonso the Good. If thou dost not instantly comply with these just demands, he defies thee to single combat to the last extremity. And so saying, the herald cast down his warder.[n]

And where is this braggart, who sends thee ? said Manfred. At the distance of a league, said the herald: he comes to make good his lord's claim against thee, as he is a true knight, and thou an usurper and ravisher.

Injurious as this challenge was, Manfred reflected that it was not his interest to provoke the marquis. He knew how well-founded the claim of Frederic was; nor was this the first time he had heard of it. Frederic's ancestors had assumed the style of princes of Otranto, from the death of Alfonso the Good without issue: but Manfred, his father, and grandfather, had been too powerful for the house of Vicenza to dispossess them. Frederic, a martial and amorous young prince, had married a beautiful young lady, of whom he was enamoured, and who had died in childbed of Isabella. Her death affected him so much, that he had taken the cross and gone to the Holy Land,[n] where he was wounded in an engagement against the infidels, made prisoner, and reported to be dead. When the news reached Manfred's ears, he bribed the guardians of the lady Isabella to deliver her up to him as a bride for his son Conrad; by which alliance he had purposed to unite the claims of the two houses. This motive, on Conrad's death, had co-operated to make him so suddenly resolve on espousing her himself; and the same reflection determined him now to endeavour at obtaining the consent of Frederic to this marriage. A like policy inspired him with the thought of inviting Frederic's champion into his castle, lest he should be informed of Isabella's flight, which he strictly enjoined his domestics not to disclose to any of the knight's retinue.

Herald, said Manfred, as soon as he had digested these reflections, return to thy master, and tell him, ere we liquidate our differences by the sword, Manfred would hold some converse with him. Bid him welcome to my castle, where, by my faith, as I am a true knight, he shall have courteous reception, and full security for himself and followers. If we cannot adjust our quarrel by amicable means, I swear he shall depart in safety, and shall have full satisfaction according to the law of arms: so help me God and his holy Trinity! – The herald made three obeisances, and retired.

During this interview Jerome's mind was agitated by a thousand contrary passions. He trembled for the life of his son, and his first idea was to persuade Isabella to return to the castle. Yet he was scarce less alarmed at the thought of her union with Manfred. He dreaded Hippolita's unbounded submission to the will of her lord: and though he did not doubt but he could alarm her piety not to consent to a divorce, if he could get access to her; yet should Manfred discover that the obstruction came from him, it might be equally fatal to Theodore. He was impatient to know whence came the herald, who with so little management had questioned the title of Manfred: yet he did not dare absent himself from the convent, lest Isabella should leave it, and her flight be imputed to him. He returned disconsolately to the monastery, uncertain on what conduct to resolve. A monk, who met him in the porch and observed his melancholy air, said, Alas! brother, is it then true that we have lost our excellent princess Hippolita? The holy man started, and cried, What meanest thou, brother? I come this instant from the castle, and left her in perfect health. Martelli, replied the other friar, passed by the convent but a quarter of an hour ago on his way from the castle, and reported that her highness was dead. All our brethren are gone to the chapel to pray for her happy transit to a better life, and willed me to wait thy arrival. They know thy holy attachment to that good lady, and are anxious for the affliction it will cause in thee – Indeed we have all reason to weep; she was a mother to our house – But this life is but a pilgrimage; we must not murmur – we shall all follow her; may our end be like hers! – Good brother, thou dreamest, said Jerome: I tell thee I come from the castle, and left the princess well – Where is the lady Isabella? – Poor gentlewoman! replied the friar; I told her the sad news, and offered her spiritual comfort; I reminded her of the transitory condition of mortality, and advised her to take the veil: I quoted the example of the holy princess Sanchia of Arragon.[n] – Thy zeal was laudable, said Jerome impatiently; but at present it was unnecessary: Hippolita is well – at least I trust in the Lord she is; I heard nothing to the contrary – Yet methinks, the prince's earnestness – Well, brother, but where is the lady Isabella? – I know not, said the friar: she wept much, and said she would retire to her chamber. Jerome left his comrade abruptly, and hasted to the princess, but she was not in her chamber. He enquired of the domestics of the convent, but could learn no news of her. He searched in vain throughout the monastery and the church, and dispatched messengers round the neighbourhood, to get intelligence if she had been seen; but to no purpose. Nothing could equal the good man's perplexity. He judged that Isabella, suspecting Manfred of having precipitated his wife's death, had taken the alarm, and withdrawn herself to some more secret place of concealment. This new flight would probably carry the prince's fury to the height. The report of Hippolita's death, though it seemed almost incredible, increased his consternation; and though Isabella's escape bespoke her aversion of Manfred for a husband, Jerome could feel no comfort from it, while it endangered the life of his son. He determined to return to the castle, and made several of his brethren accompany him, to attest his innocence to Manfred, and, if necessary, join their intercession with his for Theodore.

The prince, in the mean time, had passed into the court, and ordered the gates of the castle to be flung open for the reception of the stranger knight and his train. In a few minutes the cavalcade arrived. First came two harbingers with wands.[n] Next a herald, followed by two pages and two trumpets. Then an hundred foot-guards. These were attended by as many horse. After them fifty footmen, clothed in scarlet and black, the colours of the knight. Then a led horse.[n] Two heralds on each side of a gentleman on horseback bearing a banner with the arms of Vicenza and Otranto quarterly[n] – a circumstance that much offended Manfred – but he stifled his resentment. Two more pages. The knight's confessor telling his beads.[n] Fifty more footmen, clad as before. Two knights habited in complete armour, their beavers[n] down, comrades to the principal knight. The 'squires of the two knights, carrying their shields and devices. The knight's own 'squire. An hundred gentlemen bearing an enormous sword, and seeming to faint under the weight of it. The knight himself on a chestnut steed, in complete armour, his lance in the rest, his face entirely concealed by his vizor, which was surmounted by a large plume of scarlet and black feathers. Fifty foot-guards with drums and trumpets closed the procession, which wheeled off to the right and left to make room for the principal knight.

As soon as he approached the gate, he stopped; and the herald advancing, read again the words of the challenge.

Manfred's eyes were fixed on the gigantic sword, and he scarce seemed to attend to the cartel:[n] but his attention was soon diverted by a tempest of wind that rose behind him. He turned, and beheld the plumes of the enchanted helmet agitated in the same extraordinary manner as before. It required intrepidity like Manfred's not to sink under a concurrence of circumstances that seemed to announce his fate. Yet scorning in the presence of strangers to betray the courage he had always manifested, he said boldly, Sir knight, whoever thou art, I bid thee welcome. If thou art of mortal mould, thy valour shall meet its equal: and if thou art a true knight, thou wilt scorn to employ sorcery to carry thy point. Be these omens from heaven or hell, Manfred trusts to the righteousness of his cause and to the aid of saint Nicholas, who has ever protected his house. Alight, sir knight, and repose thyself. To-morrow thou shalt have a fair field; and heaven befriend the juster side!

The knight made no reply, but, dismounting, was conducted by Manfred to the great hall of the castle. As they traversed the court, the knight stopped to gaze at the miraculous casque; and, kneeling down, seemed to pray inwardly for some minutes. Rising, he made a sign to the prince to lead on. As soon as they entered the hall, Manfred proposed to the stranger to disarm; but the knight shook his head in token of refusal. Sir knight, said Manfred, this is not courteous; but by my good faith I will not cross thee! nor shalt thou have cause to complain of the prince of Otranto. No treachery is designed on my part: I hope none is intended on thine. Here take my gage:[n] [giving him his ring] your friends and you shall enjoy the laws of hospitality. Rest here until refreshments are brought: I will but give orders for the accommodation of your train, and return to you. The three knights bowed, as accepting his courtesy. Manfred directed the stranger's retinue to be conducted to an adjacent hospital,[n] founded by the princess Hippolita for the reception of pilgrims. As they made the circuit of the court to return towards the gate, the gigantic sword burst from the supporters, and, falling to the ground opposite to the helmet, remained immoveable. Manfred, almost hardened to preternatural appearances, surmounted the shock of this new prodigy; and returning to the hall, where by this time the feast was ready, he invited his silent guests to take their places. Manfred, however ill his heart was at ease, endeavoured to inspire the company with mirth. He put several questions to them, but was answered only by signs. They raised their vizors but sufficiently to feed themselves, and that sparingly. Sirs, said the prince, ye are the first guests I ever treated within these walls, who scorned to hold any intercourse with me : nor has it oft been customary, I ween, for princes to hazard their state and dignity against strangers and mutes. You say you come in the name of Frederic of Vicenza : I have ever heard that he was a gallant and courteous knight ; nor would he, I am bold to say, think it beneath him to mix in social converse with a prince that is his equal, and not unknown by deeds in arms. – Still ye are silent – Well! be it as it may – by the laws of hospitality and chivalry ye are masters under this roof : ye shall do your pleasure – but come, give me a goblet of wine ; ye will not refuse to pledge me to the healths of your fair mistresses. The principal knight sighed and crossed himself, and was rising from the board – Sir knight, said Manfred, what I said was but in sport : I shall constrain you in nothing : use your good liking. Since mirth is not your mood, let us be sad. Business may hit your fancies better : let us withdraw ; and hear if what I have to unfold may be better relished than the vain efforts I have made for your pastime.

Manfred, then, conducting the three knights into an inner chamber, shut the door, and, inviting them to be seated, began thus, addressing himself to the chief personage :

You come, sir knight, as I understand, in the name of the marquis of Vicenza, to re-demand the lady Isabella his daughter, who has been contracted in the face of holy church to my son, by the consent of her legal guardians ; and to require me to resign my dominions to your lord, who gives himself for the nearest of blood to prince Alfonso, whose soul God rest ! I shall speak to the latter article of your demands first. You must know, your lord knows, that I enjoy the principality of Otranto from my father Don Manuel, as he received it from his father Don Ricardo. Alfonso, their predecessor, dying childless in the Holy Land, bequeathed his estates to my grandfather Don Ricardo, in consideration of his faithful services – [The stranger shook his head] – Sir knight, said Manfred warmly, Ricardo was a valiant and upright man; he was a pious man; witness his munificent foundation of the adjoining church and two convents. He was peculiarly patronized by saint Nicholas – My grandfather was incapable – I say, sir, Don Ricardo was incapable – Excuse me, your interruption has disordered me – I venerate the memory of my grandfather – Well, sirs! he held this estate; he held it by his good sword, and by the favour of saint Nicholas – so did my father; and so, sirs, will I, come what come will. – But Frederic, your lord, is nearest in blood – I have consented to put my title to the issue of the sword – does that imply a vitious[n] title? I might have asked, where is Frederic, your lord? Report speaks him dead in captivity. You say, your actions say, he lives – I question it not – I might, sirs, I might – but I do not. Other princes would bid Frederic take his inheritance by force, if he can: they would not stake their dignity on a single combat: they would not submit it to the decision of unknown mutes![n] Pardon me, gentlemen, I am too warm: but suppose yourselves in my situation: as ye are stout knights, would it not move your choler to have your own and the honour of your ancestors called in question? – But to the point. Ye require me to deliver up the lady Isabella – Sirs, I must ask if ye are authorized to receive her? [The knight nodded.] Receive her – continued Manfred: Well! you are authorized to receive her – But, gentle knight, may I ask if you have full powers? [The knight nodded.] 'Tis well, said Manfred: then hear what I have to offer – Ye see, gentlemen, before you the most unhappy of men! [he began to weep] afford me your compassion; I am entitled to it; indeed I am. Know, I have lost my only hope, my joy, the support of my house – Conrad died yester-morning. [The knights discovered signs of surprise.] Yes, sirs, fate has disposed of my son. Isabella is at liberty. – Do you then restore her, cried the chief knight, breaking silence. Afford me your patience, said Manfred. I rejoice to find, by this testimony of your good-will, that this matter may be adjusted without blood. It is no interest of mine dictates what little I have farther to say. Ye behold in me a man disgusted with the world: the loss of my son has weaned me from earthly cares. Power and greatness have no longer any charms in my eyes. I wished to transmit the sceptre I had received from my ancestors with honour to my son – but that is over! Life itself is so indifferent to me, that I accepted your defiance with joy: a good knight cannot go to the grave with more satisfaction than when falling in his vocation. Whatever is the will of heaven, I submit; for, alas! sirs, I am a man of many sorrows. Manfred is no object of envy – but no doubt you are acquainted with my story. [The knight made signs of ignorance, and seemed curious to have Manfred proceed.] Is it possible, sirs, continued the prince, that my story should be a secret to you? Have you heard nothing relating to me and the princess Hippolita? [They shook their heads] – No! Thus then, sirs, it is. You think me ambitious: ambition, alas, is composed of more rugged materials. If I were ambitious, I should not for so many years have been a prey to the hell of conscientious scruples – But I weary your patience: I will be brief. Know then, that I have long been troubled in mind on my union with the princess Hippolita. – Oh! sirs, if ye were acquainted with that excellent woman! if ye knew that I adore her like a mistress, and cherish her as a friend – But man was not born for perfect happiness! She shares my scruples, and with her consent I have brought this matter before the church, for we are related within the forbidden degrees. I expect every hour the definitive sentence that must separate us forever. I am sure you feel for me – I see you do – Pardon these tears! [The knights gazed on each other, wondering where this would end.] Manfred continued: The death of my son betiding while my soul was under this anxiety, I thought of nothing but resigning my dominions, and retiring forever from the sight of mankind. My only difficulty was to fix on a successor, who would be tender of my people, and to dispose of the lady Isabella, who is dear to me as my own blood. I was willing to restore the line of Alfonso, even in his most distant kindred: and though, pardon me, I am satisfied it was his will that Ricardo's lineage should take place of his own relations; yet, where was I to search for those relations? I knew of none but Frederic, your lord: he was a captive to the infidels, or dead; and were he living, and at home, would he quit the flourishing state of Vicenza for the inconsiderable principality of Otranto? If he would not, could I bear the thought of seeing a hard unfeeling viceroy set over my poor faithful people? – for, sirs, I love my people, and thank heaven am beloved by them. – But ye will ask, Whither tends this long discourse? Briefly then, thus, sirs. Heaven in your arrival seems to point out a remedy for these difficulties and my misfortunes. The lady Isabella is at liberty: I shall soon be so. I would submit to any thing for the good of my people – Were it not the best, the only way to extinguish the feuds between our families, if I were to take the lady Isabella to wife? – You start – But though Hippolita's virtues will ever be dear to me, a prince must not consider himself; he is born for his people. – A servant at that instant entering the chamber, apprized Manfred that Jerome and several of his brethren demanded immediate access to him.

The prince, provoked at this interruption, and fearing that the friar would discover to the strangers that Isabella had taken sanctuary, was going to forbid Jerome's entrance. But recollecting that he was certainly arrived to notify the princess's return, Manfred began to excuse himself to the knights for leaving them for a few moments, but was prevented by the arrival of the friars. Manfred reprimanded them for their intrusion, and would have forced them back from the chamber; but Jerome was too much agitated to be repulsed. He declared aloud the flight of Isabella, with protestations of his own innocence. Manfred, distracted at the news, and not less at its coming to the knowledge of the strangers, uttered nothing but incoherent sentences, now upbraiding the friar, now apologizing to the knights, earnest to know what was become of Isabella, yet equally afraid of their knowing, impatient to pursue her, yet dreading to have them join in the pursuit. He offered to dispatch messengers in quest of her: – but the chief knight, no longer keeping silence, reproached Manfred in bitter terms for his dark and ambiguous dealing, and demanded the cause of Isabella's first absence from the castle. Manfred, casting a stern look at Jerome, implying a command of silence, pretended that on Conrad's death he had placed her in sanctuary until he could determine how to dispose of her. Jerome, who trembled for his son's life, did not dare contradict this falsehood; but one of his brethren, not under the same anxiety, declared frankly that she had fled to their church in the preceding night. The prince in vain endeavoured to stop this discovery, which overwhelmed him with shame and confusion. The principal stranger, amazed at the contradictions he heard, and more than half persuaded that Manfred had secreted the princess, notwithstanding the concern he expressed at her flight, rushing to the door, said, Thou traitor-prince! Isabella shall be found. Manfred endeavoured to hold him; but the other knights assisting their comrade, he broke from the prince, and hastened into the court, demanding his attendants. Manfred, finding it in vain to divert him from the pursuit, offered to accompany him; and summoning his attendants, and taking Jerome and some of the friars to guide them, they issued from the castle; Manfred privately giving orders to have the knight's company secured, while to the knight he affected to dispatch a messenger to require their assistance.

The company had no sooner quitted the castle, than Matilda, who felt herself deeply interested for the young peasant, since she had seen him condemned to death in the hall, and whose thoughts had been taken up with concerting measures to save him, was informed by some of the female attendants that Manfred had dispatched all his men various ways in pursuit of Isabella. He had in his hurry given this order in general terms, not meaning to extend it to the guard he had set upon Theodore, but forgetting it. The domestics, officious to obey so peremptory a prince, and urged by their own curiosity and love of novelty to join in any precipitate chace, had to a man left the castle. Matilda disengaged herself from her women, stole up to the black tower, and, unbolting the door, presented herself to the astonished Theodore. Young man, said she, though filial duty and womanly modesty condemn the step I am taking, yet holy charity, surmounting all other ties, justifies this act. Fly; the doors of thy prison are open: my father and his domestics are absent; but they may soon return: begone in safety; and may the angels of heaven direct thy course! — Thou art surely one of those angels! said the enraptured Theodore: none but a blessed saint could speak, could act, could look like thee! — May I not know the name of my divine protectress? Methought thou namedst thy father: is it possible? can Manfred's blood feel holy pity? – Lovely lady, thou answerest not – But how art thou here thyself? Why dost thou neglect thy own safety, and waste a thought on a wretch like Theodore? Let us fly together: the life thou bestowest shall be dedicated to thy defence. Alas! thou mistakest, said Matilda sighing: I am Manfred's daughter, but no dangers await me. Amazement! said Theodore: but last night I blessed myself for yielding thee the service thy gracious compassion so charitably returns me now. Still thou art in an error, said the princess; but this is no time for explanation. Fly, virtuous youth, while it is in my power to save thee: should my father return, thou and I both should indeed have cause to tremble. How? said Theodore: thinkest thou, charming maid, that I will accept of life at the hazard of aught calamitous to thee? Better I endured a thousand deaths – I run no risk, said Matilda, but by thy delay. Depart: it cannot be known that I assisted thy flight. Swear by the saints above, said Theodore, that thou canst not be suspected; else here I vow to await whatever can befall me. Oh! thou art too generous, said Matilda; but rest assured that no suspicion can alight on me. Give me thy beauteous hand in token that thou dost not deceive me, said Theodore; and let me bathe it with the warm tears of gratitude. – Forbear, said the princess: this must not be. – Alas! said Theodore, I have never known but calamity until this hour – perhaps shall never know other fortune again: suffer the chaste raptures of holy gratitude: 'tis my soul would print its effusions on thy hand. – Forbear, and begone, said Matilda: how would Isabella approve of seeing thee at my feet? Who is Isabella? said the young man with surprise. Ah me! I fear, said the princess, I am serving a deceitful one! Hast thou forgot thy curiosity this morning? – Thy looks, thy actions, all thy beauteous self seems an emanation of divinity, said Theodore, but thy words are dark and mysterious – Speak, lady, speak to thy servant's comprehension. – Thou understandest but too well, said Matilda: but once more I command thee to be gone: thy blood, which I may preserve, will be on my head, if I waste the time in vain discourse. I go, lady, said Theodore, because it is thy will, and because I would not bring the grey hairs of my father with sorrow to the grave. Say but, adored lady, that I have thy gentle pity. – Stay, said Matilda ; I will conduct thee to the subterraneous vault by which Isabella escaped ; it will lead thee to the church of saint Nicholas, where thou mayst take sanctuary. – What ! said Theodore, was it another, and not thy lovely self, that I assisted to find the subterraneous passage ? It was, said Matilda : but ask no more ; I tremble to see thee still abide here : fly to the sanctuary. – To sanctuary ! said Theodore : No, princess ; sanctuaries are for helpless damsels, or for criminals. Theodore's soul is free from guilt, nor will wear the appearance of it. Give me a sword, lady, and thy father shall learn that Theodore scorns an ignominious flight. Rash youth ! said Matilda, thou wouldst not dare to lift thy presumptuous arm against the prince of Otranto ? Not against *thy* father ; indeed I dare not, said Theodore : excuse me, lady ; I had forgotten – but could I gaze on thee, and remember thou art sprung from the tyrant Manfred ? – But he is thy father, and from this moment my injuries are buried in oblivion. A deep and hollow groan, which seemed to come from above, startled the princess and Theodore. Good heaven ! we are overheard ! said the princess. They listened ; but perceiving no farther noise, they both concluded it the effect of pent-up vapours : and the princess, preceding Theodore softly, carried him to her father's armoury ; where equipping him with a complete suit, he was conducted by Matilda to the postern-gate. Avoid the town, said the princess, and all the western side of the castle : 'tis there the search must be making by Manfred and the strangers : but hie thee to the opposite quarter. Yonder, behind that forest to the east is a chain of rocks, hollowed into a labyrinth of caverns that reach to the sea-coast. There thou mayst lie concealed, till thou canst make signs to some vessel to put on shore and take thee off. Go ! heaven be thy guide ! – and sometimes in thy prayers remember – Matilda ! – Theodore flung himself at her feet, and seizing her lily hand, which with struggles she suffered him to kiss, he vowed on the earliest opportunity to get himself knighted, and fervently entreated her permission to swear himself eternally her knight. – Ere the princess could reply, a clap of thunder was suddenly heard, that shook the battlements. Theodore, regardless of the tempest, would have urged his suit; but the princess, dismayed, retreated hastily into the castle, and commanded the youth to be gone, with an air that would not be disobeyed. He sighed, and retired, but with eyes fixed on the gate, until Matilda closing it put an end to an interview, in which the hearts of both had drunk so deeply of a passion which both now tasted for the first time.

Theodore went pensively to the convent, to acquaint his father with his deliverance. There he learned the absence of Jerome, and the pursuit that was making after the lady Isabella, with some particulars of whose story he now first became acquainted. The generous gallantry of his nature prompted him to wish to assist her; but the monks could lend him no lights to guess at the route she had taken. He was not tempted to wander far in search of her; for the idea of Matilda had imprinted itself so strongly on his heart, that he could not bear to absent himself at much distance from her abode. The tenderness Jerome had expressed for him concurred to confirm this reluctance; and he even persuaded himself that filial affection was the chief cause of his hovering between the castle and monastery. Until Jerome should return at night, Theodore at length determined to repair to the forest that Matilda had pointed out to him. Arriving there, he sought the gloomiest shades, as best suited to the pleasing melancholy that reigned in his mind. In this mood he roved insensibly to the caves which had formerly served as a retreat to hermits, and were now reported round the country to be haunted by evil spirits. He recollected to have heard this tradition; and being of a brave and adventurous disposition, he willingly indulged his curiosity in exploring the secret recesses of this labyrinth. He had not penetrated far before he thought he heard the steps of some person who seemed to retreat before him. Theodore, though firmly grounded in all our holy faith enjoins to be believed, had no apprehension that good men were abandoned without cause to the malice of the powers of darkness. He thought the place more likely to be infested by robbers, than by those infernal agents who are reported to molest and bewilder travellers. He had long burned with impatience to approve his valour. Drawing his sabre, he marched sedately onwards, still directing his steps as the imperfect rustling sound before him led the way. The armour he wore was a like indication to the person who avoided him. Theodore, now convinced that he was not mistaken, redoubled his pace, and evidently gained on the person that fled; whose haste increasing, Theodore came up just as a woman fell breathless before him. He hasted to raise her; but her terror was so great, that he apprehended she would faint in his arms. He used every gentle word to dispel her alarms, and assured her that, far from injuring, he would defend her at the peril of his life. The lady recovering her spirits from his courteous demeanour, and gazing on her protector, said, Sure I have heard that voice before? – Not to my knowledge, replied Theodore, unless, as I conjecture, thou art the lady Isabella. – Merciful heaven! cried she, thou art not sent in quest of me, art thou? And saying those words she threw herself at his feet, and besought him not to deliver her up to Manfred. To Manfred! cried Theodore – No, lady: I have once already delivered thee from his tyranny, and it shall fare hard with me now, but I will place thee out of the reach of his daring. Is it possible, said she, that thou shouldst be the generous unknown whom I met last night in the vault of the castle? Sure thou art not a mortal, but my guardian angel: on my knees let me thank – Hold, gentle princess, said Theodore, nor demean thyself before a poor and friendless young man. If heaven has selected me for thy deliverer, it will accomplish its work, and strengthen my arm in thy cause. But come, lady, we are too near the mouth of the cavern; let us seek its inmost recesses: I can have no tranquillity till I have placed thee beyond the reach of danger. – Alas! what mean you, sir? said she. Though all your actions are noble, though your sentiments speak the purity of your soul, is it fitting that I should accompany you alone into these perplexed retreats? Should we be found together, what would a censorious world think of my conduct? – I respect your virtuous delicacy, said Theodore; nor do you harbour a suspicion that wounds my honour. I meant to conduct you into the most private cavity of these rocks; and then, at the hazard of my life, to guard their entrance against every living thing. Besides, lady, continued he, drawing a deep sigh, beauteous and all perfect as your form is, and though my wishes are not guiltless of aspiring, know, my soul is dedicated to another; and although—A sudden noise prevented Theodore from proceeding. They soon distinguished these sounds, Isabella! What ho! Isabella! — The trembling princess relapsed into her former agony of fear. Theodore endeavoured to encourage her, but in vain. He assured her he would die rather than suffer her to return under Manfred's power; and begging her to remain concealed, he went forth to prevent the person in search of her from approaching.

At the mouth of the cavern he found an armed knight discoursing with a peasant, who assured him he had seen a lady enter the passes of the rock. The knight was preparing to seek her, when Theodore, placing himself in his way, with his sword drawn, sternly forbad him at his peril to advance. And who art thou who darest to cross my way? said the knight haughtily. One who does not dare more than he will perform, said Theodore. I seek the lady Isabella, said the knight; and understand she has taken refuge among these rocks. Impede me not, or thou wilt repent having provoked my resentment. – Thy purpose is as odious as thy resentment is contemptible, said Theodore. Return whence thou camest, or we shall soon know whose resentment is most terrible. – The stranger, who was the principal knight that had arrived from the marquis of Vicenza, had galloped from Manfred as he was busied in getting information of the princess, and giving various orders to prevent her falling into the power of the three knights. Their chief had suspected Manfred of being privy to the princess's absconding; and this insult from a man who he concluded was stationed by that prince to secrete her, confirming his suspicions, he made no reply, but, discharging a blow with his sabre at Theodore, would soon have removed all obstruction, if Theodore, who took him for one of Manfred's captains, and who had no sooner given the provocation than prepared to support it, had not received the stroke on his shield. The valour that had so long been smothered in his breast, broke forth at once: he rushed impetuously on the knight, whose pride and wrath were not less powerful incentives to hardy deeds. The combat was furious, but not long. Theodore wounded the knight in three several places, and at last disarmed him as he fainted by the loss of blood. The peasant, who had fled on the first onset, had given the alarm to some of Manfred's domestics, who by his orders were dispersed through the forest in pursuit of Isabella. They came up as the knight fell, whom they soon discovered to be the noble stranger. Theodore, notwithstanding his hatred to Manfred, could not behold the victory he had gained without emotions of pity and generosity: but he was more touched, when he learned the quality of his adversary, and was informed that he was no retainer, but an enemy of Manfred. He assisted the servants of the latter in disarming the knight, and in endeavouring to staunch the blood that flowed from his wounds. The knight, recovering his speech, said in a faint and faltering voice, Generous foe, we have both been in an error: I took thee for an instrument of the tyrant; I perceive thou hast made the like mistake — It is too late for excuses — I faint. — If Isabella is at hand, call her — I have important secrets to — He is dying! said one of the attendants; has nobody a crucifix about them? Andrea, do thou pray over him. — Fetch some water, said Theodore, and pour it down his throat, while I hasten to the princess. Saying this, he flew to Isabella; and in few words told her modestly, that he had been so unfortunate by mistake as to wound a gentleman from her father's court, who wished ere he died to impart something of consequence to her. The princess, who had been transported at hearing the voice of Theodore as he called her to come forth, was astonished at what she heard. Suffering herself to be conducted by Theodore, the new proof of whose valour recalled her dispersed spirits, she came where the bleeding knight lay speechless on the ground — but her fears returned when she beheld the domestics of Manfred. She would again have fled, if Theodore had not made her observe that they were unarmed, and had not threatened them with instant death, if they should dare to seize the princess. The stranger, opening his eyes, and beholding a woman, said, Art thou — pray tell me truly — art thou Isabella of Vicenza? I am, said she; good heaven restore thee! — Then thou — then thou — said the knight, struggling for utterance — seest — thy father! — Give me one — Oh! amazement!

horror! what do I hear? what do I see? cried Isabella. My father! You my father! How came you here, sir? For heaven's sake speak!—Oh! run for help, or he will expire! — 'Tis most true, said the wounded knight, exerting all his force; I am Frederic thy father — Yes, I came to deliver thee — It will not be — Give me a parting kiss, and take—Sir, said Theodore, do not exhaust yourself: suffer us to convey you to the castle. — To the castle! said Isabella: Is there no help nearer than the castle? Would you expose my father to the tyrant? If he goes thither, I dare not accompany him. — And yet, can I leave him? — My child, said Frederic, it matters not for me whither I am carried: a few minutes will place me beyond danger: but while I have eyes to dote on thee, forsake me not, dear Isabella! This brave knight — I know not who he is — will protect thy innocence. Sir, you will not abandon my child, will you? — Theodore, shedding tears over his victim, and vowing to guard the princess at the expense of his life, persuaded Frederic to suffer himself to be conducted to the castle. They placed him on a horse belonging to one of the domestics, after binding up his wounds as well as they were able. Theodore marched by his side; and the afflicted Isabella, who could not bear to quit him, followed mournfully behind.

CHAPTER 4

The sorrowful troop no sooner arrived at the castle, than they were met by Hippolita and Matilda, whom Isabella had sent one of the domestics before to advertise of their approach. The ladies, causing Frederic to be conveyed into the nearest chamber, retired, while the surgeons examined his wounds. Matilda blushed at seeing Theodore and Isabella together; but endeavoured to conceal it by embracing the latter, and condoling with her on her father's mischance. The surgeons soon came to acquaint Hippolita that none of the marquis's wounds were dangerous; and that he was desirous of seeing his daughter and the princesses. Theodore, under pretence of expressing his joy at being freed from his apprehensions of the combat being fatal to Frederic, could not resist the impulse of following Matilda. Her eyes were so often cast down on meeting his, that Isabella, who regarded Theodore as attentively as he gazed on Matilda, soon divined who the object was that he had told her in the cave engaged his affections. While this mute scene passed, Hippolita demanded of Frederic the cause of his having taken that mysterious course for reclaiming his daughter; and threw in various apologies to excuse her lord for the match contracted between their children. Frederic, however incensed against Manfred, was not insensible to the courtesy and benevolence of Hippolita: but he was still more struck with the lovely form of Matilda. Wishing to detain them by his bed-side, he informed Hippolita of his story. He told her, that, while prisoner to the infidels, he had dreamed that his daughter, of whom he had learned no news since his captivity, was detained in a castle, where she was in danger of the most dreadful misfortunes; and

Hermit — tells him where sword is

that if he obtained his liberty, and repaired to a wood near Joppa,[n] he would learn more. Alarmed at this dream, and incapable of obeying the direction given by it, his chains became more grievous than ever. But while his thoughts were occupied on the means of obtaining his liberty, he received the agreeable news that the confederate princes, who were warring in Palestine, had paid his ransom. He instantly set out for the wood that had been marked in his dream. For three days he and his attendants had wandered in the forest without seeing a human form: but on the evening of the third they came to a cell, in which they found a venerable hermit in the agonies of death. Applying rich cordials, they brought the saint-like man to his speech. My sons, said he, I am bounden to your charity — but it is in vain — I am going to my eternal rest — yet I die with the satisfaction of performing the will of heaven. When first I repaired to this solitude, after seeing my country become a prey to unbelievers [it is, alas! above fifty years since I was witness to that dreadful scene!] saint Nicholas appeared to me, and revealed a secret, which he bade me never disclose to mortal man, but on my death-bed. This is that tremendous hour, and ye are no doubt the chosen warriors to whom I was ordered to reveal my trust. As soon as ye have done the last offices to this wretched corse, dig under the seventh tree on the left hand of this poor cave, and your pains will — Oh! good heaven receive my soul! With those words the devout man breathed his last. By break of day, continued Frederic, when we had committed the holy relics to earth, we dug according to direction — But what was our astonishment, when about the depth of six feet we discovered an enormous sabre — the very weapon yonder in the court! On the blade, which was then partly out of the scabbard, though since closed by our efforts in removing it, were written the following lines—No; excuse me, madam, added the marquis, turning to Hippolita, if I forbear to repeat them: I respect your sex and rank, and would not be guilty of offending your ear with sounds injurious to aught that is dear to you. — He paused. Hippolita trembled. She did not doubt but Frederic was destined by heaven to accomplish the fate that seemed to theaten her house. Looking with anxious fondness at Matilda, a silent tear stole down her cheek; but recollecting herself, she said, Proceed, my lord; heaven does nothing in vain: mortals must receive its divine behests with lowliness and submission. It is our part to deprecate its wrath, or bow to its decrees. Repeat the sentence, my lord: we listen resigned. — Frederic was grieved that he had proceeded so far. The dignity and patient firmness of Hippolita penetrated him with respect, and the tender silent affection, with which the princess and her daughter regarded each other, melted him almost to tears. Yet apprehensive that his forbearance to obey would be more alarming, he repeated in a faltering and low voice the following lines:

> *Where'er a casque that suits this sword is found,*
> *With perils is thy daughter compass'd round:*
> *Alfonso's blood alone can save the maid,*
> *And quiet a long-restless prince's shade.*

[*message for Frederick on the sword*]

What is there in these lines, said Theodore impatiently, that affects these princesses? Why were they to be shocked by a mysterious delicacy, that has so little foundation? Your words are rude, young man, said the marquis; and though fortune has favoured you once — My honoured lord, said Isabella, who resented Theodore's warmth, which she perceived was dictated by his sentiments for Matilda, discompose not yourself for the glosing[n] of a peasant's son: he forgets the reverence he owes you; but he is not accustomed — Hippolita, concerned at the heat that had arisen, checked Theodore for his boldness, but with an air acknowledging his zeal; and, changing the conversation, demanded of Frederic where he had left her lord? As the marquis was going to reply, they heard a noise without; and rising to enquire the cause, Manfred, Jerome, and part of the troop, who had met an imperfect rumour of what had happened, entered the chamber. Manfred advanced hastily towards Frederic's bed to condole with him on his misfortune, and to learn the circumstances of the combat; when starting in an agony of terror and amazement, he cried, Ha! what art thou, thou dreadful spectre! Is my hour come? — My dearest, gracious lord, cried Hippolita, clasping him in her arms, what is it you see? Why do you fix your eye-balls thus? — What! cried

Manfred breathless – dost thou see nothing, Hippolita? Is this ghastly phantom sent to me alone – to me, who did not—For mercy's sweetest self, my lord, said Hippolita, resume your soul, command your reason. There is none here but we, your friends. – What, is not that Alfonso? cried Manfred: dost thou not see him? Can it be my brain's delirium? – This! my lord, said Hippolita; this is Theodore, the youth who has been so unfortunate – Theodore! said Manfred mournfully, and striking his forehead – Theodore, or a phantom, he has unhinged the soul of Manfred. – But how comes he here? and how comes he in armour? I believe he went in search of Isabella, said Hippolita. Of Isabella? said Manfred, relapsing into rage – Yes, yes, that is not doubtful – But how did he escape from durance in which I left him? Was it Isabella, or this hypocritical old friar, that procured his enlargement? – And would a parent be criminal, my lord, said Theodore, if he meditated the deliverance of his child? Jerome, amazed to hear himself in a manner accused by his son, and without foundation, knew not what to think. He could not comprehend how Theodore had escaped, how he came to be armed, and to encounter Frederic. Still he would not venture to ask any questions that might tend to inflame Manfred's wrath against his son. Jerome's silence convinced Manfred that he had contrived Theodore's release. – And is it thus, thou ungrateful old man, said the prince, addressing himself to the friar, that thou repayest mine and Hippolita's bounties? And not content with traversing my heart's nearest wishes, thou armest thy bastard, and bringest him into my own castle to insult me! – My lord, said Theodore, you wrong my father: nor he nor I is capable of harbouring a thought against your peace. Is it insolence thus to surrender myself to your highness's pleasure? added he, laying his sword respectfully at Manfred's feet. Behold my bosom; strike, my lord, if you suspect that a disloyal thought is lodged there. There is not a sentiment engraven on my heart, that does not venerate you and yours. The grace and fervour with which Theodore uttered these words, interested every person present in his favour. Even Manfred was touched – yet still possessed with his resemblance to Alfonso, his admiration was dashed with secret horror. Rise, said he; thy life is not my present purpose. – But tell me thy history, and how thou camest connected with this old traitor here. My lord! said Jerome eagerly. – Peace, impostor! said Manfred; I will not have him prompted. My lord, said Theodore, I want no assistance; my story is very brief. I was carried at five years of age to Algiers with my mother, who had been taken by corsairs[n] from the coast of Sicily. She died of grief in less than a twelvemonth. – The tears gushed from Jerome's eyes, on whose countenance a thousand anxious passions stood expressed. Before she died, continued Theodore, she bound a writing about my arm under my garments, which told me I was the son of the count Falconara. – It is most true, said Jerome; I am that wretched father. – Again, I enjoin thee silence, said Manfred: proceed. I remained in slavery, said Theodore, until within these two years, when attending on my master in his cruizes, I was delivered by a christian vessel, which overpowered the pirate; and discovering myself to the captain, he generously put me on shore in Sicily. But alas! instead of finding a father, I learned that his estate, which was situated on the coast, had during his absence been laid waste by the rover[n] who had carried my mother and me into captivity: that his castle had been burnt to the ground: and that my father on his return had sold what remained, and was retired into religion in the kingdom of Naples, but where, no man could inform me. Destitute and friendless, hopeless almost of attaining the transport of a parent's embrace, I took the first opportunity of setting sail for Naples; from whence within these six days I wandered into this province, still supporting myself by the labour of my hands; nor till yester-morn did I believe that heaven had reserved any lot for me but peace of mind and contented poverty. This, my lord, is Theodore's story. I am blessed beyond my hope in finding a father; I am unfortunate beyond my desert in having incurred your highness's displeasure. He ceased. A murmur of approbation gently arose from the audience. This is not all, said Frederic; I am bound in honour to add what he suppresses. Though he is modest, I must be generous – he is one of the bravest youths on christian ground. He is warm too; and from the short knowledge I have of him, I will pledge myself for his veracity: if what he reports of himself were not true, he would not utter it – and for me, youth, I honour a frankness which becomes thy birth. But now, and thou didst offend me; yet the noble blood which flows in thy veins may well be allowed to boil out, when it has so recently traced itself to its source. Come, my lord, [turning to Manfred] if I can pardon him, surely you may: it is not the youth's fault, if you took him for a spectre. This bitter taunt galled the soul of Manfred. If beings from another world, replied he haughtily, have power to impress my mind with awe, it is more than living man can do; nor could a stripling's arm—My lord, interrupted Hippolita, your guest has occasion for repose; shall we not leave him to his rest? Saying this, and taking Manfred by the hand, she took leave of Frederic, and led the company forth. The prince, not sorry to quit a conversation which recalled to mind the discovery he had made of his most secret sensations, suffered himself to be conducted to his own apartment, after permitting Theodore, though under engagement to return to the castle on the morrow, [a condition the young man gladly accepted] to retire with his father to the convent. Matilda and Isabella were too much occupied with their own reflections, and too little content with each other, to wish for farther converse that night. They separated each to her chamber, with more expressions of ceremony, and fewer of affection, than had passed between them since their childhood.

If they parted with small cordiality, they did but meet with greater impatience as soon as the sun was risen. Their minds were in a situation that excluded sleep, and each recollected a thousand questions which she wished she had put to the other overnight. Matilda reflected that Isabella had been twice delivered by Theodore in very critical situations, which she could not believe accidental. His eyes, it was true, had been fixed on her in Frederic's chamber; but that might have been to disguise his passion for Isabella from the fathers of both. It were better to clear this up. She wished to know the truth, lest she should wrong her friend by entertaining a passion for Isabella's lover. Thus jealousy prompted, and at the same time borrowed an excuse from friendship to justify its curiosity.

Isabella, not less restless, had better foundation for her

suspicions. Both Theodore's tongue and eyes had told her his
heart was engaged, it was true – yet perhaps Matilda might not
correspond to his passion – She had ever appeared insensible to
love; all her thoughts were set on heaven – Why did I dissuade
her? said Isabella to herself; I am punished for my generosity –
But when did they meet? where? – It cannot be; I have deceived
myself – Perhaps last night was the first time they ever beheld
each other – it must be some other object that has prepossessed
his affections – If it is, I am not so unhappy as I thought; if it is
not my friend Matilda – How! can I stoop to wish for the
affection of a man, who rudely and unnecessarily acquainted me
with his indifference? and that at the very moment in which
common courtesy demanded at least expressions of civility. I
will go to my dear Matilda, who will confirm me in this
becoming pride – Man is false – I will advise with her on taking
the veil: she will rejoice to find me in this disposition; and I will
acquaint her that I no longer oppose her inclination for the
cloister. In this frame of mind, and determined to open her heart
entirely to Matilda, she went to that princess's chamber, whom
she found already dressed, and leaning pensively on her arm.
This attitude, so correspondent to what she felt herself, revived
Isabella's suspicions, and destroyed the confidence she had
purposed to place in her friend. They blushed at meeting, and
were too much novices to disguise their sensations with address.
After some unmeaning questions and replies, Matilda demanded
of Isabella the cause of her flight. The latter, who had almost
forgotten Manfred's passion, so entirely was she occupied by
her own, concluding that Matilda referred to her last escape from
the convent, which had occasioned the events of the preceding
evening, replied, Martelli brought word to the convent that your
mother was dead. – Oh! said Matilda interrupting her, Bianca
has explained that mistake to me: on seeing me faint, she cried
out, The princess is dead! and Martelli, who had come for the
usual dole[n] to the castle—And what made you faint? said
Isabella, indifferent to the rest. Matilda blushed, and stammered
– My father – he was sitting in judgment on a criminal. – What
criminal? said Isabella eagerly.—A young man, said Matilda – I
believe – I think it was that young man that – What, Theodore?

said Isabella. Yes, answered she; I never saw him before; I do not know how he had offended my father – but, as he has been of service to you, I am glad my lord has pardoned him. Served me? replied Isabella: do you term it serving me, to wound my father, and almost occasion his death? Though it is but since yesterday that I am blessed with knowing a parent, I hope Matilda does not think I am such a stranger to filial tenderness as not to resent the boldness of that audacious youth, and that it is impossible for me ever to feel any affection for one who dared to lift his arm against the author of my being. No, Matilda, my heart abhors him; and if you still retain the friendship for me that you have vowed from your infancy, you will detest a man who has been on the point of making me miserable for ever. Matilda held down her head, and replied, I hope my dearest Isabella does not doubt her Matilda's friendship: I never beheld that youth until yesterday; he is almost a stranger to me: but as the surgeons have pronounced your father out of danger, you ought not to harbour uncharitable resentment against one who I am persuaded did not know the marquis was related to you. You plead his cause very pathetically, said Isabella, considering he is so much a stranger to you! I am mistaken, or he returns your charity. What mean you? said Matilda. Nothing, said Isabella; repenting that she had given Matilda a hint of Theodore's inclination for her. Then changing the discourse, she asked Matilda what occasioned Manfred to take Theodore for a spectre? Bless me, said Matilda, did not you observe his extreme resemblance to the portrait of Alfonso in the gallery? I took notice of it to Bianca even before I saw him in armour; but with the helmet on, he is the very image of that picture. I do not much observe pictures, said Isabella; much less have I examined this young man so attentively as you seem to have done.—Ah! Matilda, your heart is in danger – but let me warn you as a friend – He has owned to me that he is in love: it cannot be with you, for yesterday was the first time you ever met – was it not? Certainly, replied Matilda. But why does my dearest Isabella conclude from any thing I have said, that – She paused – then continuing, He saw you first, and I am far from having the vanity to think that my little portion of charms

could engage a heart devoted to you. May you be happy,
Isabella, whatever is the fate of Matilda! – My lovely friend,
said Isabella, whose heart was too honest to resist a kind
expression, it is you that Theodore admires; I saw it; I am
persuaded of it; nor shall a thought of my own happiness suffer
me to interfere with yours. This frankness drew tears from the
gentle Matilda; and jealousy, that for a moment had raised a
coolness between these amiable maidens, soon gave way to the
natural sincerity and candour of their souls. Each confessed to
the other the impression that Theodore had made on her; and
this confidence was followed by a struggle of generosity, each
insisting on yielding her claim to her friend. At length, the
dignity of Isabella's virtue reminding her of the preference which
Theodore had almost declared for her rival, made her determine
to conquer her passion, and cede the beloved object to her
friend.

During this contest of amity, Hippolita entered her daughter's
chamber. Madam, said she to Isabella, you have so much
tenderness for Matilda, and interest yourself so kindly in whatever affects our wretched house, that I can have no secrets with
my child, which are not proper for you to hear. The princesses
were all attention and anxiety. Know then, madam, continued
Hippolita, and you, my dearest Matilda, that being convinced
by all the events of these two last ominous days, that heaven
purposes the sceptre of Otranto should pass from Manfred's
hands into those of the marquis Frederic, I have been perhaps
inspired with the thought of averting our total destruction by
the union of our rival houses. With this view I have been
proposing to Manfred my lord to tender this dear dear child to
Frederic your father—Me to lord Frederic! cried Matilda –
Good heavens! my gracious mother – and have you named it to
my father? I have, said Hippolita: he listened benignly to my
proposal, and is gone to break it to the marquis. Ah! wretched
princess! cried Isabella, what hast thou done? What ruin has
thy inadvertent goodness been preparing for thyself, for me, and
for Matilda! Ruin from me to you and to my child! said
Hippolita: What can this mean? Alas! said Isabella, the purity
of your own heart prevents your seeing the depravity of others.

Manfred, your lord, that impious man—Hold, said Hippolita;
you must not in my presence, young lady, mention Manfred
with disrespect: he is my lord and husband, and – Will not be
long so, said Isabella, if his wicked purposes can be carried into
execution. This language amazes me, said Hippolita. Your
feeling, Isabella, is warm; but until this hour I never knew it
betray you into intemperance. What deed of Manfred authorizes
you to treat him as a murderer, an assassin? Thou virtuous and
too credulous princess! replied Isabella; it is not thy life he aims
at – it is to separate himself from thee! to divorce thee! To –
to divorce me! To divorce my mother! cried Hippolita and
Matilda at once. – Yes, said Isabella; and to complete his crime,
he meditates – I cannot speak it! What can surpass what thou
hast already uttered? said Matilda. Hippolita was silent. Grief
choked her speech: and the recollection of Manfred's late
ambiguous discourses confirmed what she heard. Excellent, dear
lady! madam! mother! cried Isabella, flinging herself at Hippolita's feet in a transport of passion; trust me, believe me, I will
die a thousand deaths sooner than consent to injure you, than
yield to so odious – oh! – This is too much! cried Hippolita:
what crimes does one crime suggest! Rise, dear Isabella; I do
not doubt your virtue. Oh! Matilda, this stroke is too heavy for
thee! Weep not, my child; and not a murmur, I charge thee.
Remember, he is *thy* father still. – But you are my mother too,
said Matilda fervently; and *you* are virtuous, *you* are guiltless!
– Oh! must not I, must not I complain? You must not, said
Hippolita – Come, all will yet be well. Manfred, in the agony
for the loss of thy brother, knew not what he said: perhaps
Isabella misunderstood him: his heart is good – and, my child,
thou knowest not all. There is a destiny hangs over us; the hand
of Providence is stretched out – Oh! could I but save thee from
the wreck! – Yes, continued she in a firmer tone, perhaps the
sacrifice of myself may atone for all—I will go and offer myself
to this divorce – it boots not what becomes of me. I will
withdraw into the neighbouring monastery, and waste the
remainder of life in prayers and tears for my child and – the
prince! Thou art as much too good for this world, said Isabella,
as Manfred is execrable – But think not, lady, that thy weakness

shall determine for me. I swear – hear me, all ye angels—Stop, I adjure thee, cried Hippolita; remember, thou dost not depend on thyself; thou hast a father. – My father is too pious, too noble, interrupted Isabella, to command an impious deed. But should he command it, can a father enjoin a cursed act? I was contracted to the son; can I wed the father? – No, madam, no; force should not drag me to Manfred's hated bed. I loathe him, I abhor him: divine and human laws forbid. – And my friend, my dearest Matilda! would I wound her tender soul by injuring her adored mother? my own mother – I never have known another.—Oh! she is the mother of both! cried Matilda. Can we, can we, Isabella, adore her too much? My lovely children, said the touched Hippolita, your tenderness overpowers me – but I must not give way to it. It is not ours to make election for ourselves; heaven, our fathers, and our husbands, must decide for us. Have patience until you hear what Manfred and Frederic have determined. If the marquis accepts Matilda's hand, I know she will readily obey. Heaven may interpose and prevent the rest. What means my child? continued she, seeing Matilda fall at her feet with a flood of speechless tears – But no; answer me not, my daughter; I must not hear a word against the pleasure of thy father. Oh! doubt not my obedience, my dreadful obedience to him and to you! said Matilda. But can I, most respected of women, can I experience all this tenderness, this world of goodness, and conceal a thought from the best of mothers? What art thou going to utter? said Isabella trembling. Recollect thyself, Matilda. No, Isabella, said the princess, I should not deserve this incomparable parent, if the inmost recesses of my soul harboured a thought without her permission – Nay, I have offended her; I have suffered a passion to enter my heart without her avowal – But here I disclaim it; here I vow to heaven and her—My child! my child! said Hippolita, what words are these? What new calamities has fate in store for us? Thou a passion! thou, in this hour of destruction—Oh! I see all my guilt! said Matilda. I abhor myself, if I cost my mother a pang. She is the dearest thing I have on earth – Oh! I will never, never behold him more! Isabella, said Hippolita, thou art conscious to this unhappy secret, whatever it is. Speak

– What! cried Matilda, have I so forfeited my mother's love that she will not permit me even to speak my own guilt? Oh! wretched, wretched Matilda! – Thou art too cruel, said Isabella to Hippolita: canst thou behold this anguish of a virtuous mind, and not commiserate it? Not pity my child! said Hippolita, catching Matilda in her arms – Oh! I know she is good, she is all virtue, all tenderness, and duty. I do forgive thee, my excellent, my only hope! The princesses then revealed to Hippolita their mutual inclination for Theodore, and the purpose of Isabella to resign him to Matilda. Hippolita blamed their imprudence, and shewed them the improbability that either father would consent to bestow his heiress on so poor a man, though nobly born. Some comfort it gave her to find their passion of so recent a date, and that Theodore had but little cause to suspect it in either. She strictly enjoined them to avoid all correspondence with him. This Matilda fervently promised: but Isabella, who flattered herself that she meant no more than to promote his union with her friend, could not determine to avoid him; and made no reply. I will go to the convent, said Hippolita, and order new masses to be said for a deliverance from these calamities. – Oh! my mother, said Matilda, you mean to quit us: you mean to take sanctuary, and to give my father an opportunity of pursuing his fatal intention. Alas! on my knees I supplicate you to forbear – Will you leave me a prey to Frederic? I will follow you to the convent. – Be at peace, my child, said Hippolita: I will return instantly. I will never abandon thee, until I know it is the will of heaven, and for thy benefit. Do not deceive me, said Matilda. I will not marry Frederic until thou commandest it. Alas! what will become of me? – Why that exclamation? said Hippolita. I have promised thee to return. – Ah! my mother, replied Matilda, stay and save me from myself. A frown from thee can do more than all my father's severity. I have given away my heart, and you alone can make me recall it. No more, said Hippolita: thou must not relapse, Matilda. I can quit Theodore, said she, but must I wed another? Let me attend thee to the altar, and shut myself from the world forever. Thy fate depends on thy father, said Hippolita: I have ill bestowed my tenderness, if it has taught

thee to revere aught beyond him. Adieu, my child! I go to pray
for thee.

Hippolita's real purpose was to demand of Jerome, whether
in conscience she might not consent to the divorce. She had oft
urged Manfred to resign the principality, which the delicacy of
her conscience rendered an hourly burthen to her. These scruples
concurred to make the separation from her husband appear less
dreadful to her than it would have seemed in any other situation.

Jerome, at quitting the castle overnight, had questioned
Theodore severely why he had accused him to Manfred of being
privy to his escape. Theodore owned it had been with design to
prevent Manfred's suspicion from alighting on Matilda; and
added, the holiness of Jerome's life and character secured him
from the tyrant's wrath. Jerome was heartily grieved to discover
his son's inclination for that princess; and, leaving him to his
rest, promised in the morning to acquaint him with important
reasons for conquering his passion. Theodore, like Isabella, was
too recently acquainted with parental authority to submit to its
decisions against the impulse of his heart. He had little curiosity
to learn the friar's reasons, and less disposition to obey them.
The lovely Matilda had made stronger impressions on him than
filial affection. All night he pleased himself with visions of love;
and it was not till late after the morning-office, that he recollected the friar's commands to attend him at Alfonso's tomb.

Young man, said Jerome, when he saw him, this tardiness
does not please me. Have a father's commands already so little
weight? Theodore made awkward excuses, and attributed his
delay to having overslept himself. And on whom were thy
dreams employed? said the friar sternly. His son blushed. Come,
come, resumed the friar, inconsiderate youth, this must not be;
eradicate this guilty passion from thy breast. – Guilty passion!
cried Theodore: can guilt dwell with innocent beauty and
virtuous modesty? It is sinful, replied the friar, to cherish those
whom heaven has doomed to destruction. A tyrant's race must
be swept from the earth to the third and fourth generation. Will
heaven visit the innocent for the crimes of the guilty? said
Theodore. The fair Matilda has virtues enough – To undo thee,
interrupted Jerome. Hast thou so soon forgotten that twice the

savage Manfred has pronounced thy sentence? Nor have I forgotten, sir, said Theodore, that the charity of his daughter delivered me from his power. I can forget injuries, but never benefits. The injuries thou hast received from Manfred's race, said the friar, are beyond what thou canst conceive. – Reply not, but view this holy image! Beneath this marble monument rest the ashes of the good Alfonso; a prince adorned with every virtue: the father of his people! the delight of mankind! Kneel, head-strong boy, and list, while a father unfolds a tale of horror, that will expel every sentiment from thy soul, but sensations of sacred vengeance.[n] – Alfonso! much-injured prince! let thy unsatisfied shade sit awful on the troubled air, while these trembling lips – Ha! who comes there? – The most wretched of women, said Hippolita, entering the choir. Good father, art thou at leisure? – But why this kneeling youth? what means the horror imprinted on each countenance? why at this venerable tomb – Alas! hast thou seen aught? We were pouring forth our orisons to heaven, replied the friar with some confusion, to put an end to the woes of this deplorable province. Join with us, lady! thy spotless soul may obtain an exemption from the judgments which the portents of these days but too speakingly denounce against thy house. I pray fervently to heaven to divert them, said the pious princess. Thou knowest it has been the occupation of my life to wrest a blessing for my lord and my harmless children – One, alas! is taken from me! Would heaven but hear me for my poor Matilda! Father, intercede for her! – Every heart will bless her, cried Theodore with rapture. – Be dumb, rash youth! said Jerome. And thou, fond princess, contend not with the powers above! The Lord giveth, and the Lord taketh away: bless his holy name, and submit to his decrees. I do most devoutly, said Hippolita: but will he not spare my only comfort? must Matilda perish too? – Ah! father, I came – But dismiss thy son. No ear but thine must hear what I have to utter. May heaven grant thy every wish, most excellent princess! said Theodore retiring. Jerome frowned.

Hippolita then acquainted the friar with the proposal she had suggested to Manfred, his approbation of it, and the tender of Matilda that he was gone to make to Frederic. Jerome could not conceal his dislike of the motion, which he covered under pretence of the improbability that Frederic, the nearest of blood to Alfonso, and who was come to claim his succession, would yield to an alliance with the usurper of his right. But nothing could equal the perplexity of the friar, when Hippolita confessed her readiness not to oppose the separation, and demanded his opinion of the legality of her acquiescence. The friar catched eagerly at her request of his advice; and without explaining his aversion to the proposed marriage of Manfred and Isabella, he painted to Hippolita in the most alarming colours the sinfulness of her consent, denounced judgments against her if she complied, and enjoined her in the severest terms to treat any such proposition with every mark of indignation and refusal.

Manfred, in the mean time, had broken his purpose to Frederic, and proposed the double marriage. That weak prince, who had been struck with the charms of Matilda, listened but too early to the offer. He forgot his enmity to Manfred, whom he saw but little hope of dispossessing by force; and flattering himself that no issue might succeed from the union of his daughter with the tyrant, he looked upon his own succession to the principality as facilitated by wedding Matilda. He made faint opposition to the proposal; affecting, for form only, not to acquiesce unless Hippolita should consent to the divorce. Manfred took that upon himself. Transported with his success, and impatient to see himself in a situation to expect sons, he hastened to his wife's apartment, determined to extort her compliance. He learned with indignation that she was absent at the convent. His guilt suggested to him that she had probably been informed by Isabella of his purpose. He doubted whether her retirement to the convent did not import an intention of remaining there, until she could raise obstacles to their divorce; and the suspicions he had already entertained of Jerome, made him apprehend that the friar would not only traverse his views, but might have inspired Hippolita with the resolution of taking sanctuary. Impatient to unravel this clue, and to defeat its success, Manfred hastened to the convent and arrived there as the friar was earnestly exhorting the princess never to yield to the divorce.

Madam, said Manfred, what business drew you hither? Why did not you await my return from the marquis? I came to implore a blessing on our councils, replied Hippolita. My councils do not need a friar's intervention, said Manfred – and of all men living is that hoary traitor the only one whom you delight to confer with? Profane prince! said Jerome: is it at the altar that thou choosest to insult the servants of the altar? – But, Manfred, thy impious schemes are known. Heaven and this virtuous lady know them. Nay, frown not, prince. The church despises thy menaces. Her thunders will be heard above thy wrath. Dare to proceed in thy curst purpose of a divorce, until her sentence be known, and here I lance her anathema at thy head. Audacious rebel! said Manfred, endeavouring to conceal the awe with which the friar's words inspired him; dost thou presume to threaten thy lawful prince? Thou art no lawful prince, said Jerome; thou art no prince – Go, discuss thy claim with Frederic; and when that is done – It is done, replied Manfred: Frederic accepts Matilda's hand, and is content to wave his claim, unless I have no male issue. – As he spoke those words three drops of blood fell from the nose of Alfonso's statue. Manfred turned pale, and the princess sunk on her knees. Behold! said the friar: mark this miraculous indication that the blood of Alfonso will never mix with that of Manfred! My gracious lord, said Hippolita, let us submit ourselves to heaven. Think not thy ever obedient wife rebels against thy authority. I have no will but that of my lord and the church. To that revered tribunal let us appeal. It does not depend on us to burst the bonds that unite us. If the church shall approve the dissolution of our marriage, be it so – I have but few years, and those of sorrow, to pass. Where can they be worn away so well as at the foot of this altar, in prayers for thine and Matilda's safety? – But thou shalt not remain here until then, said Manfred. Repair with me to the castle, and there I will advise on the proper measures for a divorce. – But this meddling friar[n] comes not thither; my hospitable roof shall never more harbour a traitor – and for thy reverence's offspring, continued he, I banish him from my dominions. He, I ween, is no sacred personage, nor under the protection of the church. Whoever weds Isabella, it shall not be father Falconara's started-up son. They start up, said the friar, who are suddenly beheld in the seat of lawful princes; but they wither away like the grass, and their place knows them no more. Manfred, casting a look of scorn at the friar, led Hippolita forth; but at the door of the church whispered one of his attendants to remain concealed about the convent, and bring him instant notice, if any one from the castle should repair thither.

CHAPTER 5

Every reflection which Manfred made on the friar's behaviour, conspired to persuade him that Jerome was privy to an amour between Isabella and Theodore. But Jerome's new presumption, so dissonant from his former meekness, suggested still deeper apprehensions. The prince even suspected that the friar depended on some secret support from Frederic, whose arrival coinciding with the novel appearance of Theodore seemed to bespeak a correspondence. Still more was he troubled with the resemblance of Theodore to Alfonso's portrait. The latter he knew had unquestionably died without issue. Frederic had consented to bestow Isabella on him. These contradictions agitated his mind with numberless pangs. He saw but two methods of extricating himself from his difficulties. The one was to resign his dominions to the marquise – Pride, ambition, and his reliance on ancient prophecies, which had pointed out a possibility of his preserving them to his posterity, combated that thought. The other was to press his marriage with Isabella. After long ruminating on these anxious thoughts, as he marched silently with Hippolita to the castle, he at last discoursed with that princess on the subject of his disquiet, and used every insinuating and plausible argument to extract her consent to, even her promise of promoting, the divorce. Hippolita needed little persuasion to bend her to his pleasure. She endeavoured to win him over to the measure of resigning his dominions; but finding her exhortations fruitless, she assured him, that as far as her conscience would allow, she would raise no opposition to a separation, though, without better founded scruples than what he yet alleged, she would not engage to be active in demanding it.

This compliance, though inadequate, was sufficient to raise Manfred's hopes. He trusted that his power and wealth would easily advance his suit at the court of Rome, whither he resolved to engage Frederic to take a journey on purpose. That prince had discovered so much passion for Matilda, that Manfred hoped to obtain all he wished by holding out or withdrawing his daughter's charms, according as the marquis should appear more or less disposed to co-operate in his views. Even the absence of Frederic would be a material point gained, until he could take farther measures for his security.

Dismissing Hippolita to her apartment, he repaired to that of the marquis; but crossing the great hall through which he was to pass, he met Bianca. That damsel he knew was in the confidence of both the young ladies. It immediately occurred to him to sift her on the subject of Isabella and Theodore. Calling her aside into the recess of the oriel window[n] of the hall, and soothing her with many fair words and promises, he demanded of her whether she knew aught of the state of Isabella's affections. I! my lord? No, my lord – Yes, my lord – Poor lady! she is wonderfully alarmed about her father's wounds; but I tell her he will do well; don't your highness think so? I do not ask you, replied Manfred, what she thinks about her father: but you are in her secrets: come, be a good girl and tell me, is there any young man – ha? – you understand me. Lord bless me! understand your highness? No, not I: I told her a few vulnerary[n] herbs and repose—I am not talking, replied the prince impatiently, about her father: I know he will do well. Bless me, I rejoice to hear your highness say so; for though I thought it right not to let my young lady despond, methought his greatness had a wan look, and a something – I remember when young Ferdinand was wounded by the Venetian.[n] Thou answerest from the point, interrupted Manfred; but here, take this jewel, perhaps that may fix thy attention – Nay, no reverences; my favour shall not stop here – Come, tell me truly; how stands Isabella's heart? Well, your highness has such a way, said Bianca – to be sure – but can your highness keep a secret? If it should ever come out of your lips—It shall not, it shall not, cried Manfred. Nay, but swear, your highness – by my halidame,[n] if it should ever be known that I said it – Why, truth is truth, I do not think my lady Isabella ever much affectioned my young lord, your son: yet he was a sweet youth as one should see. I am sure if I had been a princess – But bless me! I must attend my lady Matilda; she will marvel what is become of me. – Stay, cried Manfred, thou hast not satisfied my question. Hast thou ever carried any message, any letter? – I! Good gracious! cried Bianca: I carry a letter? I would not to be a queen. I hope your highness thinks, though I am poor, I am honest. Did your highness never hear what count Marsigli offered me, when he came a-wooing to my lady Matilda? – I have not leisure, said Manfred, to listen to thy tales. I do not question thy honesty; but it is thy duty to conceal nothing from me. How long has Isabella been acquainted with Theodore? – Nay, there is nothing can escape your highness, said Bianca – not that I know any thing of the matter. Theodore, to be sure, is a proper young man, and, as my lady Matilda says, the very image of good Alfonso: Has not your highness remarked it? Yes, yes – No – thou torturest me, said Manfred: Where did they meet? when? – Who, my lady Matilda? said Bianca. No, no, not Matilda; Isabella: When did Isabella first become acquainted with this Theodore? – Virgin Mary! said Bianca, how should I know? Thou dost know, said Manfred; and I must know; I will. – Lord! your highness is not jealous of young Theodore? said Bianca. – Jealous! No, no: why should I be jealous? – Perhaps I mean to unite them – if I was sure Isabella would have no repugnance. – Repugnance! No, I'll warrant her, said Bianca: he is as comely a youth as ever trod on christian ground: we are all in love with him: there is not a soul in the castle but would be rejoiced to have him for our prince – I mean, when it shall please heaven to call your highness to itself. – Indeed! said Manfred: has it gone so far? Oh! this cursed friar! – But I must not lose time – Go, Bianca, attend Isabella; but I charge thee, not a word of what has passed. Find out how she is affected towards Theodore; bring me good news, and that ring has a companion. Wait at the foot of the winding staircase: I am going to visit the marquis, and will talk farther with thee at my return.

Manfred, after some general conversation, desired Frederic to dismiss the two knights his companions, having to talk with him on urgent affairs. As soon as they were alone, he began in artful guise to sound the marquis on the subject of Matilda; and finding him disposed to his wish, he let drop hints on the difficulties that would attend the celebration of their marriage, unless—At that instant Bianca burst into the room, with a wildness in her look and gestures that spoke the utmost terror. Oh! my lord, my lord! cried she, we are all undone! It is come again! it is come again! – What is come again? cried Manfred amazed. – Oh! the hand! the giant! the hand! – Support me! I am terrified out of my senses, cried Bianca: I will not sleep in the castle to-night. Where shall I go? My things may come after me to-morrow. – Would I had been content to wed Francesco! This comes of ambition! – What has terrified thee thus, young woman? said the marquis: thou art safe here; be not alarmed. Oh! your greatness is wonderfully good, said Bianca, but I dare not – No, pray let me go – I had rather leave every thing behind me, than stay another hour under this roof. Go to, thou hast lost thy senses, said Manfred. Interrupt us not; we were communing on important matters. – My lord, this wench is subject to fits – Come with me, Bianca. – Oh! the saints! No, said Bianca – for certain it comes to warn your highness; why should it appear to me else? I say my prayers morning and evening – Oh! if your highness had believed Diego! 'Tis the same hand that he saw the foot to in the gallery-chamber – Father Jerome has often told us the prophecy would be out one of these days – Bianca, said he, mark my words. – Thou ravest, said Manfred in a rage: Begone, and keep these fooleries to frighten thy companions. – What! my lord, cried Bianca, do you think I have seen nothing? Go to the foot of the great stairs yourself – As I live I saw it. Saw what? Tell us, fair maid, what thou hast seen, said Frederic. Can your highness listen, said Manfred, to the delirium of a silly wench, who has heard stories of apparitions until she believes them? This is more than fancy, said the marquis; her terror is too natural and too strongly impressed to be the work of imagination. Tell us, fair maiden, what it is has moved thee thus. Yes, my lord, thank your greatness, said Bianca — I believe I look very pale; I shall be better when I have recovered myself. — I was going to my lady Isabella's chamber by his highness's order — We do not want the circumstances, interrupted Manfred: since his highness will have it so, proceed; but be brief. — Lord, your highness thwarts one so! replied Bianca — I fear my hair — I am sure I never in my life — Well! as I was telling your greatness, I was going by his highness's order to my lady Isabella's chamber: she lies in the watchet-coloured chamber, on the right hand, one pair of stairs: so when I came to the great stairs — I was looking on his highness's present here. Grant me patience! said Manfred, will this wench never come to the point? What imports it to the marquis, that I gave thee a bawble for thy faithful attendance on my daughter? We want to know what thou sawest. I was going to tell your highness, said Bianca, if you would permit me. — So, as I was rubbing the ring[n] — I am sure I had not gone up three steps, but I heard the rattling of armour; for all the world such a clatter, as Diego says he heard when the giant turned him about in the gallery-chamber. — What does she mean, my lord? said the marquis. Is your castle haunted by giants and goblins? — Lord, what, has not your greatness heard the story of the giant in the gallery-chamber? cried Bianca. I marvel his highness has not told you — mayhap you do not know there is a prophecy — This trifling is intolerable, interrupted Manfred. Let us dismiss this silly wench, my lord: we have more important affairs to discuss. By your favour, said Frederic, these are no trifles: the enormous sabre I was directed to in the wood; yon casque, its fellow — are these visions of this poor maiden's brain? — So Jaquez thinks, may it please your greatness, said Bianca. He says this moon will not be out without our seeing some strange revolution. For my part, I should not be surprised if it was to happen to-morrow; for, as I was saying, when I heard the clattering of armour, I was all in a cold sweat — I looked up, and, if your greatness will believe me, I saw upon the uppermost banister of the great stairs a hand in armour as big, as big — I thought I should have swooned — I never stopped until I came hither — Would I were well out of this castle! My lady Matilda told me but yester-morning that her highness Hippolita knows

something – Thou art an insolent! cried Manfred – Lord
marquis, it much misgives me that this scene is concerted to
affront me. Are my own domestics suborned to spread tales
injurious to my honour? Pursue your claim by manly daring;
or let us bury our feuds, as was proposed, by the intermarriage
of our children: but trust me, it ill becomes a prince of your
bearing to practice on mercenary wenches. – I scorn your
imputation, said Frederic; until this hour I never set eyes on this
damsel: I have given her no jewel! – My lord, my lord, your
conscience, your guilt accuses you, and would throw the suspicion on me – But keep your daughter, and think no more of
Isabella: the judgments already fallen on your house forbid me
matching into it.

Manfred, alarmed at the resolute tone in which Frederic
delivered these words, endeavoured to pacify him. Dismissing
Bianca, he made such submissions to the marquis, and threw in
such artful encomiums on Matilda, that Frederic was once more
staggered. However, as his passion was of so recent a date, it
could not at once surmount the scruples he had conceived. He
had gathered enough from Bianca's discourse to persuade him
that heaven declared itself against Manfred. The proposed
marriages too removed his claim to a distance: and the principality of Otranto was a stronger temptation, than the contingent
reversion of it with Matilda.[n] Still he would not absolutely recede
from his engagements; but purposing to gain time, he demanded
of Manfred if it was true in fact that Hippolita consented to the
divorce. The prince, transported to find no other obstacle, and
depending on his influence over his wife, assured the marquis it
was so, and that he might satisfy himself of the truth from her
own mouth.

As they were thus discoursing, word was brought that the
banquet was prepared. Manfred conducted Frederic to the great
hall, where they were received by Hippolita and the young
princesses. Manfred placed the marquis next to Matilda, and
seated himself between his wife and Isabella. Hippolita com-
ported herself with an easy gravity; but the young ladies were
silent and melancholy. Manfred, who was determined to pursue
his point with the marquis in the remainder of the evening,

pushed on the feast until it waxed late; affecting unrestrained gaiety, and plying Frederic with repeated goblets of wine. The latter, more upon his guard than Manfred wished, declined his frequent challenges, on pretence of his late loss of blood; while the prince, to raise his own disordered spirits, and to counterfeit unconcern, indulged himself in plentiful draughts, though not to the intoxication of his senses.

The evening being far advanced, the banquet concluded. Manfred would have withdrawn with Frederic; but the latter, pleading weakness and want of repose, retired to his chamber, gallantly telling the prince, that his daughter should amuse his highness until himself could attend him. Manfred accepted the party; and, to the no small grief of Isabella, accompanied her to her apartment. Matilda waited on her mother, to enjoy the freshness of the evening on the ramparts of the castle.

Soon as the company was dispersed their several ways, Frederic, quitting his chamber, enquired if Hippolita was alone; and was told by one of her attendants, who had not noticed her going forth, that at that hour she generally withdrew to her oratory, where he probably would find her. The marquis during the repast had beheld Matilda with increase of passion. He now wished to find Hippolita in the disposition her lord had promised. The portents that had alarmed him were forgotten in his desires. Stealing softly and unobserved to the apartment of Hippolita, he entered it with a resolution to encourage her acquiescence to the divorce, having perceived that Manfred was resolved to make the possession of Isabella an unalterable condition, before he would grant Matilda to his wishes.

The marquis was not surprised at the silence that reigned in the princess's apartment. Concluding her, as he had been advertised, in her oratory, he passed on. The door was a-jar; the evening gloomy and overcast. Pushing open the door gently, he saw a person kneeling before the altar. As he approached nearer, it seemed not a woman, but one in a long woollen weed, whose back was towards him. The person seemed absorbed in prayer. The marquis was about to return, when the figure rising, stood some moments fixed in meditation, without regarding him. The marquis, expecting the holy person to come forth, and

meaning to excuse his uncivil interruption, said, Reverend
father, I sought the lady Hippolita. – Hippolita! replied a
hollow voice: camest thou to this castle to seek Hippolita? –
And then the figure, turning slowly round, discovered to Frederic
the fleshless jaws and empty sockets of a skeleton, wrapt in a
hermit's cowl. Angels of grace, protect me! cried Frederic
recoiling. Deserve their protection, said the spectre. Frederic,
falling on his knees, adjured the phantom to take pity on him.
Dost thou not remember me? said the apparition. Remember
the wood of Joppa! Art thou that holy hermit? cried Frederic
trembling – can I do aught for thy eternal peace? – Wast thou
delivered from bondage, said the spectre, to pursue carnal
delights? Hast thou forgotten the buried sabre, and the behest
of heaven engraven on it? – I have not, I have not, said Frederic
– But say, blest spirit, what is thy errand to me? what remains
to be done? To forget Matilda! said the apparition – and
vanished.

Frederic's blood froze in his veins. For some minutes he
remained motionless. Then falling prostrate on his face before
the altar, he besought the intercession of every saint for pardon.
A flood of tears succeeded to this transport; and the image of
the beauteous Matilda rushing in spite of him on his thoughts,
he lay on the ground in a conflict of penitence and passion. Ere
he could recover from this agony of his spirits, the princess
Hippolita, with a taper in her hand, entered the oratory alone.
Seeing a man without motion on the floor, she gave a shriek,
concluding him dead. Her fright brought Frederic to himself.
Rising suddenly, his face bedewed with tears, he would have
rushed from her presence; but Hippolita, stopping him, conjured him in the most plaintive accents to explain the cause of
his disorder, and by what strange chance she had found him
there in that posture. Ah! virtuous princess! said the marquis,
penetrated with grief – and stopped. For the love of heaven, my
lord, said Hippolita, disclose the cause of this transport! What
mean these doleful sounds, this alarming exclamation on my
name? What woes has heaven still in store for the wretched
Hippolita? – Yet silent? – By every pitying angel, I adjure thee,
noble prince, continued she, falling at his feet, to disclose the

purport of what lies at thy heart – I see thou feelest for me; thou feelest the sharp pangs that thou inflictest – Speak, for pity! – Does aught thou knowest concern my child? – I cannot speak, cried Frederic, bursting from her – Oh! Matilda!

Quitting the princess thus abruptly, he hastened to his own apartment. At the door of it he was accosted by Manfred, who, flushed by wine and love, had come to seek him, and to propose to waste some hours of the night in music and revelling. Frederic, offended at an invitation so dissonant from the mood of his soul, pushed him rudely aside, and, entering his chamber, flung the door intemperately against Manfred, and bolted it inwards. The haughty prince, enraged at this unaccountable behaviour, withdrew in a frame of mind capable of the most fatal excesses. As he crossed the court, he was met by the domestic whom he had planted at the convent as a spy on Jerome and Theodore. This man, almost breathless with the haste he had made, informed his lord, that Theodore and some lady from the castle were at that instant in private conference at the tomb of Alfonso in St Nicholas's church. He had dogged Theodore thither, but the gloominess of the night had prevented his discovering who the woman was.

Manfred, whose spirits were inflamed, and whom Isabella had driven from her on his urging his passion with too little reserve, did not doubt but the inquietude she had expressed had been occasioned by her impatience to meet Theodore. Provoked by this conjecture, and enraged at her father, he hastened secretly to the great church. Gliding softly between the aisles, and guided by an imperfect gleam of moonshine that shone faintly through the illuminated windows, he stole towards the tomb of Alfonso, to which he was directed by indistinct whispers of the persons he sought. The first sounds he could distinguish were – Does it, alas, depend on me? Manfred will never permit our union. – No, this shall prevent it! cried the tyrant, drawing his dagger, and plunging it over her shoulder into the bosom of the person that spoke – Ah me, I am slain! cried Matilda sinking: Good heaven, receive my soul! – Savage, inhuman monster! what hast thou done? cried Theodore, rushing on him, and wrenching his dagger from him. – Stop, stop thy impious hand, cried

Matilda; it is my father! – Manfred, waking as from a trance, beat his breast, twisted his hands in his locks, and endeavoured to recover his dagger from Theodore to dispatch himself. Theodore, scarce less distracted, and only mastering the transports of his grief to assist Matilda, had now by his cries drawn some of the monks to his aid. While part of them endeavoured in concert with the afflicted Theodore to stop the blood of the dying princess, the rest prevented Manfred from laying violent hands on himself.

Matilda, resigning herself patiently to her fate, acknowledged with looks of grateful love the zeal of Theodore. Yet oft as her faintness would permit her speech its way, she begged the assistants to comfort her father. Jerome by this time had learnt the fatal news, and reached the church. His looks seemed to reproach Theodore; but turning to Manfred, he said, Now, tyrant! behold the completion of woe fulfilled on thy impious and devoted head! The blood of Alfonso cried to heaven for vengeance; and heaven has permitted its altar to be polluted by assassination, that thou mightest shed thy own blood at the foot of that prince's sepulchre! – Cruel man! cried Matilda, to aggravate the woes of a parent! May heaven bless my father, and forgive him as I do! My lord, my gracious sire, dost thou forgive thy child? Indeed I came not hither to meet Theodore! I found him praying at this tomb, whither my mother sent me to intercede for thee, for her – Dearest father, bless your child, and say you forgive her. – Forgive thee! Murderous monster! cried Manfred – can assassins forgive? I took thee for Isabella; but heaven directed my bloody hand to the heart of my child! – Oh! Matilda – I cannot utter it – canst thou forgive the blindness of my rage? – I can, I do, and may heaven confirm it! said Matilda – But while I have life to ask it – oh, my mother! what will she feel! – Will you comfort her, my lord? Will you not put her away? Indeed she loves you – Oh, I am faint! bear me to the castle – can I live to have her close my eyes?

Theodore and the monks besought her earnestly to suffer herself to be borne into the convent; but her instances were so pressing to be carried to the castle, that, placing her on a litter, they conveyed her thither as she requested. Theodore supporting her head with his arm, and hanging over her in an agony of despairing love, still endeavoured to inspire her with hopes of life. Jerome on the other side comforted her with discourses of heaven, and holding a crucifix before her, which she bathed with innocent tears, prepared her for her passage to immortality. Manfred, plunged in the deepest affliction, followed the litter in despair.

Ere they reached the castle, Hippolita, informed of the dreadful catastrophe, had flown to meet her murdered child; but when she saw the afflicted procession, the mightiness of her grief deprived her of her senses, and she fell lifeless to the earth in a swoon. Isabella and Frederic, who attended her, were overwhelmed in almost equal sorrow. Matilda alone seemed insensible to her own situation: every thought was lost in tenderness for her mother. Ordering the litter to stop, as soon as Hippolita was brought to herself, she asked for her father. He approached, unable to speak. Matilda, seizing his hand and her mother's, locked them in her own, and then clasped them to her heart. Manfred could not support this act of pathetic piety. He dashed himself on the ground, and cursed the day he was born. Isabella, apprehensive that these struggles of passion were more than Matilda could support, took upon herself to order Manfred to be borne to his apartment, while she caused Matilda to be conveyed to the nearest chamber. Hippolita, scarce more alive than her daughter, was regardless of every thing but her: but when the tender Isabella's care would have likewise removed her, while the surgeons examined Matilda's wound, she cried, Remove me? Never! never! I lived but in her, and will expire with her. Matilda raised her eyes at her mother's voice, but closed them again without speaking. Her sinking pulse, and the damp coldness of her hand, soon dispelled all hopes of recovery. Theodore followed the surgeons into the outer chamber, and heard them pronounce the fatal sentence with a transport equal to phrensy — Since she cannot live mine, cried he, at least she shall be mine in death! — Father! Jerome! will you not join our hands? cried he to the friar, who with the marquis had accompanied the surgeons. What means thy distracted rashness? said Jerome: is this an hour for marriage? It is, it is, cried

Theodore: alas, there is no other! Young man, thou art too unadvised, said Frederic: dost thou think we are to listen to thy fond transports in this hour of fate? What pretensions hast thou to the princess? Those of a prince, said Theodore; of the sovereign of Otranto. This reverend man, my father, has informed me who I am. Thou ravest, said the marquis: there is no prince of Otranto but myself, now Manfred by murder, by sacrilegious murder, has forfeited all pretensions. My lord, said Jerome, assuming an air of command, he tells you true. It was not my purpose the secret should have been divulged so soon; but fate presses onward to its work. What his hot-headed passion has revealed, my tongue confirms. Know, prince, that when Alfonso set sail for the Holy Land — Is this a season for explanations? cried Theodore. Father, come and unite me to the princess: she shall be mine — in every other thing I will dutifully obey you. My life! my adored Matilda! continued Theodore, rushing back into the inner chamber, will you not be mine? will you not bless your—Isabella made signs to him to be silent, apprehending the princess was near her end. What, is she dead? cried Theodore: is it possible? The violence of his exclamations brought Matilda to herself. Lifting up her eyes she looked round for her mother — Life of my soul! I am here, cried Hippolita: think not I will quit thee! — Oh! you are too good, said Matilda — but weep not for me, my mother! I am going where sorrow never dwells. — Isabella, thou hast loved me; will thou not supply my fondness to this dear, dear woman? Indeed I am faint! — Oh! my child! my child! said Hippolita in a flood of tears, can I not withhold thee a moment? — It will not be, said Matilda — Commend me to heaven — Where is my father? Forgive him, dearest mother — forgive him my death; it was an error — Oh! I had forgotten — Dearest mother, I vowed never to see Theodore more — Perhaps that has drawn down this calamity — but it was not intentional — can you pardon me? — Oh! wound not my agonizing soul! said Hippolita; thou never couldst offend me. — Alas, she faints! Help! help! — I would say something more, said Matilda struggling, but it wonnot be — Isabella — Theodore — for my sake — oh! — She expired. Isabella and her women tore Hippolita from the corse; but Theodore threatened destruction to all who attempted to remove him from it. He printed a thousand kisses on her clay-cold hands, and uttered every expression that despairing love could dictate.

Isabella, in the mean time, was accompanying the afflicted Hippolita to her apartment; but in the middle of the court they were met by Manfred, who, distracted with his own thoughts, and anxious once more to behold his daughter, was advancing to the chamber where she lay. As the moon was now at its height, he read in the countenances of this unhappy company the event he dreaded. What! is she dead? cried he in wild confusion – A clap of thunder at that instant shook the castle to its foundations; the earth rocked, and the clank of more than mortal armour was heard behind. Frederic and Jerome thought the last day was at hand. The latter, forcing Theodore along with them, rushed into the court. The moment Theodore appeared, the walls of the castle behind Manfred were thrown down with a mighty force, and the form of Alfonso, dilated to an immense magnitude, appeared in the centre of the ruins. Behold in Theodore, the true heir of Alfonso! said the vision: and having pronounced those words, accompanied by a clap of thunder, it ascended solemnly towards heaven, where the clouds parting asunder, the form of saint Nicholas was seen; and receiving Alfonso's shade, they were soon wrapt from mortal eyes in a blaze of glory.

The beholders fell prostrate on their faces, acknowledging the divine will. The first that broke silence was Hippolita. My lord, said she to the desponding Manfred, behold the vanity of human greatness! Conrad is gone! Matilda is no more! in Theodore we view the true prince of Otranto. By what miracle he is so, I know not – suffice it to us, our doom is pronounced! Shall we not, can we but dedicate the few deplorable hours we have to live, in deprecating the farther wrath of heaven? Heaven ejects us – whither can we fly, but to yon holy cells that yet offer us a retreat? – Thou guiltless but unhappy woman! unhappy by my crimes! replied Manfred, my heart at last is open to thy devout admonitions. Oh! could – but it cannot be – ye are lost in wonder – let me at last do justice on myself! To heap shame on my own head is all the satisfaction I have left to offer to offended heaven. My story has drawn down these judgments: let my confession atone – But ah! what can atone for usurpation and a murdered child? a child murdered in a consecrated place!— List, sirs, and may this bloody record be a warning to future tyrants!

Alfonso, ye all know, died in the Holy Land – Ye would interrupt me; ye would say he came not fairly to his end – It is most true – why else this bitter cup which Manfred must drink to the dregs? Ricardo, my grandfather, was his chamberlain – I would draw a veil over my ancestor's crimes – but it is in vain: Alfonso died by poison. A fictitious will declared Ricardo his heir. His crimes pursued him – yet he lost no Conrad, no Matilda! I pay the price of usurpation for all! A storm overtook him. Haunted by his guilt, he vowed to saint Nicholas to found a church and two convents if he lived to reach Otranto. The sacrifice was accepted: the saint appeared to him in a dream, and promised that Ricardo's posterity should reign in Otranto until the rightful owner should be grown too large to inhabit the castle, and as long as issue-male from Ricardo's loins should remain to enjoy it. – Alas! alas! nor male nor female, except myself, remains of all his wretched race! – I have done – the woes of these three days speak the rest. How this young man can be Alfonso's heir I know not – yet I do not doubt it. His are these dominions; I resign them – yet I knew not Alfonso had an heir – I question not the will of heaven – poverty and prayer must fill up the woeful space, until Manfred shall be summoned to Ricardo.

What remains is my part to declare, said Jerome. When Alfonso set sail for the Holy Land, he was driven by a storm on the coast of Sicily. The other vessel, which bore Ricardo and his train, as your *lordship* must have heard, was separated from him. It is most true, said Manfred; and the title you give me is more than an out-cast can claim – Well, be it so – proceed. Jerome blushed, and continued. For three months lord Alfonso was wind-bound in Sicily. There he became enamoured of a fair virgin named Victoria. He was too pious to tempt her to forbidden pleasures. They were married. Yet deeming this amour incongruous with the holy vow of arms by which he was bound, he was determined to conceal their nuptials until his return from the crusade, when he purposed to seek and acknowledge her for his lawful wife. He left her pregnant. During his absence she was delivered of a daughter : but scarce had she felt a mother's pangs, ere she heard the fatal rumour of her lord's death, and the succession of Ricardo. What could a friendless, helpless woman do? would her testimony avail? – Yet, my lord, I have an authentic writing. – It needs not, said Manfred; the horrors of these days, the vision we have but now seen, all corroborate thy evidence beyond a thousand parchments. Matilda's death and my expulsion – Be composed, my lord, said Hippolita; this holy man did not mean to recall your griefs. Jerome proceeded.

I shall not dwell on what is needless. The daughter of which Victoria was delivered, was at her maturity bestowed in marriage on me. Victoria died; and the secret remained locked in my breast. Theodore's narrative has told the rest.

The friar ceased. The disconsolate company retired to the remaining part of the castle. In the morning Manfred signed his abdication of the principality, with the approbation of Hippolita, and each took on them the habit of religion in the neighbouring convents. Frederic offered his daughter to the new prince, which Hippolita's tenderness for Isabella concurred to promote: but Theodore's grief was too fresh to admit the thought of another love; and it was not till after frequent discourses with Isabella, of his dear Matilda, that he was persuaded he could know no happiness but in the society of one with whom he could forever indulge the melancholy that had taken possession of his soul.

HIEROGLYPHIC TALES

Schah Baham ne comprenoit jamais bien que les choses
absurdes & hors de toute vraisemblance.[n]
Le Sopha, p. 5

PREFACE

As the invaluable present I am making to the world may not please all tastes, from the gravity of the matter, the solidity of the reasoning, and the deep learning contained in the ensuing sheets, it is necessary to make some apology for producing this work in so trifling an age, when nothing will go down but temporary politics, personal satire, and idle romances. The true reason then for my surmounting all these objections was singly this: I was apprehensive lest the work should be lost to posterity; and though it may be condemned at present, I can have no doubt but it will be treated with due reverence some hundred ages hence, when wisdom and learning shall have gained their proper ascendant over mankind, and when men shall only read for instruction and improvement of their minds. As I shall print an hundred thousand copies, some, it may be hoped, will escape the havoc that is made of moral works, and then this jewel will shine forth in its genuine lustre. I was in the greater hurry to consign this work to the press, as I foresee that the art of printing will ere long be totally lost, like other useful discoveries well known to the ancients. Such were the art of dissolving rocks with hot vinegar, of teaching elephants to dance on the slack rope, of making malleable glass, of writing epic poems that any body would read after they had been published a month, and the stupendous invention of new religions, a secret of which illiterate Mahomet[n] was the last person possessed.

Notwithstanding this my zeal for good letters, and the ardour of my universal citizenship (for I declare I design this present for all nations), there are some small difficulties in the way, that prevent my conferring this my great benefaction on the world completely and all at once. I am obliged to produce it in small portions, and therefore beg the prayers of all good and wise men that my life may be prolonged to me, till I shall be able to publish the whole work, no man else being capable of executing the charge so well as myself, for reasons that my modesty will not permit me to specify. In the mean time, as it is the duty of an editor to acquaint the world with what relates to himself as well as his author, I think it right to mention the causes that compel me to publish this work in numbers. The common reason of such proceedings is to make a book dearer for the ease of the purchasers, it being supposed that most people had rather give twenty shillings by sixpence a fortnight, than pay ten shillings once for all. Public-spirited as this proceeding is, I must confess my reasons are more and merely personal. As my circumstances are very moderate, and barely sufficient to maintain decently a gentleman of my abilities and learning, I cannot afford to print at once an hundred thousand copies of two volumes in folio, for that will be the whole mass of Hieroglyphic Tales when the work is perfected. In the next place, being very asthmatic, and requiring a free communication of air, I lodge in the uppermost story of a house in an alley not far from St Mary Axe;[n] and as a great deal of good company lodges in the same mansion, it was by a considerable favour that I could obtain a single chamber to myself; which chamber is by no means large enough to contain the whole impression, for I design to vend the copies myself, and, according to the practice of other great men, shall sign the first sheet myself with my own hand.

Desirous as I am of acquainting the world with many more circumstances relative to myself, some private considerations prevent my indulging their curiosity any farther at present; but I shall take care to leave so minute an account of myself to some public library, that the future commentators and editors of this work shall not be deprived of all necessary lights. In the mean time I beg the reader to accept the temporary compensation of an account of the author whose work I am publishing.

The Hieroglyphic Tales were undoubtedly written a little before the creation of the world, and have ever since been preserved, by oral tradition, in the mountains of Crampcraggiri, an uninhabited island, not yet discovered. Of these few facts we could have the most authentic attestations of several clergymen, who remember to have heard them repeated by old men long before they, the said clergymen, were born. We do not trouble the reader with these attestations, as we are sure every body will believe them as much as if they had seen them. It is more difficult to ascertain the true author. We might ascribe them with great probability to Kemanrlegorpikos, son of Quat; but besides that we are not certain that any such person ever existed, it is not clear that he ever wrote any thing but a book of cookery, and that in heroic verse. Others give them to Quat's nurse, and a few to Hermes Trismegistus,[n] though there is a passage in the latter's treatise on the harpsichord which directly contradicts the account of the first volcano in the 114th of the Hieroglyphic Tales. As Trismegistus's work is lost, it is impossible to decide now, whether the discordance mentioned is so positive as has been asserted by many learned men, who only guess at the opinion of Hermes from other passages in his writings, and who indeed are not sure whether he was speaking of volcanos or cheesecakes; for he drew so ill, that his hieroglyphics may often be taken for the most opposite things in nature; and as there is no subject which he has not treated, it is not precisely known what he was discussing in any one of them.

This is the nearest we can come to any certainty with regard to the author. But whether he wrote the Tales six thousand years ago, as we believe, or whether they were written for him within these ten years, they are incontestably the most ancient work in the world; and though there is little imagination, and still less invention in them, yet there are so many passages in them exactly resembling Homer, that any man living would conclude they were imitated from that great poet, if it was not certain that Homer borrowed from them, which I shall prove two ways: first, by giving Homer's parallel passages at the bottom of the page; and secondly, by translating Homer himself into prose, which shall make him so unlike himself, that nobody will think he could be an original writer: and when he is become totally lifeless and insipid, it will be impossible but these Tales should be preferred to the Iliad; especially as I design to put them into a kind of style that shall be neither verse nor prose; a diction lately much used in tragedies and heroic poems, the former of which are really heroic poems from want of probability, as an antico-moderno epic poem is in fact a mere tragedy, having little or no change of scene, no incidents but a ghost and a storm, and no events but the deaths of the principal actors.

I will not detain the reader longer from the perusal of this invaluable work; but I must beseech the public to be expeditious in taking off the whole impression, as fast as I can get it printed; because I must inform them that I have a more precious work in contemplation; namely, a new Roman history, in which I mean to ridicule, detect and expose all ancient virtue and patriotism, and show from original papers which I am going to write, and which I shall afterwards bury in the ruins of Carthage and then dig up, that it appears by the letters of Hanno the Punic embassador at Rome, that Scipio was in the pay of Hannibal, and that the dilatoriness of Fabius proceeded from his being a pensioner of the same general.[n] I own this discovery will pierce my heart; but as morality is best taught by showing how little effect it had on the best of men, I will sacrifice the most virtuous names for the instruction of the present wicked generation; and I cannot doubt but when once they have learnt to detest the favourite heroes of antiquity, they will become good subjects of the most pious king that ever lived since David, who expelled the established royal family, and then sung psalms to the memory of Jonathan, to whose prejudice he had succeeded to the throne.[n]

TALE 1

A new Arabian Night's Entertainment[n]

At the foot of the great mountain Hirgonqúu was anciently situated the kingdom of Larbidel. Geographers, who are not apt to make such just comparisons, said it resembled a football just going to be kicked away : and so it happened; for the mountain kicked the kingdom into the ocean, and it has never been heard of since.

One day a young princess had climbed up to the top of the mountain to gather goat's eggs, the whites of which are excellent for taking off freckles. – Goat's eggs ! – Yes – naturalists hold that all beings are conceived in an egg. The goats of Hirgonqúu might be oviparous,[n] and lay their eggs to be hatched by the sun. This is my supposition; no matter whether I believe it myself or not. I will write against and abuse any man that opposes my hypothesis. It would be fine indeed if learned men were obliged to believe what they assert.

The other side of the mountain was inhabited by a nation of whom the Larbidellians knew no more than the French nobility do of Great Britain, which they think is an island that some how or other may be approached by land. The princess had strayed into the confines of Cucurucu, when she suddenly found herself seized by the guards of the prince that reigned in that country. They told her in few words that she must be conveyed to the capital, and married to the giant their lord and emperor. The giant, it seems, was fond of having a new wife every night, who was to tell him a story that would last till morning, and then have her head cut off – Such odd ways have some folks of passing their wedding-nights ![n] The princess modestly asked, why their master loved such long stories ? The captain of the guard replied, his majesty did not sleep well. – Well! said she, and if he does not? – Not but I believe I can tell as long stories as any princess in Asia. Nay, I can repeat Leonidas[n] by heart; and your emperor must be wakeful indeed if he can hold out against that.

By this time they were arrived at the palace. To the great surprise of the princess, the emperor, so far from being a giant, was but five feet one inch in height; but being two inches taller than any of his predecessors, the flattery of his courtiers had bestowed the name of *giant* on him; and he affected to look down upon any man above his own stature. The princess was immediately undressed and put to bed, his majesty being impatient to hear a new story.

Light of my eyes, said the emperor, what is your name? I call myself the princess Gronovia, replied she; but my real appellation is the frow Gronow. And what is the use of a name, said his majesty, but to be called by it? And why do you pretend to be a princess, if you are not? My turn is romantic, answered she, and I have ever had an ambition of being the heroine of a novel. Now there are but two conditions that entitle one to that rank; one must be a shepherdess or a princess. Well, content yourself, said the giant; you will die an empress, without being either the one or the other! – But what sublime reason had you for lengthening your name so unaccountably? It is a custom in my family, said she: all my ancestors were learned men, who wrote about the Romans. It sounded more classic, and gave a higher opinion of their literature, to put a Latin termination to their names. All this is Japonese to me, said the emperor; but your ancestors seem to have been a parcel of mountebanks. Does one understand any thing the better for corrupting one's name? Oh, said the princess, but it showed taste too. There was a time when in Italy the learned carried this still farther; and a man with a large forehead, who was born on the fifth of January, called himself Quintus Januarius Fronto. More and more absurd, said the emperor. You seem to have a great deal of impertinent knowledge about a great many impertinent people; but proceed in your story: whence came you? Mynheer, said she, I was born in Holland – The deuce you was? said the emperor, and where is that? It was no where, replied the

princess spritelily, till my countrymen gained it from the sea. –
Indeed, moppet! said his majesty; and pray who were your
countrymen, before you had any country? Your majesty asks a
very shrewd question, said she, which I cannot resolve on a
sudden; but I will step home to my library, and consult five or
six thousand volumes of modern history, an hundred or two
dictionaries, and an abridgement of geography in forty volumes
in folio, and be back in an instant. Not so fast, my life, said the
emperor, you must not rise till you go to execution: it is now
one in the morning, and you have not begun your story.

My great grandfather, continued the princess, was a Dutch
merchant, who passed many years in Japan – On what account?
said the emperor. He went thither to abjure his religion, said
she, that he might get money enough to return and defend it
against Philip II.[n] You are a pleasant family, said the emperor;
but though I love fables, I hate genealogies. I know in all
families, by their own account, there never was any thing but
good and great men from father to son; a sort of fiction that
does not at all amuse me. In my dominions there is no nobility
but flattery. Whoever flatters me best is created a great lord, and
the titles I confer are synonymous to their merits. There is Kiss-
my-breech-Can, my favourite; Adulation-Can, lord treasurer;
Prerogative-Can, head of the law; and Blasphemy-Can, high-
priest. Whoever speaks truth corrupts his blood, and is ipso
facto degraded. In Europe you allow a man to be noble because
one of his ancestors was a flatterer. But every thing degenerates,
the farther it is removed from its source. I will not hear a word
of any of your race before your father: what was he?

It was in the height of the contests about the bull Unigenitus[n]
– I tell you, interrupted the emperor, I will not be plagued with
any more of those people with Latin names: they were a parcel
of coxcombs, and seem to have infected you with their folly. I
am sorry, replied Gronovia, that your sublime highness is so
little acquainted with the state of Europe, as to take a papal
ordinance for a person. Unigenitus is Latin for the Jesuits – And
who the devil are the Jesuits? said the giant. You explain one
nonsensical term by another, and wonder I am never the wiser.
Sir, said the princess, if you will permit me to give you a short

account of the troubles that have agitated Europe for these last two hundred years, on the doctrines of grace, free-will, pre-destination, reprobation, justification, &c. you will be more entertained, and will believe less, than if I told your majesty a long story of fairies and goblins. You are an eternal prater, said the emperor, and very self-sufficient; but talk your fill, and upon what subject you like, till to-morrow morning: but I swear by the soul of the holy Jirigi, who rode to heaven on the tail of a magpie, as soon as the clock strikes eight, you are a dead woman. Well, who was the Jesuit Unigenitus?

The novel doctrines that had sprung up in Germany, said Gronovia, made it necessary for the church to look about her. The disciples of Loyola – Of whom? said the emperor, yawning – Ignatius Loyola,[n] the founder of the Jesuits, replied Gronovia, was – A writer of Roman history, I suppose, interrupted the emperor: what the devil were the Romans to you, that you trouble your head so much about them? The empire of Rome and the church of Rome are two distinct things, said the princess; and yet, as one may say, the one depends upon the other, as the new testament does on the old. One destroyed the other, and yet pretends a right to its inheritance. The temporalities of the church – What's o'clock, said the emperor to the chief eunuch? It cannot sure be far from eight – This woman has gossiped at least seven hours. Do you hear, my to-morrow night's wife shall be dumb – Cut her tongue out before you bring her to our bed. Madam, said the eunuch, his sublime highness, whose erudition passes the sands of the sea, is too well acquainted with all human sciences to require information. It is therefore that his exalted wisdom prefers accounts of what never happened, to any relation either in history or divinity – You lie, said the emperor; when I exclude truth, I certainly do not mean to forbid divinity – How many divinities have you in Europe, woman? The council of Trent,[n] replied Gronovia, has decided – The emperor began to snore – I mean, continued Gronovia, that notwithstanding all father Paul has asserted, cardinal Palavicini affirms that in the three first sessions of that council – The emperor was now fast asleep; which the princess and the chief eunuch perceiving, clapped several pillows upon his face, and held them there till he expired. As soon as they were convinced he was dead, the princess, putting on every mark of despair and concern, issued to the divan, where she was immediately proclaimed empress. The emperor, it was given out, had died of an hemorrhoidal colic; but to show her regard for his memory, her imperial majesty declared she would strictly adhere to the maxims by which he had governed. Accordingly she espoused a new husband every night, but dispensed with their telling her stories, and was graciously pleased also, upon their good behaviour, to remit the subsequent execution. She sent presents to all the learned men in Asia; and they in return did not fail to cry her up as a pattern of clemency, wisdom, and virtue: and though the panegyrics of the learned are generally as clumsy as they are fulsome, they ventured to assure her that their writings would be as durable as brass, and that the memory of her glorious reign would reach to the latest posterity.

TALE 2

The King and his three Daughters

There was formerly a king, who had three daughters – that is, he would have had three, if he had had one more – but some how or other the eldest never was born. She was extremely handsome, had a great deal of wit, and spoke French in perfection, as all the authors of that age affirm, and yet none of them pretend that she ever existed. It is very certain that the two other princesses were far from beauties; the second had a strong Yorkshire dialect, and the youngest had bad teeth and but one leg, which occasioned her dancing very ill.

As it was not probable that his majesty would have any more children, being eighty-seven years two months and thirteen days old when his queen died, the states of the kingdom were very anxious to have the princesses married. But there was one great obstacle to this settlement, though so important to the peace of the kingdom. The king insisted that his eldest daughter should be married first; and as there was no such person, it was very difficult to fix upon a proper husband for her. The courtiers all approved his majesty's resolution; but, as under the best princes there will always be a number of discontented, the nation was torn into different factions, the grumblers or patriots insisting that the second princess was the eldest, and ought to be declared heiress apparent to the crown. Many pamphlets were written pro and con; but the ministerial party pretended that the chancellor's argument was unanswerable, who affirmed, that the second princess could not be the eldest, as no princess-royal ever had a Yorkshire accent. A few persons who were attached to the youngest princess took advantage of this plea for whispering that *her* royal highness's pretensions to the crown were the best of all; for, as there was no eldest princess, and as the second must be the first if there was no first, and as she could not be the second if she was the first, and as the chancellor had proved that she could not be the first, it followed plainly by every idea of law that she could be nobody at all; and then the consequence followed of course, that the youngest must be the eldest, if she had no elder sister.

It is inconceivable what animosities and mischiefs arose from these different titles; and each faction endeavoured to strengthen itself by foreign alliances. The court party, having no real object for their attachment, were the most attached of all, and made up by warmth for the want of foundation in their principles. The clergy in general were devoted to this, which was styled *the first party*. The physicians embraced the second; and the lawyers declared for the third, or the faction of the youngest princess, because it seemed best calculated to admit of doubts and endless litigation.

While the nation was in this distracted situation, there arrived the prince of Quifferiquimini, who would have been the most accomplished hero of the age, if he had not been dead, and had spoken any language but the Egyptian, and had not had three legs. Notwithstanding these blemishes, the eyes of the whole nation were immediately turned upon him, and each party wished to see him married to the princess whose cause they espoused.

The old king received him with the most distinguished honours; the senate made the most fulsome addresses to him; the princesses were so taken with him, that they grew more bitter enemies than ever; and the court ladies and petit-maîtres[n] invented a thousand new fashions upon his account – Every thing was to be à la Quifferiquimini. Both men and women of fashion left off rouge, to look the more cadaverous; their clothes were embroidered with hieroglyphics, and all the ugly characters they could gather from Egyptian antiquities, with which they were forced to be contented, it being impossible to learn a language that is lost; and all tables, chairs, stools, cabinets and couches were made with only three legs: the last, however, soon went out of fashion, as being very inconvenient.

The prince, who, ever since his death, had had but a weakly constitution, was a little fatigued with this excess of attentions, and would often wish himself at home in his coffin. But his greatest difficulty of all was to get rid of the youngest princess, who kept hopping after him wherever he went, and was so full of admiration of his three legs, and so modest about having but one herself, and so inquisitive to know how his three legs were set on, that, being the best-natured man in the world, it went to his heart whenever in a fit of peevishness he happened to drop an impatient word, which never failed to throw her into an agony of tears; and then she looked so ugly that it was impossible for him to be tolerably civil to her. He was not much more inclined to the second princess – In truth, it was the eldest who made the conquest of his affections: and so violently did his passion increase one Tuesday morning, that, breaking through all prudential considerations (for there were many reasons which ought to have determined his choice in favour of either of the other sisters), he hurried to the old king, acquainted him with his love, and demanded the eldest princess in marriage. Nothing could equal the joy of the good old monarch, who wished for nothing but to live to see the consummation of this match. Throwing his arms about the prince skeleton's neck, and watering his hollow cheeks with warm tears, he granted his request, and added, that he would immediately resign his crown to him and his favourite daughter.

I am forced for want of room to pass over many circumstances that would add greatly to the beauty of this history, and am sorry I must dash the reader's impatience by acquainting him, that notwithstanding the eagerness of the old king and youthful ardour of the prince, the nuptials were obliged to be postponed; the archbishop declaring that it was essentially necessary to have a dispensation from the pope, the parties being related within the forbidden degrees;[n] a woman that never was, and a man that had been, being deemed first cousins in the eye of the canon law.

Hence arose a new difficulty. The religion of the Quifferiquiminians was totally opposite to that of the papists. The former believed in nothing but grace; and they had a high-priest of their own, who pretended that he was master of the whole fee-simple[n] of grace, and by that possession could cause every thing to have been that never had been, and could prevent every thing that had been from ever having been. 'We have nothing to do,' said the prince to the king, 'but to send a solemn embassy to the high-priest of grace, with a present of a hundred thousand million of ingots, and he will cause your charming no-daughter to have been, and will prevent my having died, and then there will be no occasion for a dispensation from your old fool at Rome.' – How! thou impious, atheistical bag of drybones, cried the old king; dost thou profane our holy religion? Thou shalt have no daughter of mine, thou three-legged skeleton – Go and be buried and be damned, as thou must be; for, as thou art dead, thou art past repentance: I would sooner give my child to a baboon, who has one leg more than thou hast, than bestow her on such a reprobate corpse. – You had better give your one-legged infanta to the baboon, said the prince; they are fitter for one another. As much a corpse as I am, I am preferable to nobody; and who the devil would have married your no-daughter, but a dead body? For my religion, I lived and died in it, and it is not in my power to change it now if I would. – But for your part – A great shout interrupted this dialogue; and the captain of the guard, rushing into the royal closet, acquainted his majesty, that the second princess, in revenge of the prince's neglect, had given her hand to a drysalter, who was a common-councilman; and that the city, in consideration of the match, had proclaimed them king and queen, allowing his majesty to retain the title for his life, which they had fixed for the term of six months; and ordering, in respect of his royal birth, that the prince should immediately lie in state and have a pompous funeral.

This revolution was so sudden and so universal, that all parties approved, or were forced to seem to approve it. The old king died the next day, as the courtiers said, for joy; the prince of Quifferiquimini was buried in spite of his appeal to the law of nations; and the youngest princess went distracted, and was shut up in a madhouse, calling out day and night for a husband with three legs.

TALE 3

The Dice Box : A Fairy Tale

Translated from the French Translation of the Countess
DAUNOIS, *for the Entertainment of Miss* CAROLINE CAMPBELL[1]

There was a merchant of Damascus named Aboulcasem,[n] who had an only daughter called Pissimissi, which signifies *the waters of Jordan* ; because a fairy foretold at her birth that she would be one of Solomon's concubines.[n] Azaziel, the angel of death,[n] having transported Aboulcasem to the regions of bliss, he had no fortune to bequeath to his beloved child but the shell of a pistachia-nut drawn by an elephant and a ladybird. Pissimissi, who was but nine years old, and who had been kept in great confinement, was impatient to see the world ; and no sooner was the breath out of her father's body, than she got into the car, and, whipping her elephant and ladybird, drove out of the yard as fast as possible, without knowing whither she was going. Her coursers never stopped till they came to the foot of a brazen tower, that had neither doors nor windows, in which lived an old enchantress, who had locked herself up there with seventeen thousand husbands. It had but one single vent for air, which was a small chimney grated over, through which it was scarce possible to put one's hand. Pissimissi, who was very impatient, ordered her coursers to fly with her up to the top of the chimney ; which, as they were the most docile creatures in the world, they immediately did : but unluckily the fore paw of the elephant lighting on the top of the chimney, broke down the

[1] Eldest daughter of lord William Campbell. She lived with her aunt the countess of Ailesbury.[n]

grate by its weight, but at the same time stopped up the passage so entirely, that all the enchantress's husbands were stifled for want of air. As it was a collection she had made with great care and cost, it is easy to imagine her vexation and rage. She raised a storm of thunder and lightning that lasted eight hundred and four years; and having conjured up an army of two thousand devils, she ordered them to flay the elephant alive, and dress it for her supper with anchovy sauce. Nothing could have saved the poor beast, if, struggling to get loose from the chimney, he had not happily broken wind, which it seems is a great preservative against devils. They all flew a thousand ways, and in their hurry carried away half the brazen tower; by which means the elephant, the car, the ladybird, and Pissimissi got loose; but in their fall tumbled through the roof of an apothecary's shop, and broke all his bottles of physic. The elephant, who was very dry with his fatigue, and who had not much taste, immediately sucked up all the medicines with his proboscis; which occasioned such a variety of effects in his bowels, that it was well he had such a strong constitution, or he must have died of it. His evacuations were so plentiful, that he not only drowned the tower of Babel,[n] near which the apothecary's shop stood, but the current ran fourscore leagues till it came to the sea, and there poisoned so many whales and leviathans, that a pestilence ensued, and lasted three years nine months and sixteen days. As the elephant was extremely weakened by what had happened, it was impossible for him to draw the car for eighteen months; which was a cruel delay to Pissimissi's impatience, who during all that time could not travel above a hundred miles a day; for, as she carried the sick animal in her lap, the poor ladybird could not make longer stages with no assistance. Besides, Pissimissi bought every thing she saw wherever she came; and all was crowded into the car, and stuffed into the seat. She had purchased ninety-two dolls, seventeen baby-houses, six cart-loads of sugar-plums, a thousand ells of gingerbread, eight dancing dogs, a bear and a monkey, four toyshops with all their contents, and seven dozen of bibs and aprons of the newest fashion. They were jogging on with all this cargo over mount Caucasus,[n] when an immense humming-bird, who had been

struck with the beauty of the ladybird's wings, that I had forgot
to say were of ruby spotted with black pearls, sousing down at
once upon her prey, swallowed ladybird, Pissimissi, the elephant, and all their commodities. It happened that the humming-
bird belonged to Solomon; he let it out of its cage every morning
after breakfast, and it constantly came home by the time the
council broke up. Nothing could equal the surprise of his
majesty and the courtiers, when the dear little creature arrived,
with the elephant's proboscis hanging out of its divine little bill.
However, after the first astonishment was over, his majesty,
who to be sure was wisdom itself, and who understood natural
philosophy that it was a charm to hear him discourse of those
matters, and who was actually making a collection of dried
beasts and birds in twelve thousand volumes of the best fool's-
cap paper, immediately perceived what had happened; and
taking out of the side-pocket of his breeches a diamond tooth-
pick-case of his own turning, with the toothpick made of the
only unicorn's horn he ever saw, he stuck it into the elephant's
snout, and began to draw it out: but all his philosophy was
confounded, when jammed between the elephant's legs he
perceived the head of a beautiful girl, and between her legs a
baby-house, which with the wings extended thirty feet, out of
the windows of which rained a torrent of sugar-plums, that had
been placed there to make room. Then followed the bear, who
had been pressed to the bales of gingerbread and was covered
all over with it, and looked but uncouthly; and the monkey
with a doll in every paw, and his pouches so crammed with
sugar-plums that they hung on each side of him, and trailed on
the ground behind like the duchess of ********'s beautiful
breasts.[n] Solomon, however, gave small attention to this procession, being caught with the charms of the lovely Pissimissi: he
immediately began the song of songs[n] extempore; and what he
had seen — I mean, all that came out of the humming-bird's
throat — had made such a jumble in his ideas, that there was
nothing so unlike to which he did not compare all Pissimissi's
beauties. As he sung his canticles too to no tune, and God
knows had but a bad voice, they were far from comforting
Pissimissi: the elephant had torn her best bib and apron, and

she cried and roared, and kept such a squalling, that, though Solomon carried her in his arms and showed her all the fine things in the temple, there was no pacifying her. The queen of Sheba,[n] who was playing at backgammon with the high-priest, and who came every October to converse with Solomon, though she did not understand a word of Hebrew,[n] hearing the noise, came running out of her dressing-room; and seeing the king with a squalling child in his arms, asked him peevishly, if it became his reputed wisdom to expose himself with his bastards to all the court? Solomon, instead of replying, began singing; which so provoked the Sheban princess, that, happening to have one of the dice-boxes in her hand, she without any ceremony threw it at his head. The enchantress, whom I mentioned before, and who, though invisible, had followed Pissimissi, and drawn her into her train of misfortunes, turned the dice-box aside, and directed it to Pissimissi's nose; which being something flat, like madame de ********'s,[n] it stuck there, and being of ivory, Solomon ever after compared his beloved's nose to the tower that leads to Damascus. The queen, though ashamed of her behaviour, was not in her heart sorry for the accident; but when she found that it only increased the monarch's passion, her contempt redoubled; and calling him a thousand old fools to herself, she ordered her postchaise and drove away in a fury, without leaving sixpence for the servants; and nobody knows what became of her or her kingdom, which has never been heard of since.

TALE 4

The Peach in Brandy. A Milesian Tale

Fitz Scanlan Mac Giolla l'ha druig,[1] king of Kilkenny, the thousand and fifty-seventh descendant in a direct line from Milesius king of Spain, had an only daughter called Great A, and by corruption Grata; who being arrived at years of discretion, and perfectly initiated by her royal parents in the arts of government, the fond monarch determined to resign his crown to her: having accordingly assembled the senate, he declared his resolution to them, and having delivered his sceptre into the princess's hand, he obliged her to ascend the throne; and, to set the example, was the first to kiss her hand, and vow eternal obedience to her. The senators were ready to stifle the new queen with panegyrics and addresses; the people, though they adored the old king, were transported with having a new sovereign; and the university, according to custom immemorial, presented her majesty, three months after every body had forgotten the event, with testimonials of the excessive sorrow and excessive joy they felt on losing one monarch and getting another.

Her majesty was now in the fifth year of her age, and a prodigy of sense and goodness. In her first speech to the senate, which she lisped with inimitable grace, she assured them that her[2] heart was entirely Irish, and that she did not intend any longer to go in leading-strings;[n] as a proof of which she immediately declared her nurse prime-minister. The senate applauded this sage choice with even greater encomiums than the last, and voted a free gift to the queen of a million of sugar-plums, and to the favourite of twenty thousand bottles of usquebaugh.[n] Her majesty then jumping from her throne, declared it was her royal pleasure to play at blindman's buff; but such a hub-bub arose

from the senators' pushing, and pressing, and squeezing, and
punching one another, to endeavour to be the first blinded, that
in the scuffle her majesty was thrown down, and got a bump on
her forehead as big as a pigeon's egg, which set her a-squalling,
that you might have heard her to Tipperary. The old king flew
into a rage, and snatching up the mace knocked out the
chancellor's brains, who at that time happened not to have
any;[n] and the queen-mother, who sat in a tribune above to see
the ceremony, fell into a fit and miscarried of twins, who were
killed by her majesty's fright;[n] but the earl of Bullaboo, great but-
ler of the crown, happening to stand next to the queen, catched
up one of the dead children, and, perceiving it was a boy, ran
down to the king and wished him joy of the birth of a son and
heir.[n] The king, who had now recovered his sweet temper, called
him a fool and blunderer; upon which Mr Phelim O'Torture, a
zealous courtier, started up with great presence of mind and
accused the earl of Bullaboo of high treason, for having asserted
that his late majesty had had any other heir than their present
most lawful and most religious sovereign queen Grata. An
impeachment was voted by a large majority, though not without
warm opposition, particularly from a celebrated Kilkennian
orator, whose name is unfortunately not come down to us, it being
erased out of the journals afterwards, as the Irish author whom I
copy says, when he became first lord of the treasury, as he was
during the whole reign of queen Grata's successor. The argument
of this Mr Killmorackill, says my author, whose name is lost, was,
that her majesty the queen-mother having conceived a son before
the king's resignation, that son was indubitably heir to the crown,
and consequently the resignation void, it not signifying an iota
whether the child was born alive or dead: it was alive, said he,
when it was conceived – Here he was called to order by Dr
O'Flaharty, the queen-mother's man-midwife and member for
the borough of Corbelly, who entered into a learned dissertation
on embryos; but he was interrupted by the young queen's crying
for her supper, the previous question for which was carried
without a negative; and then the house being resumed, the
debate was cut short by the impatience of the majority to go
and drink her majesty's health. This seeming violence gave

occasion to a very long protest, drawn up by sir Archee Mac Sarcasm, in which he contrived to state the claim of the departed fœtus so artfully, that it produced a civil war, and gave rise to those bloody ravages and massacres which so long laid waste the ancient kingdom of Kilkenny, and which were at last terminated by a lucky accident, well known, says my author, to every body, but which he thinks it his duty to relate for the sake of those who never may have heard it. These are his words:

It happened that the archbishop of Tuum (anciently called Meum by the Roman catholic clergy), the great wit of those times, was in the queen-mother's closet, who had the young queen in her lap.[3] His grace was suddenly seized with a violent fit of the cholic, which made him make such wry faces, that the queen-mother thought he was going to die, and ran out of the room to send for a physician, for she was a pattern of goodness, and void of pride. While she was stepped into the servants' hall to call somebody, according to the simplicity of those times, the archbishop's pains increased, when perceiving something on the mantle-piece, which he took for a peach in brandy, he gulped it all down at once without saying grace, God forgive him! and found great comfort from it. He had not done licking his lips before the queen-mother returned, when queen Grata cried out, 'Mama, mama, the gentleman has eat my little brother!' This fortunate event put an end to the contest, the male line entirely failing in the person of the devoured prince. The archbishop, however, who became pope by the name of Innocent the third, having afterwards a son by his sister, named the child Fitzpatrick, as having some of the royal blood in its veins; and from him are descended all the younger branches of the Fitzpatricks of our time. Now the rest of the acts of Grata, and all that she did, are they not written in the book of the chronicles of the kings of Kilkenny?

NOTES ON TALE 4

1 Vide Lodge's Peerage of Ireland, in the Family of Fitzpatrick.[n]

2 Queen Anne in her first speech to the parliament said, her heart was entirely English.[n]

3 Some commentators have ignorantly supposed that the Irish author is guilty of a great anachronism in this passage; for having said that the contested succession occasioned long wars, he yet speaks of queen Grata, at the conclusion of them, as still sitting in her mother's lap as a child. Now I can confute them from their own state of the question. *Like a child*, does not import that she actually was a child: she only sat *like a child;* and so she might though thirty years old. Civilians have declared at what period of his life a king may be of age before he is: but neither Grotius nor Puffendorffe, nor any of the tribe, have determined how long a king or queen may remain infants after they are past their infancy.

TALE 5

Mi Li. A Chinese Fairy Tale

Mi Li, prince of China, was brought up by his godmother the fairy Hih, who was famous for telling fortunes with a tea-cup. From that unerring oracle she assured him, that he would be the most unhappy man alive unless he married a princess whose name was the same with her father's dominions. As in all probability there could not be above one person in the world to whom that accident had happened, the prince thought there would be nothing so easy as to learn who his destined bride was. He had been too well educated to put the question to his godmother, for he knew when she uttered an oracle, that it was with intention to perplex, not to inform; which has made people so fond of consulting all those who do not give an explicit answer, such as prophets, lawyers, and any body you meet on the road, who, if you ask the way, reply by desiring to know whence you came. Mi Li was no sooner returned to his palace than he sent for his governor, who was deaf and dumb, qualities for which the fairy had selected him, that he might not instil any bad principles into his pupil; however, in recompence, he could talk upon his fingers like an angel. Mi Li asked him directly who the princess was whose name was the same with her father's kingdom? This was a little exaggeration in the prince, but nobody ever repeats any thing just as they heard it: besides, it was excusable in the heir of a great monarchy, who of all things had not been taught to speak truth, and perhaps had never heard what it was. Still it was not the mistake of *kingdom* for *dominions* that puzzled the governor. It never helped him to understand any thing the better for its being rightly stated. However, as he had great presence of mind, which consisted in never giving a direct answer, and in looking as if he could, he replied, it was a question of too great importance to be resolved on a sudden. How came you to know that? said the prince. – This youthful impetuosity told the governor that there was something more in the question than he had apprehended; and though he could be very solemn about nothing, he was ten times more so when there was something he did not comprehend. Yet that unknown something occasioning a conflict between his cunning and his ignorance, and the latter being the greater, always betrayed itself, for nothing looks so silly as a fool acting wisdom. The prince repeated his question; the governor demanded why he asked – the prince had not patience to spell the question over again on his fingers, but bawled it as loud as he could, to no purpose. The courtiers ran in, and catching up the prince's words, and repeating them imperfectly, it soon flew all over Pekin, and thence into the provinces, and thence into Tartary, and thence to Muscovy, and so on, that the prince wanted to know who the princess was, whose name was the same as her father's. As the Chinese have not the blessing (for aught I know) of having family surnames as we have, and as what would be their christian-names, if they were so happy as to be christians, are quite different for men and women, the Chinese, who think that must be a rule all over the world because it is theirs, decided that there could not exist upon the square face of the earth a woman whose name was the same as her father's. They repeated this so often, and with so much deference and so much obstinacy, that the prince, totally forgetting the original oracle, believed that he wanted to know who the woman was who had the same name as her father. However, remembering there was something in the question that he had taken for royal, he always said *the king her father*. The prime minister consulted the red book or court-calendar, which was *his* oracle, and could find no such princess. All the ministers at foreign courts were instructed to inform themselves if there was any such lady; but as it took up a great deal of time to put these instructions into cypher, the prince's impatience could not wait for the couriers setting out, but he determined to go himself in search of the princess. The old king, who, *as is usual*, had left the whole management of affairs to his son the moment he was fourteen, was charmed with the prince's resolution of seeing the world, which he thought could be done in a few days, the facility of which makes so many monarchs never stir out of their own palaces till it is too late; and his majesty declared, that he should approve of his son's choice, be the lady who she would, provided she answered to the divine designation of having the same name as her father.

The prince rode post to Canton, intending to embark there on board an English man of war. With what infinite transport did he hear the evening before he was to embark, that a sailor knew the identic lady in question. The prince scalded his mouth with the tea he was drinking, broke the old china cup it was in, and which the queen his mother had given him at his departure from Pekin, and which had been given to her great great great great grandmother queen Fi by Confucius[n] himself, and ran down to the vessel and asked for the man who knew his bride. It was honest Tom O'Bull, an Irish sailor, who by his interpreter Mr James Hall, the supercargo,[n] informed his highness that Mr Bob Oliver of Sligo had a daughter christened of both his names, the fair miss Bob Oliver.[1] The prince by the plenitude of his power declared Tom a mandarin of the first class, and at Tom's desire promised to speak to his brother the king of Great Ireland, France and Britain, to have him made a peer in his own country, Tom saying he should be ashamed to appear there without being a lord as well as all his acquaintance.

The prince's passion, which was greatly inflamed by Tom's description of her highness Bob's charms, would not let him stay for a proper set of ladies from Pekin to carry to wait on his bride, so he took a dozen of the wives of the first merchants in Canton, and two dozen virgins as maids of honour, who however were disqualified for their employments before his highness got to St Helena. Tom himself married one of them,[n] but was so great a favourite with the prince, that she still was appointed maid of honour, and with Tom's consent was afterwards married to an English duke.

Nothing can paint the agonies of our royal lover, when on his landing at Dublin he was informed that princess Bob had quitted

Ireland, and was married to nobody knew whom. It was well for Tom that he was on Irish ground. He would have been chopped as small as rice, for it is death in China to mislead the heir of the crown through ignorance. To do it knowingly is no crime, any more than in other countries.

As a prince of China cannot marry a woman that has been married before, it was necessary for Mi Li to search the world for another lady equally qualified with miss Bob, whom he forgot the moment he was told he must marry somebody else,[n] and fell equally in love with somebody else though he knew not with whom. In this suspence he dreamt, '*that he would find his destined spouse, whose father had lost the dominions which never had been his dominions, in a place where there was a bridge over no water, a tomb where nobody ever was buried nor ever would be buried, ruins that were more than they had ever been, a subterraneous passage in which there were dogs with eyes of rubies and emeralds, and a more beautiful menagerie of Chinese pheasants than any in his father's extensive gardens.*' This oracle seemed so impossible to be accomplished, that he believed it more than he had done the first; which shewed his great piety. He determined to begin his second search, and being told by the lord lieutenant that there was in England a Mr Banks,[n] who was going all over the world in search of he did not know what, his highness thought he could not have a better conductor, and sailed for England. There he learnt that the sage Banks was at Oxford, hunting in the Bodleian library for a MS. voyage of a man who had been in the moon, which Mr Banks thought must have been in the western ocean, where the moon sets, and which planet if he could discover once more, he would take possession of in his majesty's name, upon condition that it should never be taxed, and so be lost again to this country like the rest of his majesty's dominions in that part of the world.

Mi Li took a hired post-chaise for Oxford, but as it was a little rotten it broke on the new road down to Henley. A beggar advised him to walk into general Conway's, who was the most courteous person alive, and would certainly lend him his own chaise. The prince travelled incog.[n] He took the beggar's advice, but going up to the house was told the family were in the grounds, but he should be conducted to them. He was led through a venerable wood of beeches, to a menagerie[2] commanding a more glorious prospect than any in his father's dominions, and full of Chinese pheasants. The prince cried out in ecstacy, Oh! potent Hih! my dream begins to be accomplished. The gardener, who knew no Chinese but the names of a few plants, was struck with the similitude of the sounds, but discreetly said not a word. Not finding his lady there, as he expected, he turned back, and plunging suddenly into the thickest gloom of the wood, he descended into a cavern totally dark, the intrepid prince following him boldly. After advancing a great way into this subterraneous vault, at last they perceived light, when on a sudden they were pursued by several small spaniels, and turning to look at them, the prince perceived their eyes[3] shone like emeralds and rubies. Instead of being amazed, as Fo-Hi, the founder of his race, would have been, the prince renewed his exclamations, and cried, I advance! I advance! I shall find my bride! Great Hih! thou art infallible! Emerging into light, the imperturbed gardener[n] conducted his highness to a heap of artificial[4] ruins, beneath which they found a spacious gallery or arcade, where his highness was asked if he would not repose himself; but, instead of answering, he capered like one frantic, crying out, I advance! I advance! Great Hih! I advance! – The gardener was amazed, and doubted whether he was not conducting a madman to his master and lady, and hesitated whether he should proceed; – but as he understood nothing the prince said, and perceiving he must be a foreigner, he concluded he was a Frenchman by his dancing. As the stranger too was so nimble and not at all tired with his walk, the sage gardener proceeded down a sloping valley, between two mountains clothed to their summits with cedars, firs, and pines, which he took care to tell the prince were all of his honour the general's own planting: but though the prince had learnt more English in three days in Ireland, than all the French in the world ever learnt in three years, he took no notice of the information, to the great offence of the gardener, but kept running on, and increased his gambols and exclamations when he perceived the vale was terminated by a stupendous bridge, that seemed composed of

the rocks which the giants threw at Jupiter's head,[n] and had not
a drop of water beneath[5] it. – Where is my bride, my bride?
cried Mi Li – I must be near her. The prince's shouts and cries
drew a matron from a cottage that stood on a precipice near the
bridge, and hung over the river. – My lady is down at Ford-
house,[6] cried the good woman, who was a little deaf, concluding
they had called to her to know. The gardener knew it was in
vain to explain his distress to her, and thought that if the poor
gentleman was really mad, his master the general would be the
properest person to know how to manage him. Accordingly,
turning to the left, he led the prince along the banks of the river,
which glittered through the opening sallows, while on the other
hand a wilderness of shrubs climbed up the pendant cliffs of
chalk, and contrasted with the verdant meads and fields of corn
beyond the stream. The prince, insensible to such enchanting
scenes, galloped wildly along, keeping the poor gardener on a
round trot, till they were stopped by a lonely[7] tomb, surrounded
by cypress, yews, and willows, that seemed the monument of
some adventurous youth who had been lost in tempting the
current, and might have suited the gallant and daring Leander.[n]
Here Mi Li first had presence of mind to recollect the little
English he knew, and eagerly asked the gardener whose tomb he
beheld before him? It is nobody's – Before he could proceed,
the prince interrupted him: And will it never be any body's? –
Oh! thought the gardener, now there is no longer any doubt of
his phrensy – and perceiving his master and the family approaching towards them, he endeavoured to get the start: but the
prince, much younger, and borne too on the wings of love, let
out full speed the moment he saw the company, and particularly
a young damsel with them. Running almost breathless up to
lady Ailesbury, and seizing miss Campbell's hand – he cried,
Who she? who she? Lady Ailesbury screamed, the young
maiden squalled, the general, cool but offended, rushed between
them, and, if a prince could be collared, would have collared
him – Mi Li kept fast hold with one arm, but pointing to his
prize with the other, and with the most eager and supplicating
looks entreating for an answer, continued to exclaim, *Who she?
who she?* The general, perceiving by his accent and manner that

he was a foreigner, and rather tempted to laugh than be angry, replied with civil scorn, Why, *she* is miss Caroline Campbell, daughter of lord William Campbell, his majesty's late governor of Carolina – Oh, Hih! I now recollect thy words! cried Mi Li – And so she became princess of China.

NOTES ON TALE 5

1 There really was such a person.

2 Lady Ailesbury's.

3 At Park-place there is such a passage cut through a chalk-hill: when dogs are in the middle, the light from the mouth makes their eyes appear in the manner here described.[n]

4 Consequently they seem to have been larger.

5 The rustic bridge at Park-place was built by general Conway, to carry the road from Henley, and to leave the communication free between his grounds on each side of the road. Vide Anecdotes of Painting.

6 The old woman who kept the cottage built by general Conway to command a glorious prospect. Ford-house is a farm-house at the termination of the grounds.

7 A fictitious tomb in a beautiful spot by the river, built for a point of view: it has a small pyramid on it.

TALE 6

A *true* Love Story

In the height of the animosities between the factions of the Guelfs and Ghibellines,[n] a party of Venetians had made an inroad into the territories of the Viscontis, sovereigns of Milan, and had carried off the young Orondates,[n] then at nurse. His family were at that time under a cloud, though they could boast of being descended from Canis Scaliger, lord of Verona. The captors sold the beautiful Orondates to a rich widow of the noble family of Grimaldi, who, having no children, brought him up with as much tenderness as if he had been her son. Her fondness increased with the growth of his stature and charms, and the violence of his passions were augmented by the signora Grimaldi's indulgence. Is it necessary to say that love reigned predominantly in the soul of Orondates? or that in a city like Venice a form like that of Orondates met with little resistance?

The Cyprian Queen, not content with the numerous oblations of Orondates on her altars, was not satisfied while his heart remained unengaged. Across the canal, over-against the palace of Grimaldi, stood a convent of Carmelite nuns, the abbess of which had a young African slave of the most exquisite beauty, called Azora, a year younger than Orondates. Jet and japan[n] were tawney and without lustre, when compared to the hue of Azora. Afric never produced a female so perfect as Azora; as Europe could boast but of one Orondates.

The signora Grimaldi, though no bigot, was pretty regular at her devotions; but as lansquenet[n] was more to her taste than praying, she hurried over her masses as fast as she could, to allot more of her precious time to cards. This made her prefer the church of the Carmelites, separated only by a small bridge, though the abbess was of a contrary faction. However, as both ladies were of equal quality, and had had no altercations that could countenance incivility, reciprocal curtsies always passed between them, the coldness of which each pretended to lay on their attention to their devotions, though the signora Grimaldi attended but little to the priest, and the abbess was chiefly employed in watching and criticising the inattention of the signora.

Not so Orondates and Azora. Both constantly accompanied their mistresses to mass, and the first moment they saw each other was decisive in both breasts. Venice ceased to have more than one fair in the eyes of Orondates, and Azora had not remarked till then that there could be more beautiful beings in the world than some of the Carmelite nuns.

The seclusion of the abbess, and the aversion between the two ladies, which was very cordial on the side of the holy one, cut off all hopes from the lovers. Azora grew grave, and pensive, and melancholy; Orondates surly and intractable. Even his attachment to his kind patroness relaxed. He attended her reluctantly but at the hours of prayer. Often did she find him on the steps of the church ere the doors were opened. The signora Grimaldi was not apt to make observations. She was content with indulging her own passions, seldom restrained those of others; and though good offices rarely presented themselves to her imagination, she was ready to exert them when applied to, and always talked charitably of the unhappy at her cards, if it was not a very unlucky deal.

Still it is probable that she never would have discovered the passion of Orondates, had not her woman, who was jealous of his favour, given her a hint; at the same time remarking, under affectation of good will, how well the circumstances of the lovers were suited, and, that as her ladyship was in years, and would certainly not think of providing for a creature she had bought in the public market, it would be charitable to marry the fond couple, and settle them on her farm in the country.

Fortunately madame Grimaldi always was open to good impressions, and rarely to bad. Without perceiving the malice of her woman, she was struck with the idea of a marriage. She loved the cause, and always promoted it when it was honestly in her power. She seldom made difficulties, and never apprehended them. Without even examining Orondates on the state of his inclinations, without recollecting that madame Capello and she were of different parties, without taking any precautions to guard against a refusal, she instantly wrote to the abbess to propose a marriage between Orondates and Azora.

The latter was in madame Capello's chamber when the note arrived. All the fury that authority loves to console itself with for being under restraint, all the asperity of a bigot, all the acrimony of party, and all the fictitious rage that prudery adopts when the sensual enjoyments of others are concerned, burst out on the helpless Azora, who was unable to divine how she was concerned in the fatal letter. She was made to endure all the calumnies that the abbess would have been glad to have hurled at the head of madame Grimaldi, if her own character and the rank of that offender would have allowed it. Impotent menaces of revenge were repeated with emphasis; and as nobody in the convent dared to contradict her, she gratified her anger and love of prating with endless tautologies. In fine, Azora was strictly locked up, and bread and water were ordered as sovereign cures for love. Twenty replies to madame Grimaldi were written and torn, as not sufficiently expressive of a resentment that was rather vociferous than eloquent; and her confessor was at last forced to write one, in which he prevailed to have some holy cant inserted, though forced to compound for a heap of irony that related to the antiquity of her family, and for many unintelligible allusions to vulgar stories which the Ghibelline party had treasured up against the Guelfs. The most lucid part of the epistle pronounced a sentence of eternal chastity on Azora, not without some sarcastic expressions against the promiscuous amours of Orondates, which ought in common decorum to have banished him long ago from the mansion of a widowed matron.

Just as this fulminatory mandate had been transcribed and signed by the lady abbess in full chapter, and had been consigned to the confessor to deliver, the portress of the convent came running out of breath, and announced to the venerable assembly, that Azora, terrified by the abbess's blows and threats, had fallen in labour and miscarried of four puppies: for be it known to all posterity, that Orondates was an Italian greyhound, and Azora a black spaniel.

POSTSCRIPT

The foregoing Tales are given for no more than they are worth: they are mere whimsical trifles, written chiefly for private entertainment; and for private amusement half a dozen copies only are printed. They deserve at most to be considered as an attempt to vary the stale and beaten class of stories and novels, which, though works of invention, are almost always devoid of imagination. It would scarcely be credited, were it not evident from the Bibliotheque des Romans, which contains the fictitious adventures that have been written in all ages and all countries, that there should have been so little fancy, so little variety, and so little novelty, in writings in which the imagination is fettered by no rules, and by no obligation of speaking truth. There is infinitely more invention in history, which has no merit if devoid of truth, than in romances and novels, which pretend to none.

EXPLANATORY NOTES

The following works are cited in the notes by short titles:

Corr.	*The Yale Edition of the Correspondence of Horace Walpole*, ed. W.S. Lewis (New Haven, 1937–83).
Ketton-Cremer, *Horace Walpole*	R.W. Ketton-Cremer, *Horace Walpole: A Biography* (New York, 1940).
OED	*A New English Dictionary on Historical Principles*, 2nd edn (Oxford, 1989).
Œuvres Complètes	*Œuvres Complètes de Voltaire* (Paris, 1877–85).
Works	*The Works of Horatio Walpole, Earl of Orford*, ed. Robert Berry [Mary Berry] (London, 1798).

Notes to Introduction

1 John Langhorne, *Monthly Review*, May 1765 (xxxii), 394.
2 *Critical Review*, January 1765 (xix), 50. See *Walpole and his Critics*, p. 155.
3 See *The Yale Edition of the Correspondence of Horace Walpole*, W.S. Lewis, ed. (New Haven, 1937–83), 30.177.
4 *Correspondence of Thomas Gray*, eds Paget Toynbee and Leonard Whibley (Oxford, 1935), II.855.
5 William Warburton, *Works of Alexander Pope* (London, 1770), iv.165–7. Warburton's comments on *Otranto* are included in a footnote to Pope's *Epistle to Augustus*.

6 Clara Reeve, *The Old English Baron* (London, 1778), pp. iii–vii. See pp. 155–6 below. Reeve's novel had originally appeared the preceding year as *The Champion of Virtue*.

7 Walter Scott, 'Introduction' to *The Castle of Otranto* (London, 1811). See pp. 157–60 below.

8 Walpole, *Correspondence*, 1.88.

9 Walpole, *Correspondence*, 41.409–10.

10 Kristina Bedford, ' "This Castle Hath a Pleasant Seat": Shakespearean Allusion in *The Castle of Otranto*', *English Studies in Canada*, xiv, 4 (1988), 415–33.

11 Walpole, *Correspondence*, 37.170.

12 William Guthrie, *Reply to the Counter-Address* (London, 1764), p. 25.

13 Guthrie, *Reply to the Counter-Address*, pp. 6–7.

14 Walpole, *Correspondence*, 38.437.

15 George E. Haggerty, 'Literature and Homosexuality in the Late Eighteenth Century: Walpole, Beckford, and Lewis' in *Studies in the Novel*, xviii, 4 (Winter, 1986), 345.

16 Haggerty, 345.

17 Haggerty, 342–3.

18 See note on the texts, pp. xxix–xxx.

19 Walpole, *Correspondence*, 2:141–2.

20 Charles Burney in *Monthly Review* 2nd ser. xxvi (October, 1798), 182. See pp. 162–63 below.

21 Walpole unaccountably sent the fourth of the stories included in the volume, 'The Peach in Brandy, A Milesian Tale' to his friend John Fitzpatrick, Lord Ossory, in December 1771, shortly after hearing of Lady Ossory's miscarriage. In the story a preserved fetus resting on a mantelpiece is mistaken for 'a peach in brandy' and swallowed by an unsuspecting archbishop.

22 Kenneth W. Gross, introduction to *Hieroglyphic Tales*, Augustan Reprint Society (1982), p. v.

The Castle of Otranto

It was printed at Naples, in the black letter, in the year 1529: The term 'black letter' refers to a form of heavy type – similar to gothic type – used by early printers. The preface continues the fiction introduced by Walpole on the title page of the first edition that *Otranto* is a 'found' text, and reproduces 'A STORY / Translated by William Marshal, Gent. / From the Original ITALIAN of / ONUPHRIO MURALTO, / Canon of the Church of St. NICHOLAS at OTRANTO' (see introduction p. xi). Walpole perhaps unconsciously named his fictional translator after one William Marshall, an actual engraver mentioned to him in a letter from William Cole, dated 2 August 1764, just days before Walpole finished the novel (*Corr.* I.71). The title page of the second edition of *Otranto* included an epigraph paraphrasing Horace's *De Arte Poetica*, 7–9: '*vanae / fingentur species, ut nec pes nec caput uni / reddatur formae*' ['idle fancies are shaped – like a sick man's dream – so that head and foot are assigned the same shape'].

If the story was written . . . not long afterwards: In AD 1095 Pope Urban II called for a Christian army to recapture the Church of the Holy Sepulchre in Jerusalem. There followed, by various reckonings, at least seven more Christian 'Crusades' against Muslim control of the Holy Land. The eighth Crusade – the last major concerted effort, led by King Louis IX of France – ended ignominiously in 1270 when the King and most of his army died of disease shortly after landing in North Africa.

. . . until the establishment of the Arragonian kings in Naples had made Spanish appellations familiar in that country: Alfonso V of Aragon, ruler of Sicily, seized Naples in 1442. The subsequent Kingdom of the Two Sicilies was won by the Spanish in 1504, and remained under Spanish rule until the nineteenth century.

Luther: Martin Luther (1483–1546) who, following his break from the Catholic Church in 1520, published a number of books and pamphlets ('books of controversy') elaborating his doctrine, which in turn prompted a great many refutations and responses.

Miracles . . . are exploded now even from romances: see introduction p. xiv.

subalterns: persons of inferior rank or status (*OED*).

*the sins of fathers are visited on their children to the third
and fourth generation*: Exodus 34.6–7: 'The LORD GOD,
merciful and gracious ... will by no means clear the guilty,
visiting the iniquity of the fathers upon the children, and
upon the children's children, unto the third and to the fourth
generation.'

saint Nicholas: the saint is himself an integral part of the
novel's fictional inspiration, and the church of St Nicholas at
the centre of the novel's action. In choosing this particular
figure, Walpole perhaps had in mind the specific career of St
Nicholas I (the 'Great'). One of the most forceful of the early
medieval popes, Nicholas defended the sanctity of marriage in
the divorce case of Lothair II of Lorraine, maintaining a
position reminiscent of that of father Jerome in *Otranto* (pp.
44–45).

It is pity ... the theatre: Walpole would, in 1768, complete
his own dramatic tragedy, *The Mysterious Mother* (see introduction p. xix).

The scene is undoubtedly laid in some real castle: Walpole
later acknowledged that his own home, the 'gothic castle' of
Strawberry Hill, 'inspired the author of the *Castle of
Otranto*'. In a letter to Madame du Deffand (*Corr.* 6.145) he
also noted that when he returned to visit Cambridge after an
absence of several years (in 1769, five years after *Otranto*
was written), he had been surprised to find how much the
university's architecture was likewise responsible for the novel's 'gothicism'.

the two kinds of romance, the ancient and the modern: see
introduction, pp. xiii–xix.

Let me ask if his tragedies ... vested in heroics: for Walpole's specific examples see *Julius Caesar* I.i; *Hamlet* II.ii, v.i.

*These touches remind one of the Grecian sculptor ... meas-
uring his thumb*: the anecdote is not identified.

*No ... this mixture of buffoonery and solemnity is intoler-
able*: Walpole refers to Voltaire's '*Remarques sur Le Cid*': '*Il
est vrai que dans presque toutes ces tragédies espagnoles il y
avait toujours quelques scènes de bouffoneries. Cet usage*

infecta l'Angleterre. Il n'y a guère de tragédie de Shakespeare où l'on ne trouve des plaisanteries d'hommes grossiers à côté du sublime des héros. A quoi attribuer une mode si extravagante et si honteuse pour l'esprit humain qu'à la coutume des princes mêmes, qui entretenaient toujours des bouffons auprès d'eux? coutume digne de barbares qui sentaient le besoin des plaisirs de l'esprit, et qui étaient incapables d'en avoir; coutume même qui a duré jusqu'à nos temps, lorsqu'on en reconnaissait la turpitude. Jamais ce vice n'avilit la scène française: il se glissa seulement dans nos premiers opéras, qui, n'étant pas des ouvrages réguliers, semblaient permettre cette indécence; mais bientôt l'élégant Quinault purgea l'opéra de cette bassesse.' ['It is true that in nearly all Spanish tragedies there are always a few episodes of clowning about. This practice infected England. There is hardly a single Shakespearean tragedy in which one doesn't find the jokes of crude men next to the sublimities of a great hero. To what can we attribute a fashion so extravagant and so unworthy of the human mind, except for the custom of princes themselves, who always employed court fools? This custom was worthy of barbarians, who felt the need for pleasures of the mind, which they were incapable of having. This very custom lasted into our own day, even when people were aware of its baseness. Never did this vice contaminate the French stage. It slipped only into our first operas which, not being works governed by the rules, seemed to allow this indecency. But soon the elegant Quinault purged the opera of this baseness.'] See *Œuvres Complètes*, iii.203.

On y voit ... mieux traité: 'Préface de l'éditeur de l'édition de 1738' to *L'Enfant Prodigue*. ['We see a mixture of the serious and the jocular, of the comic and the touching; and frequently a single scene evinces the entire range of contrasting emotions. Nothing is more common than a house in which the father is having a tirade, while the daughter, absorbed by her passion, is in tears. The other children make fun of both of them, and several parents take different roles in the scene, etc. This does not mean to say that all comedy must have humorous episodes *and* scenes which are seriously moving. There are many very good plays in which only laughter holds sway, and others which are entirely serious. Others are mixtures, and there are still others in which the more touching scenes bring us nearly to the point of tears. One must not exclude any type. But if someone were to ask me which sort is the best, I would answer: that which is handled best.'] See *Œuvres Complètes*, iii.443. Voltaire's sentimental comedy *L'Enfant Prodigue* (*The Prodigal Son*) premiered in 1736.

I am aware that the preface ... were the same person: Voltaire had himself, in fact, written the 'preface'.

Tous ces traits ... une autre espèce de simplicité: ['All of these lines are naïve, all are appropriate only to the stage, and to the moral standards recognized there. These easy familiarities may, I believe, have been well received in Athens, but Parisian audiences demand another sort of straightforwardness.'] See *Œuvres Complètes*, iv.188.

difficiles nugae: i.e. 'trifling jests', from Martial, *Epigrams*, II.86.9: *'Turpe est difficiles habere nugas, / Et stultus labor est ineptiarum'*. ['It is shameful to spend too much time with trifling jests, and hard work spent on such foolishness is stupid.']

De son appartement ... celui de la reine: See 'Commentaires sur Corneille' in *Œuvres Complètes*, xxxii.272.

ichnography: groundplan

Such as it is ... whatever rank their suffrages allot to it: i.e. Walpole suggests that the mere purchase of the volume indicates a mark of respect and honour, regardless of his readers' final aesthetic judgement ('suffrages').

Lady Mary Coke: Lady Mary Campbell (1727–1811), the youngest daughter of the second Duke of Argyll. In 1747 she made an unfortunate marriage to Thomas Coke, from whom she eventually separated. Twenty-six of Walpole's letters to her survive. In the correspondence he mockingly adopts the tone and posture of an enamoured suitor, 'a true knight ... who pretends to the honour of ... [her] hand' (*Corr.* 31.14). The dedicatory sonnet was added to the second edition of April 1765. For more information on Lady Mary Coke, see Ketton-Cremer, *Horace Walpole*, 181–3.

casque: a piece of armour to cover the head; a helmet (*OED*).

poignarded: i.e. stabbed; a 'poignard' or poniard is a 'short stabbing weapon' (*OED*) or dagger.

Lead on! cried Manfred; I will follow thee to the gulph of perdition: Manfred's language recalls *Hamlet* I.v.57–86.

disculpate: to exculpate, to clear from blame.

comprehensive: i.e. apprehensive. A malapropism which, as W.S. Lewis has noted, anticipates those of Richard Brinsley Sheridan's Mrs Malaprop in *The Rivals* (1775), but also specifically recalls the verbal confusions of Dogberry in Shakespeare's *Much Ado About Nothing*, i.e. III.iii.24–5: 'This is your charge: you shall comprehend all vagrom men.'

a pallet-bed: a small bed of straw or other coarse material.

orisons: i.e. prayers. Walpole refers later in the text (p. 44) to Hippolita's 'oratory' or small private chapel. Walpole again recalls the language of Shakespeare's *Hamlet* III.i.88–9: 'Nymph, in thy orisons / Be all my sins remember'd.'

He is no saint by the almanack: 'almanacks' or annual books of tables would commonly, since the early sixteenth century, include a 'calendar' of ecclesiastical anniversaries and a list of canonized saints.

there's no resisting one's vocation: recalls Falstaff's famous protestation in *1 Henry IV* I.ii.101–2: 'Why, Hal, 'tis my vocation, Hal, 'tis no sin for a man to labour in his vocation.'

If they are spirits ... questioning them: See *Hamlet* I.i.

let us sift him: to 'sift' someone was to examine them closely, to scrutinize them. Walpole is again recalling Shakespearean language, perhaps particularly *Hamlet* II.ii.58: 'Well, we shall sift him'.

the morning dawns apace: Cf. Shakespeare, *A Midsummer Night's Dream* I.i.2; *Julius Caesar* II.i.221; *The Tempest* v.i.64.

A by-stander often sees more of the game than those that play, answered Bianca: proverbial; alternately, 'Lookers-on see more than players.' See F.P. Wilson (ed.), *Oxford Dictionary of English Proverbs*, 3rd edn (1970), p. 483.

postern-gate: back gate or private entrance.

talisman: 'talismanic' objects and multifaceted magical trinkets containing written words and signs – rings, seals, signets, etc. – were popular objects in Eastern romances and Oriental tales. The superstitious Bianca later seems to treat the ring given to her by Manfred (p. 89) as a kind of magic charm or talisman.

of another-guess mould: of a different character altogether.

my domestic: i.e. my home, household.

bearded: opposed, defied.

it is your office to be no respecter of persons: i.e. Jerome's status as a priest dictates that he disregard the distinctions of social rank and, as Hippolita reminds him, speak to all, including Manfred, 'as [his] duty prescribes'.

related to me in the fourth degree: Manfred argues that his relationship to Hippolita is incestuous by virtue of their consanguinity or near relation; the 'degree' of a relationship is a step in the line of descent.

over-reached: overcame, got the better of.

traverse: cross, thwart.

a boarded gallery with latticed windows: i.e. a panelled room with a window of lattice work (made of crossed wood or metal).

wicket: here, a small door, allowing easy entrance and exit, within the larger door of a fortified castle.

warder: a staff or wand ... used to give the signal for the commencement or cessation of hostilities in a battle or tournament (*OED*).

he had taken the cross and gone to the Holy Land: i.e. Frederic had taken a 'holy vow of arms' and embarked on the Crusades (see p. 3 and note).

the example of the holy princess Sanchia of Arragon: Walpole here conflates the daughter of Sancho of Aragon with St Sancha (c. 1180–1229), daughter of King Sancho 1 of Portugal, who assisted the first Franciscan and Dominican friars in Portugal, and herself joined the Cistercians at Cellas in 1223.

harbingers with wands: harbingers – the individuals preceding and announcing the approach of a royal train – would carry 'wands' or staffs as signs of office.

a led horse: a spare horse, led by an attendant or groom (OED).

quarterly: on a shield divided into four parts or quarters; one side of the shield would represent the arms of Vicenza, the other the arms of Otranto (OED).

telling his beads: saying his prayers.

beavers: the lower portion of the face guard of a helmet (OED).

cartel: a written challenge.

gage: a pledge, security (OED).

hospital: a house used for the reception and entertainment of pilgrims, travellers, and strangers (OED).

vitious: legally improper, faulty.

submit it to the decision of unknown mutes: i.e. to the silent knights of the Marquis of Vicenza themselves.

Joppa: i.e. Jaffa, an ancient city port on the eastern coast of the Mediterranean, in what is now Israel.

glosing: i.e. glozing. Flattery; cajolery, deceitful blandishment, specious talk or representation (OED).

corsairs: Mediterranean pirates and privateers.

rover: a familiar name for a pirate ship.

the usual dole: i.e. the usual alms or charity.

list . . . sacred vengeance: See *Hamlet* I.v.5–25.

this meddling friar: See Shakespeare's *Measure for Measure* v.i.130–1: 'My lord, I know him. 'Tis a meddling friar; / I do not like the man ...'

the oriel window: 'the window of an oriel'; a projecting window in an upper story (*OED*).

vulnerary: having curative properties in respect of external injuries (*OED*).

I remember when young Ferdinand was wounded by the Venetian: Walpole may well have a specific historical incident in mind. Bianca's slightly hysterical recollection would also have called to the minds of eighteenth-century English readers the assassination attempt made in 1492 on Ferdinand v of Spain, as well as episodes in Jacobean dramatic tragedy (e.g. the stabbing of Ferdinand, Duke of Calabria, by Daniel de Bosola in John Webster's *The Duchess of Malfi* [1614]).

by my halidame: i.e. 'by my halidome'. A 'halidome' is a holy relic; hence, an asseveration sworn by such a relic (*OED*). Cf. Shakespeare's *Two Gentlemen of Verona*, iv.ii.132: 'By my halidome, I was fast asleep.'

watchet-coloured: light blue, sky-blue (*OED*).

... as I was rubbing the ring: the jewel or 'bawble' given to Bianca by Manfred in the previous interview (p. 89). See p. 41 and note.

The proposed marriages ... contingent reversion of it with Matilda: i.e. the possibility of forcibly claiming the title for himself was more tempting than marrying Matilda (and thus acknowledging Manfred's claim to be more legitimate than his own) and waiting for the title to revert to her upon the death of her father.

Angels of grace, protect me!: recalling *Hamlet* i.iv.39: 'Angels and ministers of grace defend us!'

Hieroglyphic Tales

Schah Baham ne comprenoit jamais bien que les choses absurdes & hors de toute vraisemblance. Le Sopha, p. 5:

['The only thing Shah Baham ever really understood well were things that were absurd and beyond belief.'] Claude-Prosper Jolyot de Crebillon (1707–77) published his erotic Oriental tale and social satire, *Le Sopha*, in 1745.

illiterate Mahomet: the divine revelations contained in the *Koran*, the sacred text of Islam, were related to the prophet Mahomet by the angel Gabriel. They were then committed to memory and recited verbatim to his relatives and companions. Mahomet, himself illiterate, would then engage a scribe to commit the revelations to writing.

St Mary Axe: church in central London, near Aldgate, dating from the twelfth century; the area around the church was largely residential in the eighteenth and early nineteenth centuries.

Hermes Trismegistus: Greek name (meaning 'thrice great') applied to the supposed author or source of 'Hermetic' writings, works of revelation dating from about the third century AD.

Hanno the Punic embassador at Rome ... the same general: i.e1. Walpole's feigned 'history' would show two Roman patriots of the second Punic War – Marcus Fabius Buteo and, more significantly, Scipio Africanus – to have been hirelings in the pay of the empire's most formidable enemy, the Carthaginian general Hannibal.

David ... succeeded to the throne: the story of the Biblical King David is related in 1 Samuel 6.13–1 Kings 2.12. David honoured his beloved friend Jonathan (a son of the first King of Israel, Saul) with a dirge in which he sings, 'I am distressed for you my brother Jonathan; very pleasant you have been to me; your love to me was wonderful, passing the love of woman' (2 Samuel 1.26).

A new Arabian Night's Entertainment: 'The merit of an Hieroglyphic Tale consists of its being written extempore and without any plan, as the first four of these litteraly [sic] were.' Walpole's manuscript note to his first edition copy.

oviparous: i.e. produce their young by means of eggs.

The giant ... wedding-nights: recalling the frame story of the *Arabian Nights' Entertainments*, in which the sultan Schahriar resolves each morning to kill the wife he had married on the preceding day. His 'reign of terror' is finally stopped by the inventive (and memorially gifted) Scheherazade.

Leonidas: Richard Glover (1712–85), MP for Weymouth and an opponent of Sir Robert Walpole, published his nine-volume epic *Leonidas* in 1737. Complaining in a letter to his frequent correspondent Horace Mann of the 'woefully insipid' verse written for the English stage, Walpole nevertheless admits that he 'had rather have written the most absurd lines in [Nathaniel] Lee than *Leonides*' (*Corr.* 19.27).

Philip II: (1527–98), King of Spain and Portugal and champion of the Roman Catholic Church.

the bull Unigenitus: the bull of Pope Clement VI, issued on 27 January 1343, which approved the teaching that the efficacy of Papal Indulgences ('the remission by the Church of temporal penalty due to forgiven sins') was owing to the accumulated 'merits' ('man's right to be rewarded for work done by God') of the Church itself. See F.L. Cross, ed. *The Oxford Dictionary of the Christian Church*, 2nd edn (Oxford, 1974), p. 1400.

Ignatius Loyola: (?1491–1556), Spanish theologian and, as Gronovia points out, founder of the Society of Jesus in Paris, in 1534.

The council of Trent: ecumenical council (1545–63), the decrees of which embodied the ideals of the Counter-Reformation.

petits-maîtres: fops, dandies.

related within the forbidden degrees: see p. 46 and note.

fee-simple: absolute possession.

Aboulcasem: the name of Walpole's character recalls that of the generous hero of 'The History of Aboulcasem of Basra' in the *Persian Tales* (1714).

Solomon's concubines: King Solomon is said in the Bible (1 Kings 11.3) to have had 700 wives and 300 concubines.

Azaziel, the angel of death: the Arabic angel of death is usually called 'Azreal', although Walpole may deliberately be recalling the name Azaziel as another name for the seraph Semyaza, 'the leader of the evil angels who fell, or one of the leaders'. See Gustav Davidson, *A Dictionary of Angels* (London, 1967), p. 64.

Eldest daughter of lord William Campbell. She lived with her aunt the countess of Ailesbury: Caroline Campbell (1764–89), then living with her aunt, Lady Ailesbury. See introduction p. xxv.

the tower of Babel: the construction and subsequent abandonment of the Tower of Babel is related in Genesis 11.1–9.

mount Caucasus: fabled mountain, considered in eighteenth-century tales of fantasy such as the *Arabian Nights' Entertainments* to be the boundary of the 'habitable world'.

the duchess of ********'s beautiful breasts: 'The duchess of Kingston, the celebrated Miss Chudleigh'; manuscript note from Walpole's first edition copy; i.e. Elizabeth Chudleigh (1720–88), self-styled Duchess of Kingston. Walpole's description here recalls a passage in his correspondence in which he details the entrance of the Duchess at a 1749 masquerade 'so naked that you would have taken her for Andromeda' (*Corr.* 20.49).

the song of songs: i.e. the 'Song of Solomon' or 'Canticle of Canticles', Old Testament book attributed to King Solomon.

The queen of Sheba: the visit of the Queen of Sheba to King Solomon is related in 1 Kings 10.1–3.

though she did not understand a word of Hebrew: 'Lady Mary Coke who could not speak a word of French went twice to Vienna to see the Empress Queen and passed several months there'; Walpole's manuscript note to his first edition copy. See also p. 13 and note.

Pissimissi's nose ... being something flat, like madame de ********'s: 'Miss Whitwell, wife of Count Welderan, the Dutch minister'; obWalpole's manuscript note to his first edition copy. Anne Whitwell (1721–96) was married to Jan Walrad, Count von Welderan, Dutch envoy to England 1762–80.

leading-strings: 'Geo 3d on his accession declared that he wd [sic] not be governed by his ministers as his Grandfather had been, and to prove it made Lord Bute Prime Minister'; Walpole's manuscript note to his first edition copy.

usquebaugh: whiskey.

knocked out the chancellor's brains, who at that time happened not to have any: 'Henry Bathurst Lord Apsley was Lord Chancellor when this tale was written'; Walpole's manuscript note to his first edition copy. Walpole in his correspondence refers to Bathurst as an 'old woman' and a 'wig-block' (*Corr.* 28.239).

miscarried of twins, who were killed by her majesty's fright: 'Lady Ossory had miscarried just then of two sons'; Walpole's note, omitted from *Works*. Walpole had sent a copy of 'The Peach in Brandy' to Lord Ossory on 4 December 1771, not long after receiving the news of Lady Ossory's miscarriage (See introduction p. xxi; also p. 124 and note).

wished him joy of the birth of a son and heir: 'The housekeeper, as soon as lord Ossory came home, wished him joy of a son and heir, though both the children were born dead'; Walpole's note, omitted from *Works*.

Vide Lodge's Peerage of Ireland, in the Family of Fitzpatrick: 'This tale was written for Anne Liddel, Countess of Ossory, wife of John Fitzpatrick earl of Ossory. They had a daughter Anne, the subject of this story'; Walpole's note, omitted from *Works*. Anne Liddel (1738–1804), Countess of Upper Ossory (formerly Duchess of Grafton), was a close friend of Walpole's and one of the chief recipients of his correspondence detailing London social life.

Queen Anne in her first speech to the parliament said, her heart was entirely English: In a speech delivered to Parliament on 11 March 1702, three days following her accession to the throne, Queen Anne declared that 'she knew her heart to be entirely English'.

Confucius: Chinese philosopher (551–479 BC).

supercargo: An officer on board a merchant ship whose business it is to superintend the cargo and the commercial transactions of the voyage (*OED*).

Tom himself married one of them: 'Alluding to the famous Miss Chudliegh, who married the Duke of Kingston while Maid of Honour to the Princess Dowager of Wales, which post she retained tho [*sic*] married to Mr Augustus Hervey who was a *Seaman* and who was suspected of having connived at her marrying the Duke that he might himself get rid of her, and marry some other woman, which he attempted'; Walpole's manuscript note to his first edition copy. See p. 120 and note.

the moment he was told to marry somebody else: 'Alluding to a certain Prince who had been in love with Lady Sarah Lennox at the time he consented to marry another person'; Walpole's manuscript note to his first edition copy. George III allegedly had a love affair with Sarah Lennox prior to his marriage to Charlotte Sophia in 1761.

Mr Banks: 'The Gentleman who discovered Otaheite, in company with Dr Solander'; Walpole's note, omitted from *Works*. Sir Joseph Banks (1743–1820), botanist and president of the Royal Society. Banks travelled with Dr Daniel Solander (1736–82) in Captain Cook's expedition to the South Seas on board the *Endeavour*. They docked at Tahiti ('Otaheite'), where Banks made a thorough exploration of the island, in April 1769.

incog.: i.e. incognito, a popular eighteenth-century abbreviation.

the imperturbed gardener: 'Copeland, the gardiner, a very grave person'; Walpole's note, omitted from *Works*.

the rocks which the giants threw at Jupiter's head: In the 'Gigantomachy' of Greek mythology, a race of earth-born Giants attacked the Gods, advancing and hurling at Zeus (i.e. Jupiter) and his son Herakles boulders and entire trees. Zeus eventually defeated the Giants, burying some under entire islands.

daring Leander: hero of Greek legend who nightly swam – and eventually drowned while swimming – the Hellespont to be with his beloved Hero.

At Park-place ... the manner here described: Park Place was the Berkshire seat of Walpole's cousin and close friend Henry Seymour Conway (see introduction p. xxi).

the factions of the Guelfs and Ghibellines: the two opposing factions in Italian politics in the Middle Ages; the Guelfs supported papal authority, the Ghibellines the Holy Roman Empire.

Orondates: the name of Walpole's character recalls that of Oroondates, Prince of Scythia, hero of Gauthier de Costes de La Calprenede's *Cassandra: the fam'd Romance* (1652).

jet and japan: 'jet' is polished black marble; 'japan' is a black varnish of exceptional hardness.

lansquenet: a card game of German origin.

the Bibliotheque des Romans: i.e. *Bibliothèque universelle des romans* (1775–8), a multi-volume anthology of novels ranging from ancient Greek romances to more recent fiction including the most popular imaginary voyages and Oriental tales.

WALPOLE AND HIS CRITICS

The Castle of Otranto

1. *Critical Review*, June 1765 (xix), 469. A review of the second
   edition.

We have already reviewed the *Castle of Otranto* and we then
spoke of it in terms pretty near the character given by the
author. He solves, by his preface to this edition, the phenomenon
for which we could not account, by his diffidence as to his
success; and he asks pardon of his readers, for having offered it
to them under the borrowed personage of a translator. He says
that it is an attempt to blend two kinds of romance, the ancient
and modern; and besides many ingenious reasons to justify his
undertaking, he brings the authority of Shakespear's practice,
who, in his *Hamlet* and *Julius Caesar*, (he might have added
many other of his plays) has blended humour and clumsy jests
with dignity and solemnity.

Notwithstanding the high opinion we have of this writer's
acquaintance with whatever relates to his subject, we cannot but
think if Shakespear had possessed the critical knowledge of
modern times, he would have kept these two kinds of writing
distinct, if the prepossessions and habits of the age could have
suffered him.

2. from Clara Reeve, preface to *The Old English Baron* (1778),
   iii–vi.

... This Story is the literary offspring of the *Castle of Otranto*,
written upon the same plan, with a design to unite the most
attractive and interesting circumstances of the ancient Romance
and the modern Novel, at the same time it assumes a character

and manner of its own, that differs from both; it is distinguished by the appellation of a Gothic Story, being a picture of Gothic times and manners [. . .] Having, in some degree, opened my design, I beg leave to conduct my reader back again, till he comes within view of the *Castle of Otranto*; a work which, as already has been observed, is an attempt to unite the various merits and graces of the ancient Romance and the modern Novel. To attain this end, there is required a sufficient degree of the marvelous, to excite the attention; enough of the manners of real life, to give an air of probability to the work; and enough of the pathetic, to engage the heart in its behalf.

The book we have mentioned is excellent in the last two points, but has a redundancy in the first; the opening excites the attention very strongly; the conduct of the story is artful and judicious; the characters are admirably drawn and supported; the diction polished and elegant; yet, with all these brilliant advantages, it palls upon the mind (though it does not upon the ear); and the reason is obvious, the machinery is so violent, that it destroys the effect it was intended to excite. Had the story been kept within the utmost *verge* of probability, the effect had been preserved, without losing the least circumstance that excites or detains the attention.

For instance; we can conceive, and allow for, the appearance of a ghost; we can even dispense with an enchanted sword and helmet; but then they must keep within certain limits of credibility: A sword so large as to require an hundred men to lift it; a helmet that by its own weight forces a passage through a court-yard into an arched vault, big enough for a man to go through; a picture that walks out of its frame; a skeleton ghost in a hermit's cowl: – When your expectation is wound up to the highest pitch, these circumstances take it down with a witness, destroy the work of imagination, and, instead of attention, excite laughter. I was both surprised and vexed to find the enchantment dissolved, which I wished might continue to the end of the book; and several of its readers have confessed the same disappointment to me: the beauties are so numerous, that we cannot bear the defects, but want it to be perfect in all respects.

3. from Walter Scott, introduction to *The Castle of Otranto* (1811).

Romantic narrative is of two kinds – that which, being in itself possible, may be matter of belief at any period ; and that which, though held impossible by more enlightened ages, was yet consonant with the faith of earlier times. The subject of *The Castle of Otranto* is of the latter class. Mrs Radcliffe, a name not to be mentioned without the respect due to genius, has endeavoured to effect a compromise between those different styles of narrative, by referring her prodigies to an explanation, founded on natural causes, in the latter chapters of her romances. To this improvement upon the Gothic romance there are so many objections, that we owe ourselves inclined to prefer, as more simple and impressive, the narrative of Walpole, which details supernatural incidents as they would have been readily believed and received in the eleventh or twelfth century. In the first place, the reader feels indignant at discovering he has been cheated into a sympathy with terrors which are finally explained as having proceeded from some very simple cause ; and the interest of a second reading is entirely destroyed by his having been admitted behind the scenes at the conclusion of the first. Secondly, the precaution of relieving our spirits from the influence of supposed supernatural terror, seems as unnecessary in a work of professed fiction, as that of the prudent Bottom, who proposed that the human face of the representative of his lion should appear from under his masque, and acquaint the audience plainly that he was a man as other men, and nothing more than Snug the joiner. Lastly, these substitutes for supernatural agency are frequently to the full as improbable as the machinery which they are introduced to explain away and to supplant. The reader, who is required to admit the belief of supernatural interference, understands precisely what is demanded of him ; and, if he be a gentle reader, throws his mind into the attitude best adapted to humour the deceit which is presented for his entertainment, and grants, for the time of perusal, the premises of which the fable depends. But if the author voluntarily binds himself to account for all the wondrous occurrences which he introduces, we are entitled to exact that the explanation shall be natural, easy, ingenious, and complete. Every reader of such works must remember instances in which the explanation of mysterious circumstances in the narrative have proved equally, nay, even more incredible, than if they had been accounted for by the agency of supernatural beings. For the most incredulous must allow, that the interference of such agency is more possible than that an effect resembling it should be produced by an inadequate cause. But it is unnecessary to enlarge further on a part of the subject, which we have only mentioned to exculpate our author from the charge of using machinery more clumsy than his tale from its nature required. The bold assertion of the actual existence of phantoms and apparitions seems to us to harmonize much more naturally with the manners of feudal times, than any attempt to reconcile the superstitious credulity of feudal ages with the philosophic scepticism of our own, by referring those prodigies to the operation of fulminating powder, combined mirrors, magic lanthorns [*sic.*], trap-doors, speaking trumpets, and such like apparatus of German phantasmagoria.

It cannot, however, be denied, that the character of the supernatural machinery in *The Castle of Otranto* is liable to objections. Its action and interference is rather too frequent, and presses too hard and constantly upon the same feelings in the reader's mind, to the hazard of diminishing the elasticity of the spring upon which it should operate. The fund of fearful sympathy which can be afforded by a modern reader to a tale of wonder, is much diminished by the present habits of life and mode of education. Our ancestors could wonder and thrill through all the mazes of an interminable metrical romance of fairy land, and of enchantment, the work perhaps of some

> Prevailing poet, whose undoubting mind
> Believed the magic wonders which he sung.

But our habits and feelings and belief are different, and a transient, though vivid, impression is all that can be excited by a tale of wonder even in the most fanciful mind of the present day. By the too frequent recurrence of his prodigies, Mr Walpole ran, perhaps, his greatest risk of awakening *la raison froide*, that cold common sense, which he justly deemed the greatest enemy of the effect which he hoped to produce. It may be added also, that the supernatural occurrences of *The Castle of Otranto* are brought forward into too strong day-light, and marked by an over degree of distinctness and accuracy of outline. A mysterious obscurity seems congenial at least, if not essential, to our ideas of disembodied spirits, and the gigantic limbs of the ghost of Alphonso, as described by the terrified domestics, are somewhat too distinct and corporeal to produce the feelings which their appearance is intended to excite. This fault, however, if it be one, is more than compensated by the high merit of many of the marvellous incidents in the romance. The descent of the picture of Manfred's ancestor, although it borders on extravagance, is finely introduced, and interrupts an interesting dialogue with striking effect. We have heard it observed, that the animated figure should rather have been a statue than a picture. We greatly doubt the justice of the criticism. The advantage of the colouring induces us decidedly to prefer Mr Walpole's fiction to the proposed substitute. There are few who have not felt, at some period of their childhood, a sort of terror from the manner in which the eye of an ancient portrait appears to fix that of the spectator from every point of view. It is, perhaps, hypercritical to remark (what, however, Walpole of all authors might have been expected to attend to), that the time assigned to the action, being about the eleventh century, is rather too early for the introduction of a full-length portrait. The apparition of the skeleton hermit to the prince of Vicenza was long accounted a master-piece of the horrible; but of late the valley of Jehosophat could hardly supply the dry bones necessary for the exhibition of similar spectres, so that injudicious and repeated imitation has, in some degree, injured the effect of its original model. What is most striking in *The Castle of Otranto*, is the manner in which the various prodigious appearances, bearing each upon the other, and all upon the accomplishment of the ancient prophecy, denouncing the ruin of the house of Otranto, gradually prepare us for the grand catastrophe. The moon-light vision of Alphonso dilated to immense magnitude, the astonished group of spectators in the front, and the shattered ruins of the castle in the back-ground, is briefly and sublimely described [. . .]

The persons indeed are rather generic than individual, but this was in a degree necessary to a plan calculated rather to exhibit a general view of society and manners during the times which the author's imagination loved to contemplate, than the more minute shades and discriminating points of particular characters. But the actors in the romance are strikingly drawn, with bold outlines becoming the age and nature of the story. Feudal tyranny was, perhaps, never better exemplified, than in the character of Manfred. He has the courage, the art, the duplicity, the ambition of a barbarous chieftain of the dark ages, yet with the touches of remorse and natural feeling, which preserve some sympathy for him when his pride is quelled, and his race extinguished. The pious monk, and the patient Hippolita, are well contrasted with this selfish and tyrannical prince. Theodore is the juvenile hero of a romantic tale, and Matilda has more interesting sweetness than usually belongs to its heroine. As the character of Isabella is studiously kept down, in order to relieve that of the daughter of Manfred, few readers are pleased with the concluding insinuation, that she became at length the bride of Theodore. This is in some degree a departure from the rules of chivalry; and however natural an occurrence in common life, rather injures the magical illusions of romance. In other respects, making allowance for the extraordinary incidents of a dark and tempestuous age, the story, so far as within the course of natural events, is happily detailed, its progress is uniform, its events interesting and well combined, and the conclusion grand, tragical, and affecting.

4. from Edith Birkhead, *The Tale of Terror: A Study of the Gothic Romance* (1921), 16–20.

To Horace Walpole, whose *Castle of Otranto* was published on Christmas Eve, 1764, must be assigned the honour of having introduced the Gothic romance and of having made it fashionable. Diffident as to the success of so 'wild' a story in an age devoted to good sense and reason, he sent forth his mediaeval tale disguised as a translation from the Italian of 'Onuphrio Muralto', by William Marshall. It was only after it had been received with enthusiasm that he confessed the authorship. As he explained frankly in a letter to his friend Mason: 'It is not everybody that may in this country play the fool with impunity'. That Walpole regarded his story merely as a fanciful, amusing trifle is clear from the letter he wrote to Miss Hannah More reproving her for putting so frantic a thing into the hands of a Bristol milkwoman who wrote poetry in her leisure hours. *The Castle of Otranto* was but another manifestation of that admiration for the Gothic which had found expression fourteen years earlier in his miniature castle at Strawberry Hill, with its old armour and 'lean windows fattened with rich saints'. The word

'Gothic' in the early eighteenth century was used as a term of reproach. To Addison, Siena Cathedral was but a 'barbarous' building, which might have been a miracle of architecture, had our forefathers 'only been instructed in the right way'. Pope in his *Preface to Shakespeare* admits the strength and majesty of the Gothic, but deplores its irregularity. In *Letters on Chivalry and Romance*, published two years before *The Castle of Otranto*, Hurd pleads that Spenser's *Faerie Queene* should be read and criticised as a Gothic, not a classical, poem. He clearly recognises the right of the Gothic to be judged by laws of its own. When the nineteenth century is reached the epithet has lost all tinge of blame, and has become entirely one of praise. From the time when he began to build his castle, in 1750, Walpole's letters abound in references to Gothic, and he confesses once: 'In the heretical corner of my heart I adore the Gothic building'. At Strawberry Hill the hall and staircase were his special delight and they probably formed the background of that dream in which he saw a gigantic hand in armour on the staircase of an ancient castle. When Dr Burney visited Walpole's home in 1786 he remarked on the striking recollections of *The Castle of Otranto*, brought to mind by 'the deep shade in which some of his antique portraits were placed and the lone sort of look of the unusually shaped apartments in which they were hung'. We know how in idle moments Walpole loved to brood on the picturesque past, and we can imagine his falling asleep, after the arrival of a piece of armour for his collection, with his head full of plans for the adornment of his cherished castle. His story is but an expansion of this dilettante's nightmare. His interest in things mediaeval was not that of an antiquary, but rather that of an artist who loves things old because of their age and beauty.

5. from R.W. Ketton-Cremer, *Horace Walpole: A Biography* (1940), 214–16.

[...] It is impossible to feel that Walpole achieved his aim of blending ancient romance and the contemporary novel. He had passed his life in observing the subtler shades of human character, and recorded them in his letters; but he could not create character. His figures speak the language of the novel of his day, and exhibit the contemporary emotions. Matilda and Isabella talk and behave, amid a welter of ghosts and portents, as

Clarissa Harlowe or Sophia Western would have done. But the delicate shades of character, given to their heroines by Richardson and Fielding, are lacking in Walpole's novel. All the actors in *The Castle of Otranto* are reduced to the simplest terms – the wicked and ambitious baron, the valiant and high-minded youth, the chaste and amiable maidens. Yet in spite of this simplification, which was perhaps inevitable, the reader is still left with a painful sense of incongruity. For example, Theodore finds Isabella in the forest, whither she has fled after a series of frightful occurrences at the castle, and offers to escort her into the deeper recesses of the cavern where she is seeking refuge. The following dialogue then takes place. ' "Alas! what mean you sir?" said she. "Though all your actions are noble, though your sentiments speak the purity of your soul, is it fitting that I should accompany you alone into those perplexed retreats? Should we be found together, what would a censorious world think of my conduct?" – "I respect your virtuous delicacy," said Theodore; "nor do you harbour a suspicion that wounds my honour. I meant to conduct you into the most private cavity of these rocks; and then, at the hazard of my life, to guard their entrance against every living thing. Besides, lady," continued he, drawing a deep sigh, "beauteous and perfect as your form is, and though my wishes are not guiltless of aspiring, know, my soul is dedicated to another" ' [. . .] Certainly the blending of supernatural events and Gothic savagery with the *beaux sentiments* of his own day was the least successful feature of Walpole's novel.

Hieroglyphic Tales

1. Charles Burney, *Monthly Review* (xxvi), 182. From a review of Walpole's collected *Works*.

It must be allowed that our author had a great deal of fancy, or, rather, that he had a great many *odd fancies*. In the *Hieroglyphic Tales*, many of his allusions are extremely sarcastic, personal, and sometimes profane. In the preface [. . .] we have a sneer at the clergy, and at the Mosaic account of creation. There seems also [. . .] to be a stroke at the *Hermes* of the late Mr Harris, and a knock at King David [. . .]

Tale 1. Plato's Atlantis – 'Goat's eggs! yes – this is my

supposition – no matter whether I believe it myself or not. I will write against and abuse any man that opposes my hypothesis. It would be fine indeed if learned men were obliged to believe what they assert'. Exactly the case with the author's *Historic Doubts*. He wrote with fury against everyone who opposed them. – Fairy Tales – Leonidas – Councils – the late Emperor and Empress of Russia – are here his butts.

The 2nd tale, if it means anything, is a ridicule on the marriage of Princess Mary with the Prince of Orange – on Princess Anne – and on the Revolution of 1688.

Tale 3. More Bible-ridicule.

Tale 4. Ridicule on the present King's first speech in Parliament, in which his majesty said that 'his heart was English' : – on Lord Bute, his nurse, and prime minister : – more sarcasms against courts; – and more profaneness. These are not skilful imitations of Voltaire.

Tale 5. The late King, the Prince of Wales, and his consort, (Brunswickers,) are all here typified.

The 6th Tale is the most unobjectionable of the number. The suspense is artfully protracted, and the sarcasms are fair.

2. from Kenneth W. Gross, introduction to Horace Walpole's *Hieroglyphic Tales* (1980), iv–v.

The great Augustan satirists, as W.K. Wimsatt observed, were 'laughing poets of a heightened unreality', but even their most extreme fantasies of disorder contain implicit poles of moral sense and literary decorum or set up a steady system of allusion by which to measure the inversions of a Cave of Spleen or a Cave of Dulness. A constitutive intellectual drama outlines the most outlandish projects of Swift's imperturbable madmen, such as the idea of finding capable politicians, preachers, and journalists in the lower reaches of Bedlam. But Walpole's brief narratives tend to liberate the fantasies of satire from the bondage of ideas. That is to say, his tales make use of the exaggerated, ironic fictions of satire as much as the more self-consistent magical devices of fairy tales, but their bizarre, mannerist surfaces seem continually to deny the possibility of a concealed intellectual skeleton. Despite a wealth of literary and historical allusion, and many *moments* of sharp, ironic criticism, Walpole's hieroglyphics do not invite us to read them as ciphers of an integrated satiric argument.

Peter Sabor's volume *Horace Walpole: The Critical Heritage* in Routledge & Kegan Paul's *Critical Heritage Series* (London, 1987), noted in the bibliography, gives an excellent overview of the erratic and often contradictory responses to Walpole's life and writings, ranging from the appearance of his *Letter from Xo Ho, a Chinese Philosopher at London* (1757), to the earliest anecdotes and collections of his letters first published in the early and mid nineteenth century. Many of the pieces extracted here may be consulted in their entirety in Sabor's volume. Serious and considered responses to the *Hieroglyphic Tales* remain scarce; the contemporary judgement noted above and the introduction by Kenneth Gross to the facsimile text first published by the Augustan Reprint Society in 1982 (also excerpted above) are among the very few critical documents concerning that text.